They sat there, staring at each other.

Billie felt her body pressing toward him, though she didn't move at all. The muscles of his jaw clenched while his gaze swept up to her hair and then down over her face, as much a caress as if done by his hand. Her breath choked in her throat as the longing rushed through her veins.

Damn! Linc wanted to grab her to him. He wanted . . . he wanted a lot of things at once, but it mostly came down to that one thing he had to tell her or he'd burst.

"You're good for the kids," he ground out, deep and low. "You're the best thing that's happened around here in a long time . . . and I'm glad you took on the job as housekeeper."

Housekeeper.

He knew it, and knew she knew it—they'd have to keep things cool between them if she was to stay. And he wanted her to stay. . . .

Dear Reader,

Welcome to Silhouette **Special Edition** . . . welcome to romance. Each month Silhouette **Special Edition** publishes six novels with you in mind—stories of love and life, tales that you can identify with—romance with that little "something special" added in.

And this month is no exception to the rule. May 1991 brings *No Quarter Given* by Lindsay McKenna—the first in the thrilling WOMEN OF GLORY series. Don't miss more of this compelling collection coming in June and July. Stories by wonderful writers Curtiss Ann Matlock, Tracy Sinclair, Sherryl Woods, Diana Stuart and Lorraine Carroll (with her first **Special Edition!**) round out this merry month.

In each Silhouette **Special Edition**, we're dedicated to bringing you the romances that you dream about—the type of stories that delight as well as bring a tear to the eye. And that's what Silhouette **Special Edition** is all about—special books by special authors for special readers!

I hope you enjoy this book and all of the stories to come.

Sincerely,

Tara Gavin
Senior Editor

CURTISS ANN MATLOCK
Heaven in Texas

Silhouette Special Edition

Published by Silhouette Books New York

America's Publisher of Contemporary Romance

A special thanks to Rhonda Wallace
for so generously sharing her time and knowledge.

We build our own ladders
to climb to the sky
—Ella Wheeler Wilcox

SILHOUETTE BOOKS
300 East 42nd St., New York, N.Y. 10017

HEAVEN IN TEXAS

Copyright © 1991 by Curtiss Ann Matlock

ISBN: 0-373-09668-2

First Silhouette Books printing May 1991

CURTISS ANN MATLOCK,

a self-avowed bibliophile, says "I was probably born with a book in my hand." When not reading or writing—which is almost constantly—she enjoys gardening, canning, crocheting and motorcycling with her husband and son. Married to her high school sweetheart, the author is a navy wife and has lived in eight different states within a sixteen-year period. The nomadic Matlocks finally settled in Oklahoma, where Curtiss Ann is busy juggling two full-time careers—as homemaker and writer.

OKLAHOMA

ARK.

NEW MEXICO

Clovis ●

● Lubbock

Wichita Falls ●

● Heaven

Fort Worth ● ● Dallas

LA.

Tyler ●

● El Paso

TEXAS

● Waco

Austin ⭐

Houston ●

San Antonio ●

Victoria ●

Corpus Christi ●

Gulf of Mexico

MEXICO

PADRE ISLAND

Underlined places are fictitious.

Prologue

What She Lost...

"Can't leave that girl outside with it snowing like this, now can we, Miss Ballinger?" The doorman, his hat slightly askew as always and a bright smile on his pudgy face, held open the gilt-trimmed glass door.

Billie returned his wink. "We certainly can't—thanks, Harry." She breezed through the door in a flurry of cashmere, Zoe prancing beside her on a leash, and hurried across the marble floor to the elevators. Dogs weren't allowed in the building, but Harry always made an exception for the queenly little collie.

Billie brushed snowflakes from her royal blue cape, pressed the elevator call button twice and moved from one foot to the other.

Oh, Jonathan was going to scold. He always did—and was perfectly right to, of course. She *was* given to overspending.

But when she told him, he'd understand, she thought, warming with the memory of the exquisite pen-and-ink drawing she'd arranged to purchase. At the last minute she had succeeded in finding the perfect gift for Marc and Lisa's engagement.

Billie loved buying gifts; it was one of her favorite things in the world to do. It was also the main thing that sent her running continuously to the offices of Jonathan Bledsoe, personal accountant. She always needed extra cash.

She mentally planned her persuasions. "It's perfect, Jonathan," she would say. "You know how much Marc and Lisa love originals. And my gift must be special—I want to show them how happy I am for them. I want Marc to know how much I approve of his heart's desire, how I'll always love him as a brother."

That last part she wouldn't say, she thought as she stepped through the elevator doors. But it was the true reason this gift was so important to her, why she was willing to pay the exorbitant price—and to brave Jonathan to do it.

With Zoe padding beside her, she hurried eagerly down the carpeted hallway to Jonathan's offices. Odd. The double doors were open. Voices floated out into the hall. Oh, she hoped he wasn't in the midst of some big office do.

She stepped through the doorway with Zoe and was surprised to see a policeman talking to Carol, Jonathan's secretary. Why, Carol was crying... and there sat Oriana Jordan, sobbing. Ray Jordan sat beside her, looking for all the world like a figure in a wax museum.

Curious, and with rising apprehension, Billie slowly advanced, tugging a nervous Zoe along, and peered through the open door into Jonathan's private office. The inner sanctum looked as if a tornado had hit it. Several men were searching through the enormous desk and mahogany cabinets. And then she saw Marc. What in the world was he doing here, looking as if the wind had been knocked from him?

Marc caught sight of her. "Billie..." He strode forward. "I was just going to call you."

Her breath caught in her throat. "What is it? Has something happened to Jonathan?"

Marc nodded, and his expression turned hard. "Jonathan is gone. Skipped out," he clarified as Billie slapped a hand over her mouth. "He has skipped town—probably the country—and has taken every damn bit of his clients' money with him." His eyes filled with fury. "He's taken your entire trust fund, Billie."

Chapter One

What She Found...

The car up and died on her just this side of Heaven. It coughed, sputtered, chugged, clanked, and then flat out died, just as Marc had predicted, which made the situation all the more infuriating.

A hand across her middle to hold her fluid silk blouse away from any grime that might jump up and get her, Billie leaned over and gazed into the black depths of the engine. But staring at it changed nothing. She couldn't fix it, couldn't even guess what was wrong.

"Damn!"

She hissed the rare oath, drew back and aimed a kick at the shiny fender. Her foot stopped in midair, and she lowered it to the ground. She couldn't, even now, do anything that might scratch the finish.

She stood there, gazing at the car. It had belonged to her father, this 1955, candy-apple-red Thunderbird. He'd loved it. At his death it had become hers, and she loved it mostly because it had been his and she'd loved him. And also because of the way she felt when driving it—unique, happy, lofty, rather as if she was the Good Queen of the World.

Flopping down on the bumper, feeling decidedly un-queenly, she braced her feet in the gravelly grass alongside the blacktop that led off into nowhere in both directions.

Slowly lifting her head, she once again gazed up at the sign.

Heaven. That's what the reflective green-and-silver state marker about fifteen feet in front of her said. It was also noted in very small print on the map.

Heaven. Right here in west Texas.

She stared at the sign and then at the surrounding coun-tryside.

This was the most godforsaken land she could imagine. She'd passed only one farmhouse in twenty miles—twenty miles that had seemed like a hundred. Here it would be easy to believe in the world's being flat. Beneath the gold of an evening sun, row upon row of some deep green bushy stuff stretched forever north and south, and the blacktopped road stretched forever east and west.

She swept the surroundings again with blurring vision. Oh, Lord, she was in the middle of nowhere. Alone. She had less than three hundred dollars in cash in her purse. No credit cards.

Her bottom lip trembled, and, sitting there on that hard bumper, she thought of how her father used to point out that her lips pouted a good five minutes before she ever broke out crying. He used to tell her to go ahead and let it out, not to keep it bottled up, because all she did was create a painful volcanic explosion when she finally did give way. But Billie didn't like to cry. Crying only stopped up her nose, and she hated a stopped-up nose worse than just about anything.

Slowly, with the reluctance of a cat needing to cross a muddy river, she rose, went around to the car door and slid inside. She was without choice in the situation.

Sucking in a trembling breath, she riffled through the pile of stuff in the opposite seat, found the tissues and blew her nose on one, hard. She dug out her purse, dabbed on a bit of lipstick, took up her coat, then paused to stick a pack-age of Twinkies snack cakes into each pocket and two more into her purse—her stash in case of emergency. The clock in the dash read seven-thirty-five; the sun would set inside an hour.

Outside, the breeze was rising, bringing a damp chill to the sultry air. To the west, purple clouds gathered in front of the sun. She hesitated, heartily wishing she didn't have to leave her beloved Thunderbird. Firmly she pushed down the lock, shut the door and turned away.

Hooking her purse strap over her shoulder, she stuffed her hands into her coat pockets and started off toward the distant buildings. She glanced again at the sign as she passed. Heaven. Obviously the people who'd settled this part of the country had a sense of humor. Or a great longing to be somewhere else.

Well, *she* certainly wished to be somewhere else. And she would have been if she hadn't gotten that crazy notion to see Billy the Kid's grave! Or if she hadn't started on this stupid trip in the first place. Or if she'd followed Marc's advice, instead of being carried away with pride and principles and an insane sense of daring. Or if Jonathan Bledsoe had dropped dead before he'd robbed her blind.

With every step, which became increasingly painful in the expensive Italian boots that were not made for walking, Billie cursed Jonathan to a life of a thousand plagues.

By the time she reached the distant buildings, Billie had defined sixty-five of those plagues and had fallen into an awkward, pigeon-toed limp.

Heaven, she saw, appeared a place where time had stopped somewhere back around 1945. Two mobile homes, one brown, one faded turquoise, the turquoise one boasting a cockeyed overstuffed living room chair just outside the front door, sat near a couple of small white clapboard dwellings just off the two-lane highway. A drooping chain-link fence, minus its gates, surrounded a grouping of curiously shaped buildings with odd pipes jutting from one to another. The sign on the wide gable of the tallest structure proclaimed it the Heavener Gin and Elevator. A squatty building next to it had the words Heavener Feed and Seed painted on the large front window. It all had a rather desolate look, not a soul in sight.

Heavener. This godforsaken settlement's founding family? That would explain the town name. They must have thought they were being cute.

A group of homemade billboards off the side of the highway advertised the Holy Land Baptist Church, Forman's Irrigation Wells, and Paula's Beauty Boutique. All the arrows pointed south, and Billie wondered how far.

"Lord," she murmured, "if you have a mechanic in this town of yours who can fix my car, I'll give up Twinkies for six months and donate the money saved to charity." Well, three months, she amended. It was no use promising what she couldn't deliver.

She drew her coat together—the closest thing to armor she had at the moment—needing shelter in this strange and foreign land.

Limping, she continued toward the building straight in front of her—Snow's Café, the lettering on the large front window announced. The aroma of cooking brought her stomach to life, and the two shiny, late-model pickups parked in the gravel lot gave her hope.

Hand on the knob, she caught sight of two more small signs identifying the café as also being the official post office and bus stop. The meager connections to destinations beyond this lonesome place were somehow reassuring, familiar.

A brass bell jingled merrily when she entered the café. The burly, balding man behind the counter twisted his head from the television set high in a rear corner. His bushy iron-gray eyebrows rose, and he came fully around to stare at her. Quick as a wink, his gaze swept her from head to toe and back up again. The three other men in the café, all sitting together in one booth, did likewise.

"Evenin', ma'am." The bushy-eyebrowed man came down the length of the counter, running a thumb beneath his bright red suspenders. He did not exude friendliness.

"Good evening."

Billie hesitated between a seat at the counter or one of the maroon vinyl booths. With the man staring questioningly at her from the counter, she slid onto one of the red-topped stools.

"I make the best onion burgers in the county, if you're havin' to decide." The counterman braced himself stiff-armed against the counter and raised one iron-gray, bushy eyebrow.

"Oh, you always say that, Fred," someone from the booth cackled. They were elderly men with weathered faces that had seen at least sixty years of sun and wind.

The bushy-eyebrowed man didn't laugh.

"That sounds fine," Billie murmured. "And coffee, too, please."

She thought he was about to say, "Comin' right up," but he simply gave a curt nod.

With surprisingly graceful movements, he swung around and took up the glass coffeepot and a cup and saucer. Seemingly all in one motion he plunked the cup and saucer in front of Billie and began pouring the coffee. His expression remained decidedly dour.

The three elderly men continued to stare at her, and she became highly aware of her windblown hair and the shiny rhinestones on her designer denim coat—a style currently chic in Reno but making her feel strangely garish here. She felt as much an oddity as if she'd worn sneakers to a charity ball.

Slowly she spooned a heaping teaspoonful of sugar into her coffee, stirred, then set the spoon aside and folded her hands in her lap. She considered taking off her coat, but felt it equal at that moment to taking off her clothes.

She gazed at the red suspenders crossing Fred's back, then glanced about, taking in the stainless steel appliances, the shelf of real Coke glasses, the jukebox music selectors at each booth. The walls were a sparkling white enamel at least five coats thick. A huge stuffed marlin arched above the back door. To her right was the entry to what was grandly labeled the U.S. Post Office.

She looked again at the red suspenders crossing Fred's wide back. "My car has broken down, and I was wondering if there's a garage nearby."

Out of the corner of her eye she caught the farmers' ripe curiosity—they suddenly resembled cranes in workshirts. Fred gave the onions on the grill a shuffle, then turned.

"Thought I hadn't heard a car pull up. I always hear the cars. How far away are you?"

Billie couldn't decide if he were about to be friendly or not; his face and voice were devoid of emotion.

"Out by the town sign to the west," she answered, inclining her head.

"Well..." He pointed south with the spatula. "Closest place is Larry's about three miles south. But he came down with the measles on Thursday and ain't fixin' nothin' right now."

"Larry cain't fix much of anythin' anyway," one of the old men put in.

So, Billie thought, it didn't look as if she would be giving up Twinkies. She gripped the coffee cup with both hands and looked into the dark brew as she raised it to her lips. She wouldn't call Marc. He couldn't help her anyway. She was on her own.

Fred turned back to poke the burger and onions. One of the old gentlemen called loudly, "The only other garage is away over in Moorestown. Carter there is real handy. He fixes all my vehicles, and I don't have any complaints a'tall."

"You say that like you have a fleet, George. You only have the truck and car," another man in the booth teased his friend. He raised his voice to Billie. "Where he's talkin' about is twenty miles away. And this is Saturday, and that garage won't open until Monday mornin', little darlin'."

Something within Billie jumped at the term "little darlin'" and the appreciative way the old man was looking at her. Then the factual information quietly entered her mind.

She downed the rest of her coffee. The last of the sun's rays splashed red-gold on the countertop.

"Is there a motel anywhere nearby? Perhaps I could take a bus...." She included the three in the booth with her question.

"Over in Moorestown," one of them answered.

"Nope." Fred set the famous onion hamburger in front of her. "I didn't make fries. You didn't say you wanted fries, so I didn't make 'em. And that motel in Moorestown's been closed for a year."

"You don't say?" said one of the old cronies.

"I think you're mistaken about that," put in another. "I'm sure it was there when the wife and I went to visit her sister last month."

"Naw...Fred's right, little darlin'," said the third. He leaned back and picked at his teeth with a toothpick. "That place is closed. There was a fire, and it was cheaper for them to just fold up."

"Where is the nearest motel?" She looked at Fred.

"When you're gettin' into Lubbock."

Lubbock. That was at least fifty miles away.

"About fifty-five miles on down the road," Fred elaborated, as if in answer to her thoughts. "And there won't be a bus through here until Monday around noon."

He stared at her, and she saw he had unexpectedly gentle eyes beneath those bushy eyebrows. He gestured.

"Eat that while it's hot, gal. Onions don't taste right when they get cold."

She gazed at the hamburger. Then, not wanting to offend, she picked it up and took a bite, though she wasn't certain she could swallow past the lump in her throat.

She was stuck, in Heaven, where buses didn't run on the weekends, where there weren't any hotels or mechanics, where the post office was in a café and where the men still called a woman little darlin'. This was probably one of those times she'd look back on later and have a great laugh over. Someday.

If she ever got to someday.

Whatever was she going to do?

It was going to rain tonight, and Linc intended to get this final plowing done and his cotton laid by. And he intended to do it while he could without Tommy and Toby hanging around his legs. Since Kit had gone back to school, that's how Linc had to spend most of his days—with his two youngest stuck to him like leeches. He'd spent most of yesterday and part of today plowing this damn field, his largest, and he vowed to finish tonight, by God. He wasn't going to risk the rain turning the soil into a bog. No, sir, he wasn't, even if it was going to take him half a night of plowing.

He bore down on the fence and turned the giant tractor right at the last minute. He could handle the speed, he told the nagging inner voice. He'd been driving a tractor for better than twenty-five years.

He checked the gauges, glanced at the sky and cursed life and the weather all at the same time. Either it was feast or famine. Why in hell didn't he just chuck it all and head for the city?

Because he had four kids who needed feeding and clothing, he thought caustically. Denise had left him holding that bag when she'd cut out, and now the third housekeeper inside a year had up and deserted him—and right before schooltime, too! Turned sixty-two and started collecting her social security, so she'd lit out for Florida to live in one of those fancy condos and play canasta and meet old farts. Which she'd said would be a lot more pleasant than taking care of his kids.

Well, maybe his kids weren't model specimens, but she hadn't been any winner as a housekeeper, either.

Damn it all to hell, anyway. Now his choices for housekeeper were down to Coralee Hutch, who did everything out of a warped sense of Christian duty and whom the kids were convinced was a witch, or a drill sergeant of a woman who'd had Tommy crying within five minutes, or an old man who wanted to bring his mother with him. It was quite plain that housekeepers didn't grow on fence posts out here.

The rumble of the tractor engine had just made a disturbing change when Linc spied the familiar battered white pickup shooting down the rutted lane alongside the fence. Dust billowed up behind; the headlights bounced in front.

"Damn!" Linc whispered. If that boy thought he was going to get a license after his birthday and go driving around the highways like that, he'd better think again. And what in hell could be so all-fired important for him to come ripping out here and leave his brothers and sister? Of course, if the radio in the tractor hadn't been broken, the boy wouldn't have had to drive out from the house—and that was Sam Tate's fault, and Linc was going to call him on it!

Linc brought the tractor to a halt at the end of the field in front of the pickup. Again he caught a slightly different engine noise. As he listened, Kit scrambled up the side of the tractor.

"Uncle Fred says he needs to see you right away," Kit said, raising his cracking adolescent voice over the idling engine and the rising wind.

"What for?" Linc cocked an ear to the engine. Was that damn carburetor clogged again? Lord knew he couldn't afford trouble now—not now!

"Somethin' important is all he told me."

"And I'm supposed to stop everything here?" Linc shouted. "Fred must have said what he needed." The boy probably hadn't been paying attention.

"He didn't say anything but that I was to tell you he needed you now," Kit shouted back, hunching his shoulders. "I told him you were out in the field and wouldn't want to stop, but he told me to tell you. I'm just doin' what he said."

What in hell could Fred need with him? Linc fumed. He shook his head. "I've got to get this plowin' finished. It may rain so much we can't get back into the field for a week!" Anything short of Fred being on his deathbed could wait.

Uncertainty and worry flitted across his son's young face, though he nodded and turned away.

"Wait." Linc pushed open the door, thinking that he ought to have his head examined. "Are your sister and the boys occupied?"

Kit nodded quickly. "They're watchin' television."

"Okay. Keep this thing goin' till I get back."

Kit slipped onto the cushion, gripped the wheel and bobbed his head as Linc barked directions at him.

"Watch your rows. Don't get cockeyed because you're paying more attention to the damn radio than to your job. And watch your speed—you're not at the Indy, and I want cotton left in this field. You hear me?"

Kit nodded, his tightening jaw revealing how he felt about being told what to do. Linc ignored it. The boy had to learn to take orders and do right; he was way older than Linc had been when he'd done most of the family plowing.

Linc slammed the door and jumped from the tractor. As he sent the pickup speeding out of the field, he wondered why his uncle would have need of him. That Fred hadn't ever called him like this was what had made Linc change his mind about going, and was what put the small knot of worry in his gut now.

He sped the eight miles into Heaven and skidded to a stop beside the café, sending fine gravel spraying. He hit the ground sprinting and burst through the doorway, only to find Fred standing behind the counter, gazing up at the television, just like always. Somehow Linc had expected the old man to be doubled over in pain, to have a broken leg, or to have been taken hostage by a crazed killer... something!

"What in the hell's the problem, Fred?" He jerked the hat from his head and ran his fingers through his damp hair. "I know Kit told you I was out in the field!"

Fred's characteristically dour expression didn't change. He swept out his arm, and Linc followed the gesture. His gaze came to rest on a striking young woman sitting at the end of the counter, staring at him. Linc blinked and took a second look.

Hair waving to her shoulders like glimmering sun-ripe wheat, eyes as blue and wide as a Texas winter sky and legs that stretched to the Gulf. Every male cell in his body stood up and took notice.

"Linc, this is Miss Billie Ballinger," Fred said in his gruff voice.

For a second Linc could only stare at her, a warmth spreading through his groin and up into his chest. She was one hell of a beautiful woman. And dressed to kill. She was straight out of one of those fancy New York fashion magazines Denise always used to have her nose stuck in. This thought instantly squelched his stupid flash of male hormones and returned him to his good senses. God save us all from pretty women, was his motto.

He gave her a terse nod. She gave him a tight smile. Linc looked back at Fred.

"So what's the emergency?"

Fred nodded at the woman. "Her car broke down at the west end of town, and as mayor, you're in charge of the welfare of residents and visitors alike."

Linc couldn't believe what he heard. He glanced at the woman, feeling a sharp dislike. A broken-down car was the emergency!

"Damn it all to hell, Fred!" He smacked his hat against his leg, then shook it at the old man. "Don't go throwin' that mayor business at me. My name only got down for that job because I was the only man not at the yearly meeting to refuse. And for this you don't need a mayor—call Larry." He turned to go.

"Can't call Larry," Fred said. "Larry's down with the measles. Got 'em from his daughter. His wife said he could hardly lift his head from the pillow."

Linc paused and turned back. "Then call someone from Carter's over in Moorestown."

"I did that. No answer—not at Carter's home number either." Fred braced his arms against the counter. "Theo Lopez went down and had a look and says the fuel pump's gone out. He's pretty handy with engines, you know. Main trouble is there's nobody west of Lubbock goin' to have a fuel pump for a '55 *Thunderbird* settin' on their shelves."

That gave Linc pause. "A '55 *Thunderbird?*" He glanced from his uncle to the woman. She'd slid from the stool and was slipping on a coat. As she searched for the arm of the coat, her thin blouse stretched tight over her breasts. Full, rounded breasts. She pulled the coat closed—one of those trendy, long denim coats city people liked to call dusters, decorated with rhinestones and white, blue and gold beading. The kind that cost an arm and a leg from some specialty boutique.

"Yes," she said, speaking for the first time. "And I'm sure you wouldn't have a spare fuel pump for it on any of your shelves either. I'm sorry you were troubled." She laid several bills on the counter. "Thank you so much, Fred. You've been very helpful." She flashed the older man a smile, gave Linc a bare glance, then swished out the door. The bell jingled as it closed.

"You've gone and insulted her," Fred said.

"I didn't say anything to her."

"That's just it—you were too busy complainin' about being inconvenienced. And swearing. You'd better get along after her."

"Why should I do that?" Guilt nagged at Linc, but, by damn, she wasn't his concern! "I don't have time for this, Fred. I want to get my cotton laid by and only have one field left to plow in order to do that—and I've gotta get it done before the rain and while Kit's there to watch the twins."

"What happened to your hired help?"

"I let the choppers go yesterday, end of the week. They got work farther south. Eldon's up at his daddy's funeral in Amarillo, and Joe picked this weekend to fall off the wagon." Which had been one more kink in things, Linc thought hotly.

Fred shook his head. "Poor Joe. Thought he had demon rum licked. Aw, a few hours one way or 'nother ain't gonna hurt your crop, Linc," Fred said cavalierly. Wasn't no skin off his back. "And that little gal ain't got nowhere to go but back to her car, and she can't stay there all night. Not in a durn two-seater and it fixin' to storm," he added.

"And why don't you go after her?"

"Because I'm not the mayor."

"Oh, sh—!" Linc jammed his hat on his head and bit back the curse.

"Go down there and give her a lift to Lubbock."

"I got work to do. And I'm not runnin' any chauffeur service. You do it."

"You know I can't drive at night with my eyesight. Besides, I hold this place open 'til ten—have for twenty-five years."

Linc took a deep breath, rested a hand on his belt. Calm down and think, he told himself. This is a simple problem; solve it in two minutes and get back to the field. Lord only knew what kind of job Kit was doing. Probably plowin' up cotton plants instead of weeds.

"She headin' for Lubbock?"

Fred nodded. "Headin' thata way."

"Maybe there's friends or family there she could call to come get her."

Fred was already shaking his head. "She's on her way down to the Gulf."

Linc sighed. "Okay—I'll go get her, and you let her stay at your place for the night. Then me, or you, or someone will take her to Lubbock tomorrow."

Fred's eyes widened, and he shook his head. "No, sir. I'm a single man, livin' alone with one bed and a settee."

"You're sixty-eight, Fred." When Fred's expression didn't change, he added, "And who's to know?"

"I'm still a man." Fred fixed him with a level eye. "And Gracie Hendricks can spit from her porch to mine. She watches me like a hawk—she's jealous, you know. I ain't riskin' riling her."

"Then stick Miss . . . her with Gracie."

"Gracie wouldn't open her door a crack to that gal. She'd accuse her of being an ax murderer or somethin'. You know how Gracie can be."

Fred wasn't exaggerating there, Linc thought. If it hadn't been for Fred—hell, the entire community—taking care of Gracie and putting up with her eccentric ways, she would have gone to the state home years ago.

"What about Theo? You said he was here."

"He was passing through, headin' west to his son's place. Josh was here, too, but he lost his license 'cause he can't see but about five feet, then there was George, but he and his wife had a party to go to."

Fred hadn't fully finished his saga when Linc headed for the door. Standing there arguing wasn't getting him back to his field. "Okay, I'll handle it!" He stalked from the café, muttering obscenities under his breath.

The woman had been a damn fool to be traveling across this area in such an old car anyway, Linc thought as he jumped into his pickup and slammed the door. She deserved to suffer the consequences of being stupid. And why was a woman like that driving such an old car? And why out here in the middle of nowhere—nowhere at least for the likes of her?

His headlights caught her gleaming hair and the rhinestones of that long denim coat. She was limping, as if she'd stepped in a hole or something.

He pulled to a stop. She kept on walking.

Linc opened the door, poked up out of the seat and called to her over the windshield. "It's me—Linc Snow." He stopped then because he didn't know what else to say.

She kept on walking. And he knew damn well she'd heard him.

A big gust of wind pushed on the door, and it pinched him under the arm. He cursed her because of it. A handful of raindrops splattered on his hat. He flopped back into the seat and slammed the door, thinking that it wouldn't hurt her none to spend the night in her car. The image of the two seats of a sporty '55 Thunderbird flashed through his mind. It wouldn't be comfortable—but then, what did he care? He didn't even know her, and she wasn't his responsibility.

"Damn!"

Pressing the accelerator, he drove on down the road until he came upon the vehicle on the shoulder of the opposite side. He did a quick three-point turn in the middle of the road, then pulled up behind the stalled car and found himself nearly blinded by chrome and lollipop-red gleaming like a precious gemstone in his headlights. Hardly the "old" car he'd imagined.

Her movements caught his eye. He watched her shadowy figure limping forward out of the dimming twilight and into the glare of his headlights.

He got out of the pickup and walked toward her.

Chapter Two

Billie glanced at the shadowed figure walking toward her in the glare of his truck's headlights. Cowboy hat on his head, well-worn jeans hugging his legs down to his boots. Tall, lean, he sank down into his hips and walked with a stride formidable in its laziness.

She refused to look again. Refused to acknowledge the disagreeable man who minutes ago had made her feel like a lowly, beggarly vagrant. A humiliating thorn in his side. Why in the world he had come out here when he'd so obviously not wanted to be bothered with her?

She dug into her handbag, searching for the keys. That they eluded her made her all the more angry. She felt stupid—she didn't want to look it. The wind blew dust in her face, and a raindrop plopped on her nose.

The man—Mr. Somebody Snow—stopped beside the rear wheel, his body cutting off the worst of the headlights' glare, just as Billie's fingers closed around the keys. Pulling them out, she kept her gaze on the lock of the driver's door.

"Are you plannin' to spend the night in your car?" he asked.

Recognizing the absurdity of the situation, she turned her head toward him. He *was* there, after all. They were the only two people standing beside a deserted highway, at night, on the edge of a storm, and to pretend otherwise was simply too ludicrous and childish a thing to do.

"Yes." What else did he think she was going to do? Walk to Lubbock and perhaps get there by next week?

He rubbed the side of his shadowed nose and shifted his stance. As if he was maybe just a wee bit uncertain, she thought with a twinge of satisfaction as she inserted the key and turned it.

"This thing only has two bucket seats, doesn't it? Might be hard sleepin'."

"I'm not a very big person."

She opened the door and was swinging her purse from her shoulder when he cleared his throat and stepped forward, draping his arm along the rooftop, as if to stop her from getting inside.

"Look…" He rubbed the side of his nose again. "I can't take time to drive you into Lubbock tonight, but you're welcome to stay at my house, and tomorrow I'll find someone to get you to the city or take you myself." Reluctance echoed in his voice and vibrated from his body.

Billie clenched her jaw, staring at the leather driver's seat. This man had a harsh face and a harsh manner, yet she wasn't afraid of him; he wasn't like that. And however dubious the offer, it nevertheless appeared her only alternative to staying the night in her car. And if she said no, could she be assured of finding anyone the following day to take her to Lubbock?

"No thanks," she said anyway, knowing full well pride was going before good sense. Oh, yes, she was her father's daughter!

She flung her purse inside and bent to follow, forcing the man to jerk upright out of the way.

He placed a restraining hand on the door and bent down again, jutting his face forward. "This is real stupid. Just come on to my house. I've got a houseful of family *and* an extra room. I am the mayor," he said sarcastically, "if you're worried about my character. Tomorrow I'll get you to a motel in Lubbock.''

Billie thought darkly and without compliment that she'd known a few mayors in her time. "I appreciate the offer, Mr. Snow, but no thank you. There's no need for you to trouble yourself." She yanked the door closed.

"Suit yourself," came his muffled voice through the window, and then he was walking back to his truck.

She gazed straight ahead. Raindrops splattered on the windshield; lightning flashed in the black sky to the south. A car was a good place to be in an electric storm—wasn't it? But what if there was a tornado?

Despair washed over her as she stared out at the unfamiliar land. It had turned quite black, a tomb-like black, with no porch lights or street lamps, neon signs, windows' glow—nothing but black, making her feel as if her eyesight were failing. She suddenly wanted to change her mind and go with the man. He had a house. A bed with covers to pull over her head.

But in order to do that, she'd have to jump out right that instant and chase after him. Tell him she'd changed her mind. Say that to that pompous man, a stranger who didn't want to be bothered with her. She had never felt more alone, more a stranger in a strange land in her entire life. And this was Heaven?

Light flashed across the dash as the pickup behind her pulled out onto the road. Leaving.

However, to her amazement, the truck didn't pass, but stopped beside her. The passenger door flew open, and the man sat there in the dim glow of the interior light staring at her with a questioning gaze. Linc, she remembered suddenly. His name was Linc Snow. He was giving her one last chance.

Billie took it. With one hand she opened the car door and with the other grabbed both her purse and the handles of the small overnight bag on the floorboards.

She hesitated and looked over at the man in the pickup. Oh, wasn't there some other choice?

"If you don't come," he said then, "Fred will never let me hear the end of it. He's my uncle, and I have to see him a lot. And I'll feel like a heel later and have to come back anyway.''

He sounded as if the prospects were more than he could bear, and that it was all her fault. But it was good enough to salvage a bit of her pride. She slammed the door closed, then tossed her bags into the pickup seat and joined them with as much grace as possible, which proved to be darn little since she had to scramble up into the high seat as she would up a mountainside.

"Do you need to get a suitcase or anything from the trunk?"

"Nope." She shook her head, shut the door with a firm click, and the light went out.

With one quick glance toward the dark shadow that was Linc Snow, she folded her coat closed and pulled her bags close to where she sat at the far edge of the seat. He shifted, and the truck started quickly forward, the momentum pressing her back into the seat. Billie stared straight ahead, scarcely breathing, and decided morosely that her life had become one big, unmanageable calamity waiting to happen.

The town of Heaven was left behind while the narrow highway eerily disappeared into the darkness ahead of them. And Billie rode alone with a man she did not know, going to stay at his house which was somewhere out in the blackness of this desolate land. He sat on his side, and she sat as far to the other side as possible. The silence rang in her ears.

It had come to this, she thought, her imagination taking flight. She was in the *Twilight Zone*. These people were all aliens, and she was being taken to their lair. She would disappear. Without a trace. Marc would call his parents' cottage when Billie didn't telephone as she'd promised to do by Sunday night. He'd call the police when she didn't answer after his fourth call. Of course, the police would do nothing for at least twenty-four hours. Marc would hire private detectives, who wouldn't even come to Heaven because no one knew she'd gone out of her way to visit Billy the Kid's grave. In the end, no one would ever know.

"It's about seven more miles out to my place." Linc Snow's sharp voice caused her to jump and glance at him.

"Oh."

His arm stretched forward in a curious motion, and Billie saw he was reaching for a microphone hanging in the shadows just below the dash. "Unit One calling base. Ronnie . . . Ronnie, come in," he said in a low voice and waited as a crackling static came from the radio near his knee. Then again, more sternly, "Ronnie, pick up."

"Yes, Daddy." A small, breathless voice answered a half-minute later.

"Everything all right there?"

"Fine, Daddy."

"I'll be there in a few minutes."

"Okay," came the soft reply. Linc Snow replaced the microphone, sat back and leaned his elbow on the window edge of the door, driving with one hand.

The truck's engine hummed loudly as older ones did— rather like the low roar of a small plane. And for the first time, Billie realized the whole truck rattled—the windows, the glove box, the gear shift knob. She smelled the musty odor of old dust and drew her legs up slightly, her arms closer, as if she could compress her body and keep it from touching anything.

She sneaked a look at Linc Snow. He drove fast but sat relaxed, his hand resting lazily upon the wheel. He obviously knew this road well. His profile showed a rather large, straight nose and firm square jaw. He was lean, hard-muscled, angular. Handsome in that rustic way. And oddly, he was one of those rare men who made her distinctly aware of her sensual self.

She recalled his eyes from before: deep-set beneath thick brows, frowning, intense. His mouth was a hard line, too. Belligerent. That was it, and the sense of belligerence remained with him still.

"I'm sorry to be such an inconvenience. I appreciate your help," she said. No matter his manner—or the state of his vehicle—he had extended a helping hand, and she should not prove ungrateful. She'd been taught that courtesy was about equal to godliness, and it'd been proven in her experience that a person could most definitely attract more bees with honey than vinegar. And what Billie wanted more than anything at that moment was a bit of friendliness to help her through this horrible situation.

"It's okay."

Two short, clipped words, which didn't invite conversation. She added taciturn to her assessment of him.

Billie turned her head to gaze out past her own reflection to the blackness beyond. It was all so foreign to her. She thought longingly of the house back in Reno she'd lived in for eight years, the rooms where soft light glowed when the sun set. The darkness beyond her wide expanses of patios had been beautiful then, adorned with the diamond brightness of thousands of distant lights.

"It's so very black out there. Like a cave without end," she said, forgetting for a moment that the man clearly wanted no conversation.

"No streetlights out here," he said tersely.

His tone served to kill any lingering hope Billie had for friendly conversation with the man. Under normal circumstances she wouldn't have given up. The taciturn Mr. Linc Snow would have been a challenge. But at the moment Billie was tired and utterly defeated.

She endured the silence by wondering what Mrs. Linc Snow would be like and prayed she would prove more hospitable than her husband. She worried over abandoning her precious T-bird in the midst of nowhere and mentally apologized to her father for doing so. She wondered how much a fuel pump would cost and thought of the blank spaces in her wallet where her credit cards had been and the cash that was all the money she had in the world. And she was distinctly aware of the stranger behind the wheel.

When he turned off the highway, Billie saw the lights of a house glimmering far down the graveled lane. Like the light at the end of a tunnel. She peered forward eagerly, yet with trepidation. Still, she reasoned, meeting this man's family couldn't be much worse than the strained drive.

The house that came into clear view, bathed in the glow of a tall pole lamp, was quite a surprise. It was white, two stories, with a porch stretching across the front and wrapping on around the side, and accented with Victorian

scrollwork. Perfectly manicured bushes formed a neat out-
line along the base of the foundation.

The graceful house seemed in stark contrast to the hard
man who pulled the pickup to a stop in front of the two-car
garage attached to the rear of the house by a screened porch.
Without a word, he got out of the truck. He didn't come
around to open the door for her but walked with that
clipped stride toward the house. Billie hurried to follow. At
least he paused at the step to wait and opened the screen
door for her to go first. He didn't look at her, though, as if
he hadn't time, didn't want to.

He ushered her across the porch and into an enormous
kitchen. Billie blinked in the bright light. There were country oak cabinets and pretty wallpaper. And a large round
table that held a messy jumble. Linc Snow moved across the
room and called, "Ronnie...boys!"

Billie glanced around and thought oh, my heaven! Then
she immediately put on a politely agreeable expression and
tried not to stare.

Still, there was no way not to see things. The jumble on
the table was dirty dishes from at least one meal but more
likely two. There was scarcely an inch of counter space or
chair space in what appeared to be a very nice kitchen-
family room area that wasn't littered with something.
Newspapers and clothing and half-empty glasses and snack
bags and toys and trash, two overflowing bags of it.

Linc Snow raked his fingers through his hair—thick, rich
mahogany brown hair with a circle indentation made by his
worn cowboy hat—then gestured with his hat toward an
opened doorway at the back of the room. "The guest
room's through here."

He started to lead the way but was stopped by a call.

"Daddy?"

Billie turned to see a young girl appear in the shadows of
the archway that led to a hallway. She gazed at Billie with
large, round eyes, her gaze moving abruptly from Billie's
face downward across her coat and back again.

"Ronnie." Linc Snow moved toward the girl and gazed
down at her. His face was stern. "Everything all right here?
Where are your brothers?"

"Watching TV upstairs. We're fine, Daddy."

He nodded and swung around to Billie. "This is my daughter, Rhonda. Ronnie, Miss . . . ah . . ." He'd forgotten her name.

"Ballinger," Billie finished for him and smiled at the child. "Billie Ballinger."

The girl's expression was more one of suspicious speculation than shyness. She arched her left eyebrow and regarded Billie much as if she thought the newcomer might be about to steal the family silver. She didn't return Billie's smile. Like father, like daughter, Billie thought.

"Ah . . . Miss Ballinger's car broke down over in Heaven, and she'll be staying the night. You show her the guest room and take care of her, okay?" He stepped toward the door and jammed his hat on his head.

"The housekeeper's room?" The girl looked highly uncertain.

"That's the guest room. And do those dishes like I told you to hours ago. Your brother'll be back in a few minutes and help you with things—so don't get into anything." He looked at Billie. "Everything you need can probably be found in the guest room. If not, the kids will get it for you. I have to get back to work, but I'll see you in the mornin' and we'll get you to Lubbock."

And then he was out the door, with no more introduction or explanation to his family than that, leaving Billie standing there, with her two bags hanging from her hands, gazing at a small girl who viewed Billie with as much friendly invitation as one did a government tax auditor.

A movement caught her eye. Two small, dark-headed, wide-eyed boys appeared on either side of Rhonda Snow, peeking around her waist and staring at Billie as if she were an apparition from the other side of midnight. If Billie had ever felt out of place, it was nothing compared to now.

Linc let the porch door bang after him and hurried to the pickup. Fleeing was what he was doing, though he acknowledged and rejected such a notion at the same time.

The memory of Billie Ballinger's face came with him, as did a faintly accusing voice. He'd have stayed and been more polite if he could have afforded to, he told the voice. Ronnie could handle it until Kit got there.

A beautiful woman, he thought, as he shifted into reverse and pressed the accelerator. He recalled the pale skin of her neck as it had led downward into her blouse. Beneath that coat he knew she had a body that just wouldn't quit. There were some women whose every movement exuded a distinct sensuality, and she was one of them. His mind considered this odd phenomenon and then played around with snatches of sexual fantasies—for about thirty seconds.

He was brought up short by the gathering warmth in his gut when he realized his fantasies were centering on a woman preparing to spend the night in his house. He wondered at his reaction to her—a reaction he hadn't experienced in longer than he could remember. He recalled her face again, and it was as if a cold wave splashed over him. God save him from a pretty woman.

Heading through the gate and out toward the east fields, he suddenly felt very tired. Very old. What could that woman be? Twenty-five at the most. He was thirty-five this year. Didn't sound so old, but he felt it.

A fine mist formed over his windshield. Was it going to rain or wasn't it? Earlier that year the rains had been plentiful—too much so. They'd washed most of the cotton seed clean to hell and had held up the wheat harvest. Then, just like some malicious devil had shut off the faucet, the rain had stopped and wind had blown and blown. Still, Linc had planted extra cotton because his gut instincts told him this was going to be a good year, both for quality cotton and a market for it.

Oh, a number of the old geezers maintained Linc had planted too late, or that he was crazy to go so all out. But Linc didn't listen to them. He was a gambler, as was any farmer, he guessed. He was gambling almost everything on this being a good year.

Dear God, let it be, he thought, though he never did really feel God was about to rearrange the universe for him.

It seemed he couldn't ever get ahead, couldn't ever stop battling—the weather, the economy, his own baser, weaker self. Again his mind played with faint, sensual thoughts. It had been over six months since he'd held a woman in his arms. He thought of Rita and how she'd felt, soft and spongy; he liked a woman with meat on her. But he'd been wise to keep his distance from Rita. He had totally quit going to the lumberyard over in Moorestown where she worked just so he wouldn't run into her. Didn't want her gettin' ideas.

Sex wasn't a requirement of life, he told himself hotly. Sex only led to a lot of trouble—either to a woman makin' a lot of demands, or to children to provide for, or to foolish feelings that tied a man's heart and guts into knots. It was a damn weakness, was what it was.

But for all those clear thoughts, Linc sometimes still experienced an ache so bad that he thought he'd die if he didn't find a way to stop it. And he knew full well having sex would do that, if only for a short while. He wondered, and not for the first time, if men and women hadn't been one of God's jokes on the world. And if blond women hadn't been one of God's jokes on him, because he certainly seemed to have a weakness for them.

For a split second he recalled Denise brushing her silky golden hair in front of the dressing table mirror. Sitting there in a slinky lace gown and doing her one hundred strokes, no matter how late, no matter if he was waiting for her in bed or the babies were crying. His thoughts turned to Billie Ballinger's silky hair, and he imagined how it would feel on his chest.

Cursing, he brought his wayward thoughts into line.

He spied the tractor to the far side of the field, running smoothly, and realized that worry over his son had lingered in the back of his mind.

This had to be only the third or fourth time he'd ever left Kit alone on the tractor, and the first at night. Still, the boy was doing okay. He was old enough, had enough experience with driving a tractor to handle it, Linc reminded himself.

However, if raising four kids had taught Linc anything, it had taught him that kids could do the craziest things for no reason. He couldn't ever remember being like that. Wild, crazy. He recalled his father's stern, forbidding face. His father had maintained that man was put on this earth to work. Linc had discovered that he had to work, and work hard, to get ahead.

When Kit climbed down from the tractor cab, Linc was struck by how tall his son had become. His eyes came to Linc's nose now. When had that happened?

"How's she runnin'?" Linc asked.

"Okay. Seems to choke up every so often, but nothin' comes of it."

Linc nodded and climbed up onto the tractor.

"Was Uncle Fred all right?"

"Oh . . . yeah. Woman's car broke down in town, and she needed a place to stay tonight." He spoke as he slipped into the seat and glanced over the gauges. "She'll be stayin' in the guest room. You go back and help your sister with it all. And you two get that kitchen cleaned up—it looks like a pigsty."

"Dad?"

Linc looked down to see Kit lingering beside the tractor, hands stuffed into his pockets.

"Tomorrow's Sunday. I won't be in school, and you'd have plenty of time to finish the plowin' then while I watch the twins—or Ronnie can watch them while I help you. She does okay. I told John maybe I could get over there for a while tonight."

Linc shook his head. "I've been trying to finish all week, and I'll do it tonight—before that comin' rain. This is a sight more important than foolin' around with hot rods."

Kit protested. "It's Saturday night, Dad. All the kids are hangin' out—and I've got to stay home and look after my stupid brothers and sister."

"Yep. That's about the size of it. Ronnie gets herself and the boys into too much trouble when we leave her alone."

In the time since the damn housekeeper had cut out, his precious daughter had crashed the lawn tractor into the garage wall, nearly poisoned Toby with some concoction in the kitchen, and freed the ants from an ant farm—a farm that hadn't even belonged to them. And those were just the incidents Linc knew of. "Now get on back to the house and see to our guest, your brothers and sister, *and* the kitchen like I told you."

His tone brooked no nonsense, and though he could fairly see Kit biting back a retort, the boy said nothing more and turned to stride off to the pickup.

That he should have praised his son's plowing flickered through Linc's thoughts, and then he started the tractor down the field, eyes focused on the ground ahead, ears listening closely to the engine much as a doctor would listen to a heartbeat.

The soil illuminated by the bright lights was a dead-gray color, the cotton plants an odd black-green dotted sparsely with white dots. But in his mind, Linc saw the rich dark loam and vibrant green plants as they were when lying beneath a bright Texas sun. He loved the earth, even when it wasn't kind to him as had been the case this year. This was his world, one he could understand.

Billie quickly decided that Linc Snow's children were very much like him. They were not given to smiles and seemed to have little knowledge of the art of polite conversation.

The girl, Rhonda, had simply said, "The room's back here." With a lofty toss of her braids, she'd led the way like a queen with her entourage.

She was slender, wearing a baggy sweatshirt and faded jeans that fell over the heels of her high-styled tennis shoes. She had a round pixie face and freckles splattered across her nose. Both her cool green eyes and the set of her shoulders indicated a person on guard against the world. And, except for the pine colored braids, she could have been mistaken for a boy.

The little boys, identical twins, had their father's dark, thick hair and cowlick in the front. One wore a red shirt, the other blue, as if a symbol for telling them apart. They were beautiful children, but oh, so solemn.

However, Billie had to admit that her experience with children was very limited. Perhaps all children acted this way toward strangers, having been instructed, and rightly so, to beware. And no doubt it wasn't every day their father brought home a stranger to spend the night.

As the children led the way through an adjoining, large and very messy laundry room, Billie wondered what was in store for her. It seemed as if no one ever washed clothes; perhaps they just stockpiled them here and bought new.

The girl opened the door to a guest room befitting a princess, or at least a high-ranking teacher. Billie stopped just inside the door and gazed about in amazement.

The room was large enough for a sitting area with a small sofa and a huge, snuggle-down-into wingback chair. There was a cherrywood coffee table in front of the sofa and a high tea table beside the chair. The carpet was a fine blushing beige, the plush kind that was wonderful in bare feet.

And the bed! A classic, it had four graceful, acorn-topped posts pointing to the ceiling and was covered in a lovely flowered spread and accented with lacy crocheted pillows. There was a chest and dresser with mirror to match the bed, draperies that matched the bedspread, and framed prints that continued the colors of greens, roses, blues. The room spoke of comfort and elegance and was certainly more reflective of a home in Virginia than in west Texas, Billie thought.

"Rita helped Daddy fix it up like this," Rhonda said. "She's a friend of our dad's."

Billie looked around to find the girl studying her with an odd intensity. At Billie's look, the child averted her face and pranced over to flop on the bed, bouncing up and down.

"Our last housekeeper quit and went to live in Florida. To play cards with old farts, Daddy said. Daddy's trying to get a new housekeeper now, but it ain't easy around here. No one likes to take care of us. We're a trial."

So apparently there was no Mrs. Snow. No wonder the house was a wreck.

Billie gazed at the child and knew the girl was trying to be big and bad. "Do you all work at being a trial or is it a natural talent?" she asked.

The child met her gaze and smirked. "Our last housekeeper said we were born trouble. Guess we're just lucky."

"It's got a big bafroom." One of the little boys ran to the end of the room, pointing. "See?" He looked very proud. "Our daddy made it."

Billie laid her bags on the bed and dutifully walked over to admire the bathroom. With all its ceramic tile and gleaming chrome, it was worthy of admiration. "It is lovely." She smiled at him, and he gave her a grin. He really was a cute little guy.

"She's seen bathrooms before, air-brain." Rhonda pushed forward, displeased at losing attention. "That's Tommy," she said as if it were very tiresome to do so, pointing at the boy who'd now lost his smile. "And that's Toby." Toby remained near the door and stared at Billie. "They're only four," she said in a lofty tone.

Billie couldn't think what she should say.

"Well—there's the TV, and you can use it." Rhonda shrugged, pushed little Tommy ahead of her to the door.

Tommy twisted around. "You wanna have some hot choc'late, lady? Ronnie's gonna make us some."

His sister gave him a quick shove and frowned over her shoulder at Billie. "I am not. I'm not supposed to turn on the stove. My brother'll be here in a few minutes, if you want hot chocolate or coffee or anything."

"I think I have all I need, thank you."

"Okay." Another shrug and Rhonda herded her brothers out of the room.

The moment the door closed there came the sounds of hushed whispers and running footsteps disappearing into the far rooms.

A real crackerjack rascal, her father would have said of Rhonda Snow, Billie thought. The term was one of mixed criticism and admiration.

Well.... She held her coat to her for a moment, then slowly, reluctant to let go of the shield, dared to slip out of it. She laid it on the bed, drew a Twinkie from one of the pockets, and moved to sit in the enormous wingback chair. Expertly she opened the packaged cake and munched on it while she gazed about.

The room *was* lovely. A longing for all she'd lost swept through her. Her own beloved house, the last one she'd lived in with her father, her bedroom with its fireplace, her library full of books, her pets, her late-model Mercedes with its mobile phone and her credit cards. And oh, her European coffeemaker—she'd love it right now.

A flash of lightning shone through the window, and Billie rose to gaze out. A tall pole lamp illuminated a yard with a silvery glow. Rain ran down the glass in rivulets. Not a hard rain, but full drops now. She was glad to be inside a house. Inside this sweet room, she thought with satisfaction and closed the drapes with a flourish.

She went to the bed and unzipped her overnight bag. One night, she thought as she pulled out her nightgown, robe, and slippers. That was all she'd be here, and it really wasn't so bad. She had all the comforts of a very nice hotel room. Actually, it greatly resembled a room she'd had in a seashore inn in France once, and she smiled, glancing around. Her own bath, television, radio...

She gazed at the telephone beside the bed. She was sorely tempted to call Marc. After his recriminations, he'd be sympathetic. He'd be there for her, if only over the telephone wire. She wouldn't be so awfully alone.

But no, she mustn't do that. She'd leaned on Marc enough. Once they'd been lovers, almost married. But, while a special friendship remained, the intimate relationship had been over long ago. Now Marc and Lisa were engaged. And Lisa was her friend, too. Billie wanted them both to be happy; they were perfect for each other. She wouldn't continue imposing on either one of them—it was way past time she stood on her own feet.

Loneliness again reared its nagging head. Marc had Lisa, Lisa had Marc, all of her friends had someone, even if temporarily. Even Billie's pets all had loving companions now. And homes to share with a loved one. Billie's life had been ripped to shreds, but the world continued to turn. People having people, people needing people. But no one needed her, and she had no one of her own. No one waited for her. She had no place in the world.

With swift turns she started the shower running into the tub, stepped in and rubbed her body with her favorite scented soap. She should enjoy the soap, she told herself, because it was expensive and when this bar was gone there would be no more.

And then the tears came. She could allow them while the water pelted her head and washed them away down the drain. The running water covered the sound of her sobs; she didn't turn it off until she knew she could stop the tears.

Coming out of the bathroom, she thought with anticipation of settling into the beautiful bed, eating another of the Twinkie cakes, and watching some good comedy on television. She'd released the tie belt of her robe and was reaching for her nightgown on the bed, when suddenly a ripple moved beneath the gown.

"Ohh!"

Billie, heart racing ninety miles an hour, drew back her hand and stared at the tiny lump that moved first one way and then skittered back again. It was as if her gown had a spirit in it. A lost and confused spirit, for now it moved in another direction.

Not taking her gaze from the lump, she retied the sash of her robe. The lump was small, about the size of her cupped palm. And elongated—like a mouse.

At the same time that she came to that conclusion a tiny white mouse poked his pointy nose and beady eyes from beneath the gown, looked at Billie for a fraction of a second while she stared, dumbfounded, at him, then raced across the bed and down the side.

Quickly Billie moved, searching the floor. Where had he gone? She most definitely did *not* wish to be in bed and that critter join her.

When the movement of his tail caught her eye, she saw the little rodent had taken shelter in her slipper. The tail disappeared and the nose reappeared. A very clean white mouse, a pet, not the barn variety. The darling Rhonda with the arched eyebrow came to mind.

Chapter Three

When Billie opened the door, Rhonda fell in at her feet.

Billie stared down, and the girl stared up. It was most definitely a toss-up as to who was more surprised. Then, looking every inch the thief caught with her hand in the collection plate, Rhonda slowly picked herself up off the floor.

"Were you waiting for something?" Billie asked sweetly. She glanced beyond the girl to the light of the kitchen shining through the laundry room. There came the sounds of rock music and water running, pans clanking.

"I, uh..." With her eyes focused on Billie's hand, the girl rubbed her palms down her baggy sweatshirt. "I just was wonderin' if you needed anything."

"No, thank you," Billie said. "Has your father come home?"

Wide-eyed, the girl shook her head. "My brother. He's...he's in the kitchen."

"I see."

Again came the grand stare off. Billie waited for the girl to speak.

Rhonda inclined her head toward Billie's hand. "Did you find him in your room?"

"What? Oh, this little guy?" Billie looked at the rodent she grasped gently yet securely. "Why, yes I did." She focused the child with an unwavering gaze. "Underneath my nightgown."

Rhonda swallowed. "He...he got away from me, and I've been looking for him."

"He's yours, then?"

The girl gave a nervous nod and licked her lips. Then she knotted her eyebrows. "I'm usually the only one who can catch him."

"Oh, I didn't catch him. I invited him to come to me for a few crumbs of Twinkie. He liked it." Billie deliberately beamed at the mouse, as if she found him the most fascinating and adorable creature in all the world.

Rhonda stared at her.

"Well, here he is then."

Billie handed the mouse over, and the child took him with extreme care, then lifted suspicious eyes to Billie.

"Good night," Billie said.

The child, looking highly skeptical, nodded and walked quietly away through the dim laundry room. She looked a very small, subdued child, without a hint of rascal left.

Billie closed the door quietly and rested against it. A sliver of regret tugged at her. That child had expected her to scream with terror and call for help, and Billie had gone and ruined her fun.

However, the regret passed quickly enough. The idea that she could have found herself sharing her robe with a mouse was not a pleasant thought.

Linc didn't awake until after six-thirty. That was sleeping in over an hour for him, and he did it because it'd been nearly two by the time he'd gotten to bed the previous night. He dozed for a few minutes, then rolled to his back—or almost to his back. Toby was there to prevent him.

Linc shifted so he could look at his son. The boy slept deeply, long dark eyelashes touching his creamy cheek, his thumb stuck loosely in his mouth. Linc pulled the thumb from Toby's mouth and the blanket up over his legs. His arm hovered there with the strong, fearful urge to hug the boy. He didn't. He wanted to, but he didn't, couldn't explain why he rarely could bring himself to touch any of his children.

Toby and Tommy had been an accident. He and Denise had two children already and certainly hadn't needed any more. Denise had wanted to abort them, but he'd persuaded her not to. And now sometimes Linc was at a loss as to what to do with them. He thought of a brief description of an adult he'd heard once: an adult is the one who cleans up the puke. It was apt. An adult, which he was supposed to be, certainly didn't have all the answers.

Of all his kids, Toby seemed to have the most trouble living without a mother. Tommy suffered, too, though he was able to cope by fastening onto Rhonda.

"What you need is a wife," his brother Wes had told him. Wes was good at handing out free advice, both Wes and his sharp-tongued wife Ginny, but not at providing any help that could possibly mean work on their part. Neither could be bothered to look after the kids even for an afternoon.

Wife? Oh, no. Never again, Linc thought. Not on his life. He wasn't going through that pain again.

Quietly he forced his stiff body out of the bed and found Tommy curled in a ball at the foot. It was a miracle the kid hadn't fallen off. He hoisted Tommy up beside his brother and tucked the covers around both of them. Tommy murmured but didn't wake.

Linc paused and stood there in his jockey shorts, gazing down at the boys. His sons. Pride and protectiveness swelled within him. Then he winced. It appeared he was going to have to rehire Coralee Hutch as housekeeper. Ronnie and the boys hated her. And Linc couldn't blame them. It could be said that Coralee Hutch had a heart of gold—cold and hard.

In the bathroom, he washed his face and, thinking of their guest downstairs, decided to shave, then slapped on some of his good after-shave. He also chose a blue-and-brown plaid shirt the housekeeper had ironed before she'd left. After all, he would be driving into the city that day.

He wondered for a few minutes about Billie Ballinger— *her* as he termed her. Woman traveling alone. Didn't think she was married. There hadn't been a ring on her finger. He'd been pretty rude last night, was sorry, but couldn't change it. He'd had his reasons, and they were damn good ones. No profit in being attracted to the woman.

Linc felt good, felt as if he could take his first clean breath in weeks. At last he'd gotten the cotton laid by. He'd done what he could and done it well; it was up to nature now. Through the window he saw a silvery glow of a morning heavy with a rainy mist. Summer clung tenaciously, but fall was pushing in fast. They'd had a heavy rain, turning the fields to mud just as he'd feared, but that no longer mattered because he'd gotten his job done.

He started to whistle as he dressed, then broke off. It wasn't likely that the boys would awaken, but he was taking no chances. The mornings were precious to him. With four children, early morning was his only chance to be completely alone, to drink his coffee in peace and read the paper. And to ensure this he carried his boots down the hall, walked softly in his sock feet and was careful to miss the floorboards that squeaked.

He was going down the stairs and anticipating working the Sunday paper's crossword puzzle when he caught the faint odor of something that smelled suspiciously like coffee. He rounded the newel and saw a shaft of light falling into the hall.

Someone in the kitchen. Damn! Irritation mingled with the calm voice of reason within him. He'd thought Kit and Ronnie asleep. Or it could be *her*. Whoever it was, he resented this intrusion into his time—but perhaps no one was there and the light had simply been left on, the coffee scent left over.

No such luck. Billie Ballinger sat at the table. He paused and, for just an instant, the sharp ache of dreams long ago crushed and buried, opened in his chest.

She looked up and saw him. A welcoming smile crossed her face, then faded into uncertainty. Well, her uncertainty was better than his, he told himself hotly, then suddenly remembered he still held his boots in his hand. He set them to the floor and began to put them on then and there, immediately regretting it because he wobbled like a tipsy stork.

"Good morning," she said quietly.

"'Mornin'."

He gave her a brief glance, then focused downward and softly stamped his left foot to press his heel into the boot. However, the brief glance was enough to see that she looked exactly as she had the previous evening—very good. And damn it! She was reading his newspaper. He hated for anyone to get to his paper before him!

"I took the liberty of making coffee and toast. I hope you don't mind."

She'd woken up worried and hungry and in great need of a cup of coffee. She still felt in need of a cup of coffee because the packaged variety in Mr. Snow's cupboard fell far short of the kind she used to buy—the rich beans Mr. Rose ground only when she was ready to leave the store so it would be as fresh as possible.

"Not at all," he replied.

But he seemed to mind. A night's sleep didn't appear to have improved his disposition any. The man was forbidding to say the least. And also very much a man.

That thought came as she swept her gaze across his lean muscled back. It came also as an amusing surprise, as was the sudden sharp awareness of him. She'd experienced such sexual awareness in the past—but never at this time of the morning. Or with such a grouch of a man. She hid a smile in her cup. Human beings were an odd bunch.

He poured himself a cup of coffee and took the chair across from her. Somehow Billie knew it was his accustomed chair. Something in the way he slid into the seat and leaned forward on the table spoke of comfort and familiarity. He became a bit less forbidding. He was simply a grump. Or a man carrying around an aching heart.

"You're up mighty early," he said, more of an accusation than friendly chitchat.

"I'm an early riser by nature, and I usually catch a nice nap in the afternoon."

"Nap? Nice if you have the time."

Meaning, of course, that it was a frivolous thing to do. "Yes," she agreed. "It is." She didn't think it frivolous. And feeling the need to defend herself for taking naps seemed rather silly. She pushed the neatly reassembled paper toward him. "I heard it land on the porch. That's convenient, it being delivered all the way up the drive. I never could get my paper delivered any farther than my driveway entry—usually in the gutter there."

"Friend of Kit's—my oldest son—delivers the Sunday paper. The rest of the week it's stuck in the box down by the road."

He had deeply tanned hardworking hands. Blunt fingers stained with dirt that he probably couldn't get out. Strong hands.

He singled out the classified section, and Billie took that as a cue to cut the conversation. She was willing; she wasn't much company before two cups of coffee either. She took up the comics.

Linc found the right page, folded the paper in half and laid it on the table, sipping his coffee and scanning the headings until he found the domestics section. There it was: his ad. Seemed an unnecessary and silly thing to do to look up his own ad, and to circle it as he did then with a pencil, but he always did. As if he'd find an answer to it printed right below or the telephone would immediately ring when he read it. Still, he'd paid for it, and he wanted to make certain it was there, that the telephone number was correct. It was, but they'd spelled his name Link. Didn't matter.

He tossed the page and pencil aside and rose to get more coffee, bringing the pot back to pour some into her cup. He kept thinking *her* or *she;* Miss Ballinger seemed too formal and Billie too familiar. Far too familiar. Her head was bent; she was reading the comics, which figured somehow. He caught the bare hint of an expensive perfume, not heavy, just there, a part of her. He gazed at her hair. It was like silk waving enticingly. It'd been a long time since he'd filled his hands with a woman's hair.

She looked up when he poured the coffee into her cup. "Thanks." Her smile was the sun coming out from behind the clouds.

"Sure." He nodded and moved to sit back down. He felt easier now about having his special private time invaded. It wasn't so bad.

"Did you get done with what you were doing last night?" she asked as she stirred an enormous spoonful of sugar into her coffee. He took his black, and just the thought of so much sugar made his teeth ache.

"Yep." He nodded, feeling the satisfaction of a job well done flow over him again.

"What do you grow?" She gazed at him over the rim of her cup, her expression curious.

"Cotton, mostly. Some wheat and corn, bit of alfalfa."

Her gaze dropped to his hands, then moved back to his face, studying him. "Do you do a lot of work at night?" It clearly puzzled her. "I mean, I just never heard much about farmers doing that."

He smiled. There was a lot about farming that wouldn't be found in glossy magazines.

"An awful lot of farming is done after dusk-thirty," he said. "That's why tractors have big headlights on 'em. I wanted to make one last pass at the weeds before the rain. Some rains—like last night—turn the fields into a bog that's even too much for the tractor. I won't be able to take the tractor back into the field for several days at least. But it doesn't matter now, 'cause I've done the last of the fooling with the cotton 'til harvest. It's not too good to be disturbin' the plant once it starts flowering."

"I'm sorry to have interrupted you. You did get it all done, then?" Her eyebrows knotted with deep concern.

"It's done."

"Good."

Then he realized they were both staring at each other. That she was looking at him with the same interest that he was looking at her.

He averted his eyes and took a deep swallow of coffee, then asked, "What do you do?"

She didn't answer immediately, kept her gaze on the table. "Nothing at the moment. I'm between jobs."

Linc got the distinct impression she didn't want to talk about it, so he didn't press. It wasn't his business. He wondered, though. She wore a small gold ring on one of her little fingers, no wedding band, as he'd thought before, no evidence of having worn one. Her hands were soft, her fingernails long and carefully manicured—not the hands of a woman who did a lot of anything, he didn't think. But he figured her silky blouse and that fancy, rhinestone-studded denim coat she'd been wearing couldn't have come off the rack. She'd paid plenty for them. The curiosity that sprang hard and strong within surprised him.

"Fred said something about you headin' down to the Gulf," he said.

She nodded. "A friend has lent me a cottage on Padre Island."

"Pretty nice down there—you ever been?" He wondered if her "friend" was a guy. It figured.

"Yes . . . a number of times. It's lovely."

"The coast had a pretty bad oil spill a while back. Damaged miles of beach property."

"I know," she said, nodding and sipping her coffee. "But it all stayed north of Patty's place, thank heaven."

So the friend was a woman.

"I really do thank you for putting me up and taking me into Lubbock," she said then. Her eyes were the color of the sky in winter—clear, perfect blue. "I really wouldn't have liked staying the night in my car."

"It's no problem. Like I said, we had the room." Wary of the vibrations sparking between them—and, by damn, he didn't think it was all one-sided on his part—he mentally took a step backward and physically sat back in his chair.

"What do you suppose it's going to cost to have my car towed into Lubbock?"

"Oh . . ." He shrugged. ". . . at least twenty-five just for the truck to come out, then probably a dollar a mile to tow in. Not less than sixty-five dollars, I'd guess."

She grew pensive as she digested his words. "Is a fuel pump a very expensive thing to have repaired?" Her eyes darkened.

"Probably about thirty-five dollars for the part, if they can get one to fit a T-bird of that era. I imagine, though, there's modifyin' that can be done to get one to fit. The labor is what'll cost the most."

She didn't say anything, and Linc wondered about her.

"Dad?"

It was Kit's voice, and, catching an edge of excitement in his tone, Linc started up from his chair. "Yeah?"

Kit came trotting through the doorway and abruptly halted, as if he'd been smacked between the eyes with a two-by-four. The boy apparently hadn't met the woman last night. His eyes riveted on Billie Ballinger and gave definition to the term bug-eyed adolescent with hormones on overdrive. And maybe memory, too, because in that instant it occurred to Linc what the boy might see—that this woman looked like Denise. No, Linc decided immediately. That wasn't the look on Kit's face by a long shot. Linc took a deep breath and hoped his son didn't make a complete fool of himself—and his father.

She smiled at his son. "Hello."

"Ah . . . hello," Kit managed and swiped at his hair that was all awry from sleep. He looked as if he'd just sprung from the bed and wore faded denims and a white T-shirt that Linc was willing to bet he'd slept in.

"Kit, this is our houseguest of last night, Miss Billie Ballinger."

His eyes still glued on her, the boy walked forward and somehow managed to trip on his own big, bare feet. Much to her credit, she ignored it, stuck out her hand in the same way she probably would have to the President himself.

"Nice to meet you, Kit."

"Uh . . . nice to meet you." Linc's son shook her hand and kept hold of it until she gently eased away.

"Do you want some coffee?" Linc asked him.

"Ah, yeah." Kit pretty well recovered himself then. "But, Dad . . ." He twisted and pointed to the side porch door.

"Larry's tow truck just pulled in our drive towin' this really neat Thunderbird . . . bright red . . ."

Before Kit finished speaking, Linc was striding toward the door. Billie Ballinger came right at his heels. Just as he reached the door and glanced through the window, he saw Uncle Fred opening the screen door of the porch. George Beasley was with him.

Billie quickly followed Linc Snow through the door and out onto the porch. There sat her precious car, rear end hooked up to a tow truck. It looked so pitiful, forlorn, embarrassed. But it was safe, and she was astoundingly glad to see it.

"Larry's tow truck was just sittin' there," Fred explained. "He said he didn't care if we used it. He don't care about much of anythin' but calamine lotion at this point. George came out to give me a lift." He nodded to George, who remained on the other side of the screen.

"Oh, thank you, Fred . . . George." She smiled at each one and felt foolish tears burning back of her eyes. George grinned in return. Fred quirked his lips into what might or might not be a smile, but his eyes twinkled.

Fred gestured and held the screen door for her. "Didn't know when you'd be able to get a tow truck out here, and didn't think it was such a good idea to leave a car like this 'un out on the side of the road. Not much mischief goes on around here, but you can't tell 'bout people passin' through. Where do you want her?" He looked at Linc.

"Right there's okay."

"Figured so."

Fred got inside the tow truck, and the cable slowly began to lower the T-bird's rear bumper.

"Wow! This yours, Miss Ballinger?" Kit, now in a denim jacket and untied tennis shoes, bounced around the Thunderbird, bending and inspecting the vehicle with the enthusiasm of youth.

"Yes." Billie grinned. She folded her arms and hugged her waist against the chilly air and stood gazing at the car. Yes, she thought proudly. She'd saved this prize from the auction block; it'd been the one thing she'd refused to sell, even when the IRS had started breathing down her neck. In the end Marc had made everything turn out right, and she was still able to enjoy being the Good Queen of the World from time to time.

"What year is it?" Kit asked.

"The first year they were made—1955. Original V-8 engine and leather interior, has every possible accessory. Cost my father over $3,000 then."

"Bet it's worth a lot more now." The boy's eyes were wide with awe.

"Yes...considerably more." She turned. "I'll get the keys, and you can sit in it."

"I'll get them, Miss Ballinger...where are they?" Like a jackrabbit, the boy was already heading for the house.

"My purse—on the table by the bed."

There followed considerable inspection and admiration of the vehicle. Even Fred bent his tall frame behind the wheel and recalled for his eager young grandnephew the time he'd first seen a Thunderbird back in 1955. It'd always seemed odd to him that the thing had only two seats—rather a gyp for the money. Rhonda and the twins, too, who came from the house still dressed in their footie pajamas, took a turn. Only Linc stood back, reserved. And very alone, Billie thought. She wondered again about a Mrs. Snow and if she'd died. Why else would the man be alone with his children?

Fred and his friend George, declined staying for breakfast; George wanted to attend a farm auction up near Clovis, and Fred had agreed to join him for the drive. "Old men don't need to be driving on these back roads alone—nor young ladies, either," he said, wagging a finger at Billie.

The only payment he'd allow Billie to make was ten dollars to pay Larry for the tow truck's gas, nothing more. Touched by his generosity, Billie wanted so much to repay him. Something of worth to share with him. All she had was herself, and heaven knew at the moment that wasn't much. Yet, when she lifted on tiptoe and gave the old man a kiss on his cheek, his expression made her feel grand.

"You get to Heaven again—" he winked "—you come to the café, gal."

"I certainly will, Fred. And I'll have fries the next time."

* * *

In the kitchen, while Linc began cooking breakfast, Billie sat at the table with the children. Kit eagerly brought Billie a cup of fresh coffee, and Rhonda and the twins enjoyed hot chocolate.

"Hot chocolate is Toby's favorite thing," Tommy told Billie seriously.

They were both such serious little boys, she thought. And she felt the odd need to be equally so. "Is it?" She looked at Toby, who sat beside his brother in the same chair. Their chins barely peeked above the rim of the table.

The boy nodded. Billie realized she'd never heard him speak.

"Your dad sure took good care of that car," Kit said and leaned forward on the table. "It looks just like it came off the line."

"Yes. Cars were his business." She smiled at his eagerness. "He had a car dealership back in the days when he bought the T-bird. Later he went into dealing in special and rare vehicles. He would often find antique ones and have them fully restored, then offer them for sale. Other times someone would engage him to find a certain vehicle and remake it how they wanted it."

"He must have known a lot about cars," Kit said with admiration.

"Well…he knew about their design and how each should look. But he didn't get into fixing them himself. He hired that done. He did a great deal of research to be able to make the car look absolutely authentic, but he wasn't mechanical at all. He probably wasn't certain of the difference between a wrench or pair of pliers."

She chuckled, and Kit smiled. He was a handsome youth. His hair was fair, a light brown, and his eyes were blue. Probably drove the girls crazy at school. Not much resemblance to his father, she thought—except maybe for the hint of a cowlick to the side of his forehead.

"O-our da-daddy c-c-can," Toby said, and it was clearly difficult for him. He immediately averted his eyes to his cup, and a hush fell over the kitchen. So stuttering was why the boy remained so quiet, Billie thought.

"I imagine your daddy can fix just about anything, can't he?" she asked, paying no heed to his speech and wanting to give him a chance to say more.

He bobbed his head. He cast those at the table a hesitant glance, then said, "Ye-s. A-and Kit, t-too." He sent his older brother a bare smile, and Kit returned it.

"I haven't been able to fix that carburetor on the tractor," Linc said from the stove, frowning.

"I like messin' with engines," Kit said shyly. He started to say more when his sister drew his attention.

Rhonda had slipped from the room and reappeared, flopping into her chair. She started to set a cage on the table, then glanced at her father and settled it into her lap. "Do you like mice, Miss Ballinger?" She regarded Billie with that suspicious raised eyebrow again.

"I never thought deeply about *liking* them," Billie replied.

"Most people are scared of them."

Billie shrugged. "My mother always rather liked them, and we had several when I was a kid."

"Your mother?" Clearly nonplussed, Rhonda stuck out her chin and gazed at Billie with eyes as round as dinner plates.

"My mother was on the board of the national People for Animal Welfare," Billie said dryly. "When I was a kid, we had animals coming and going—not just dogs and cats but things like geese and snakes. I never did like snakes, though."

"These are my mice." The girl lifted the cage, and for a split second Billie recognized something of herself in the child. The wonder and pleasure in living creatures. "That one there's Whitie. You met him last night," the girl said in a rushed whisper. "Wanna hold 'im again?"

"Don't you get him out of there!" Linc commanded from over at the stove.

"Aw, Dad . . . she likes mice."

"Does your mother still let you have a lot of animals?" little Tommy suddenly injected very seriously.

"My mother's been dead a long time," she told him softly, wondering at the intensity of his eyes.

"O-our..."

"Our mother is gone, too," Tommy said, breaking into his brother's speech.

"Yeow! Damn!" Linc dropped the pan of canned biscuits he'd taken from the oven and shook his fingers, having obviously burned them.

"No, don't do that," Billie said when he reached to put butter on the burn. She jumped up and came around the table.

"Why not?"

"Because you're supposed to put it in cold water." She began running water in the sink. The doctor had told Billie that once when she'd scorched her hand.

The silly man glared at her. Looking down to see two huge red welts on two of his fingers, she grabbed his hand, stuck the burns beneath the running water, and held them there.

"Why didn't you use a hot pad?" she said.

"I did—it was just in the other hand," he fired back. "And I've always put grease on a burn."

"Modern medicine has made great strides in burn treatment since you learned to do that."

"She's right, Dad," Kit said, digging into the freezer for ice cubes.

Billie watched the water run over Linc's fingers and then her gaze slipped to her hand closed over the top of his. It was starkly pale against his sun-darkened skin. She was holding his hand; her thigh was brushing his. And they'd actually barked at each other, this stranger and her. She'd corrected and criticized him in his very own house. In front of his own children.

She looked up to find his face only inches from her own. His eyes were a startling green with vibrant gold flecks, and they were staring at her. Angry. And hot. And not all from anger.

Chapter Four

She let go of his hand and stepped away.

"Here, Dad. Stick your hand in this bowl." Kit shoved a bowl of ice at him. Linc took the bowl and pushed it and his hand beneath the running water.

Rhonda poked forward to look at his hand and said, "Mrs. Oakley taught us to use ice water for burns." Clearly they all knew more than he did.

Linc gazed at his hand and kept seeing *hers* closed around it.

The twins had to be shown. "I-it's o-o-okay?" Toby asked with frightened eyes, and Linc assured him it was.

Kit helped Linc get breakfast on the table. Toby insisted on clinging to Linc's leg until his sister and brother and Billie Ballinger appeared to be having such a good time with the mouse that he had to go see, too.

The woman actually held each mouse and *crooned* to them. Together, she and the kids discussed how mice were very tiny and hairless when born, about how they made their nests when in the wild—wild walls of a house, Linc thought—and what they ate. He wondered how a woman like her knew all these things.

During breakfast, Ronnie listed for Billie Ballinger her favorite animals. Kit talked about the old jumble of junk that he and his friend John thought of as the hot rod they were building, and even Tommy and Toby managed to have their say. Somewhere in there *she* told the kids to call her Billie and that it was short for Wilhelmina.

Wilhelmina? Linc observed her over the rim of his coffee cup. Blond hair, nearly the color Denise's had been, that waved against her cheeks, and blue, blue eyes. A perfect nose, and lips that tilted upward at the corners. Probably because she smiled a lot. Bubbled, and it was annoying.

As he set his cup on the table, he swept them all with a quick, casual glance. They were talking to Billie Ballinger, listening to her. Carrying on conversation. He could've dropped dead right there in his chair and no one would have noticed.

The next instant her gaze came around and met his. Linc immediately averted his eyes, pushed back his chair, and stacked his and the twins' plates. They'd finished breakfast; it was time he got the ball rolling. He had a lot to do that day besides sit around a table and watch his children and Wilhelmina Ballinger having a good time.

"Hey, Dad, why don't we give a shot at fixing Billie's car?" Kit said.

Linc sent the dishes clattering into the sink.

"We can probably get it goin', Dad." The kid was about to rocket out of his seat. "I'll bet I can get a fuel pump we can make fit from one of the cars over at John's." He turned back to *her.* "I have this friend whose dad keeps a lot of old cars around. It's not a real junkyard, but he has collected a lot of parts."

It was a real junkyard, Linc thought and covertly studied Billie Ballinger.

No, was his immediate reaction to the proposal. Everything inside him told him so. It would interrupt his life. He wouldn't get any of his paperwork done, wouldn't get a chance to fiddle with the tractor carburetor, again, wouldn't have time for his crossword puzzle.

And *she'd* be around here all day long then.

Quite suddenly he hated like hell to face the paperwork or to fiddle with the tractor carburetor, and he could always do the crossword puzzle later that evening. The chance for an afternoon of doing something unexpected, something that had nothing to do with the farm, seemed very attractive. And spending a few more hours with Billie Ballinger didn't seem all that intolerable, either. Hell, it wasn't anything at all.

But then she said, "No...I don't think so. You've done enough for me already. I couldn't impose further."

Before Linc could speak, Kit was saying how it wouldn't be any trouble and how good he was with cars. The boy would give up dinner for a week just to fiddle around with as grand a specimen as that T-bird. Which went to show how Linc was muffing it as a father, he thought dryly. And no doubt the thought of amateurs messing around with her classic made her blood run cold.

"Kit," he said in a voice that got his son's attention. "Miss Ballinger has a trip to continue on. She doesn't need two people who can *maybe* fix her car. She needs a qualified mechanic to repair it with the proper part, not something rigged up. Now, let's get crackin' so she can get a tow truck out here to haul the T-bird to the city this afternoon."

And that was that. Linc had his business to attend to; she had hers. For a few minutes there he'd forgotten that.

He turned away from the faces at the table and continued cleaning up the kitchen. He heard her mention luggage in her trunk and Kit volunteer, then hurry out to get it. The telephone rang. Ronnie and the twins scuffled, each trying to be first to answer it. Linc wondered if he'd ever get things caught up around the house and the farm.

"Dad..." Ronnie's small voice quivered with cold anger. "...it's Coralee Hutch. She says this is the only time she can talk to you."

Linc paused and winced. Damn! He hadn't wanted the kids to know he was talking to Coralee Hutch.

"I'll tell her we're too busy right now." And she began to do just that.

"Ronnie!" He hastily grabbed a towel for his wet hands, and strode across the room. His kids stared at him, and he was as conscious of Billie Ballinger's presence as he would have been a sharply focused camera following his movements.

"Here's Daddy, Mrs. Hutch," Ronnie said in a rude voice, then held the receiver out to him. Sending him a scorching glance, she moved a bare three inches away, staring up at him. Hand to the hip, hard dare glinting in her eyes.

"Hello, Mrs. Hutch. Give me a second while I change phones." He covered the speaker and hissed, "Hang this one up when I get on the office extension, Ronnie." And he wouldn't allow funny business. His daughter nodded, though her jutting chin and accusing eyes didn't give an inch.

Billie, replacing the butter and jams into the refrigerator, thought of what a lovely house this was, or what she'd seen of it. She'd taken a few steps into the hallway that morning before Linc had come down, stealthy steps, feeling as if she were a Peeping Tom. She'd seen mostly white walls and lots of polished oak woodwork. It even had hardwood floors, not common these days. The entire house was built along the traditional lines of a hundred years ago. Solid, old-fashioned and comfortable for a family.

A wealth of old memories, long-forgotten dreams, stirred in her chest. Her mother had died when she was nine; Billie couldn't truthfully say she remembered her. Her mother had been a casual parent at best, having made a career of the good causes to which she was devoted. Billie's father, Michael Ballinger, had been wonderful, the best a father could be, and yet with him, too, the roles of parent and child had often been reversed. Billie had always longed for a full family, for brothers and sisters to argue and laugh with. And a homey house to live in, love in. It was at times, rare times, thankfully, when she had occasion to be around children that she was confronted with her infertility. She'd come to terms with that cruel fact years before, suspected even that she might not have been the greatest mother in the world.

Yet still, her foolish human heart couldn't entirely give up the dream of having a family of her own.

Closing the refrigerator door, she suddenly realized the room had become very quiet. She turned and located the twins on their knees on the couch, peering over the back and staring with white, solemn faces at their sister. Rhonda stood staring back at them, her face, too, a pasty white, her jaw clamped hard.

Something was very wrong, Billie thought, sharp concern slipping down her spine, her gaze flying to the telephone. The phone call. Had something happened? Some relative fallen ill?

She started to ask, then stopped, moving instead to clean the final dishes from the table. Her sudden urge of protectiveness had no place here. She was a stranger in this home, a guest passing through. An intruder plopped here by a strange twist of fate but leaving at any moment. Then she glanced at little Ronnie and the twins again and thought how they certainly needed something—and she was the only one there.

Kit came in the door. "I set your suitcases on the porch. We'll put them in the Suburban when we leave." He stopped and looked at his sister.

"Dad's talking to Coralee Hutch," the girl pronounced as if declaring he were talking to the devil.

The two shared a mutual expression of despair. Kit's jaw muscle worked, and his head swung around at the echo of their father's footsteps approaching through the hallway.

Whoever was Coralee Hutch? Partly uncertain as just what to do and partly curious, Billie stood there.

Linc Snow paused in the entryway, flicked a glance to each of his children and to Billie, then walked over to lift a ring of keys from a rack hung near the back door. His hard face revealed no emotion. "You kids brush your teeth and let's get going."

"You're hiring her again, aren't you?" Rhonda spit the words at him and clenched her fists.

This was not a good time to be plunked down in the midst of this household, Billie thought, and she decided immediate retreat was the most polite choice given the awkward circumstances. She headed for the guest room, recalling how Linc Snow hadn't wanted to be bothered with her. She'd blamed him for his inhospitable attitude, and she'd been wrong to do that. This was apparently a bad moment for this family, for the sky wasn't blue if there wasn't trouble here.

"Yes, Ronnie, I am." Linc Snow's voice, low but quite distinct, reached her in the laundry room, and Billie paused in the guest room doorway.

"Dad..." Kit began, but his sister burst into his speech. "We've had her already, and we don't want her again. You said we would get somebody else."

Billie heard the fury in the child's voice and took hold of the doorjamb. She thought she should probably close the door, but she didn't. No one *knew* she was standing there listening.

"I've tried to get someone else, Ronnie. You know that. I've had an ad in the paper every day for four weeks. The only other people to apply have been totally unacceptable."

"Coralee Hutch isn't acceptable," the child said, stumbling over the last word. But there was no hesitancy in her voice, no quivering before the man whom Billie quite clearly imagined glaring with equal fury at the child. "I'd rather have an old wino or person with half a brain than to have her."

A crackerjack rascal, Billie thought. And probably one trial for any housekeeper.

"Mrs. Hutch will come and stay during the week and return to her sister's on the weekends." Linc Snow's voice vibrated with strained patience. "We've got to have someone here to look after Tommy and Toby during the day so I can work, Ronnie. I've got a living to earn."

"You could hire someone to work for you and *you* take care of us," the child screamed. "But you won't do that! I hate Coralee Hutch! I hate her! And I won't have her...I won't!"

The pain in the girl's voice sent a sharp chill across Billie's chest. She clutched the doorjamb.

"She will be coming, Ronnie, and that's the end of it," Linc Snow said in a low, steely voice. "Now, you kids do like I said and get ready to go into Lubbock."

Silence. Then the sound of footsteps running away into the house, stomping up the stairs.

"I'll stay home with the kids, Dad."

That was Kit, and imagining his youthful, tender face, Billie laid her head on her hand that still clung to the door-jamb.

"You will all come. We'll *all* take Miss Ballinger to a hotel and then go to a movie together and have a good afternoon." It was a command to have fun, and Billie could just see Linc Snow's stubbornly set jaw—the one his daughter had so clearly inherited. "Now help your brothers."

Heavy, deliberate footsteps, the back door opening and closing with a hard rattle. Kit hollering at the twins, "You heard Dad!" and footsteps scampering away.

There wasn't much for her to do. She had all her things together in her overnight bag and purse, just as when she'd come. She slipped into her denim coat, straightened the collar and looked around the room. She guessed this was where the dreaded Coralee Hutch would stay, and she didn't like it. Anyone children could dislike as much as that couldn't be very nice.

She picked up her bags and walked out of the room. In the kitchen she paused, wondering if she should take a moment for more cleaning up. It seemed a way to repay her host, something she was *capable* of doing. She would leave the table set right, she thought, and reached for the cloth to wipe up. She stacked the woven place mats back in the middle of the table and placed the holder for salt and pepper shakers and napkins atop them. Finding a small pair of slippers in a chair, she set them out in the open.

As she again refolded the newspaper that had been tossed to the floor beside Linc Snow's chair, she saw a large circle penciled on one of the pages of the classifieds, under domestics. *Wanted: live-in housekeeper for single man and four children. Private room and bath, gd sal, benfts, Heaven area.* Then there was his name, spelled Link, and telephone number.

Billie gazed at the ad for a long moment, thinking that it was probably the admission of the Heaven area that scared applicants away. Perhaps if he advertised the lovely room, he'd have better luck. Unless word of Linc Snow himself had gotten around. Or his daughter, who was the spitting image of him.

Linc had the garage door open and was putting Billie Ballinger's suitcases into the back of the Suburban when she stepped out of the house. He heard the kitchen door softly open and close, the screen door creak before he looked over at her. What had just gone on in his kitchen wasn't any of her business, and he didn't care what she thought. And he wished she hadn't been there and heard. He didn't like people to be privy to his private life.

Her footsteps made a soft crunching sound on the gravel and stopped close to him. He caught sight of her expensive blue boots and those legs that stretched to the Gulf. He stood and looked straight into her eyes before he caught himself.

"We'll take off soon as the kids come down," he said, extending his hand for the tote bag she carried. She handed it over.

The Suburban was only a year old, metallic brown, with plush velour seats and every conceivable luxury offered. Linc felt an absurd prick of pride at producing it to drive her into the city. He didn't miss the surprise that flickered in her eyes as she looked over both the Suburban and the shiny late-model Ford stretch-cab pickup parked there beside it. She'd probably thought their only vehicle was the farm truck she'd ridden in last night. Well, it didn't matter what she thought, anyway, he thought as he slammed the double doors.

She'd walked a few feet down the drive and stood there looking around. He stared at her hair. Denise's hair had been that same length when they'd gotten married. And silky like that, nice against the palm of his hand.

He walked out to join her. The sky glowed as if lit by a giant fluorescent light, the sun burning through the clouds. Raindrops sparkled on everything. The scents of fresh, wet earth and the nearby boxwood bushes were strong in the uncommonly still air. And *her* scent came to him, too.

"You have a beautiful place here, Mr. Snow."

"We like it."

"How far away to your nearest neighbor?"

"About a mile that way. Can't see it because there's a dip in the land."

She turned her head toward him, slanted her eyes. "For a child to hate someone so vehemently as your daughter does this Hutch woman, there must be a reason." The statement that was more of a question vibrated in the air.

Anger flashed across his shoulders. It was on the tip of his tongue to tell her it wasn't any of her damn business. He stopped himself, rubbing the side of his nose. He knew what she was thinking, and he wouldn't have anyone, especially *her,* thinking he'd turn his kids over to the care of some monster. And maybe it was to her credit that she'd spoken, he thought grudgingly. He took a breath and gazed off down the drive.

"Coralee Hutch isn't Aunt Bea of Mayberry. She doesn't allow eating anywhere but the kitchen, the kids have to take their shoes off when they come in the door and clean their rooms daily. She believes that idleness is the devil's workshop and that television and video games are right up there with the seven deadly sins. She believes children should be seen and not heard and that they have to be whipped into line or they're all in danger of goin' to hell."

He looked her in the eyes. "She is a hard woman and wouldn't win any Miss Jolly awards, but she's not abusive. She's never laid a hand on any of my children—on any children that I know of."

"Are you certain of that?"

"Yes, ma'am, I am. Ronnie would have been the first to shout it to the housetops if Coralee ever stepped out of line in such a way."

She seemed to digest this. Then she nodded. "I imagine Rhonda is quite a match for Ms. Hutch." Her lips twitched, and her eyes crinkled.

"Oh, she can pretty well hold her own." She could, and Linc was proud of that, though he wasn't about to let on to anyone.

At the sound of the kitchen door opening, they both turned. Kit hustled the twins out and across the porch.

"Where's Ronnie?" Suspicion tugged at Linc.

"I figured she was out here already."

"She's not. Go back in and hurry her up."

Linc swore under his breath. He'd known he hadn't heard the last of Ronnie's displeasure over Coralee Hutch. No doubt his daughter was going to strive to make life difficult for everyone in her resentment of the situation. He would gladly leave them all here at the house while he drove into Lubbock, except for one thing—he didn't want to make that drive alone with *her*. He wasn't certain why he didn't and halfway recognized the feeling as foolish, but there it was. And by damn, his kids were always plaguing him to take them to a movie in the city!

By the time Kit came out of the house, Linc had a knot of irritation in his stomach. That knot grew to the size of a bowling ball when Kit said he couldn't find his sister. Commanding everyone to help look, Linc strode into the house, calling and searching for his precious daughter and wishing secretly to run and hide himself.

To leave and never come back. It worked for some people.

The term high and low applied to the search. Billie went with the twins and looked in small places on the grounds, while Kit and Linc Snow checked the tree house in the backyard and two big barns down the lane behind the house, even climbing around in the hay bales and tractors and equipment. Not finding the child in any of these places, Linc Snow took one pickup to search the blacktopped highway, and Kit took the other down the farm road farther away to a couple of places he thought his sister might go.

Tommy and Toby led Billie everywhere they could think their sister might hide. That included the doghouse, for a dog that had since run away, the shed saved especially for baby calves when they had any, and the shed where feed and yard tools were kept. They checked beneath the porch and behind bushes and through the garage.

Then finally, when she was alone, Billie came upon the girl in the one place no one had thought to look—the guest room. The room that would soon belong to Coralee Hutch.

The girl sat on the floor, easily hidden from view in the generous space between the bed and the wall. Walking by and seeing her came as a surprise. Billie stared at her, and Rhonda stared back.

Slowly Billie went over to sit on the edge of the bed. How typical it was that none of them had thought to look in this room, she thought. It was the most obvious of hiding places, so therefore the best.

"You were awfully clever to hide in here, Ronnie," she said. Somewhere during all that time of hearing Linc Snow and the boys calling the girl's name, the child had become Ronnie to Billie, too.

Her face jerked upwards, as if surprised that her choice of hiding place could be thought clever by anyone. Then she shrugged. "Yeah. I guess." Wallowing in dejection, she gazed at her feet and pulled at a string hanging from her sock. When Billie didn't say anything for long seconds, she cocked her head and peered up. "Is Daddy really mad?"

Billie thought. "Have you ever seen one of those Spanish bullfights on TV? I saw a real one once in Spain. Well, I think your dad is the spitting image of one of those bulls. He's not only angry, he's frightened."

The child's head sunk lower so that all Billie could see was the part in her hair and the tip of her nose. And while she stared at her, Billie had again the oddest sensation of seeing herself in this girl. She'd been a crackerjack rascal, too.

For reasons particular to her, this child felt as Billie had—different, set apart, lacking. Her heart went out to the girl, and the same urge that prompted her to save every stray animal that crossed her path made her want to help now.

Only Ronnie was a child, not an animal, and Billie didn't quite know how. She had no idea what to say. She thought then to look at what she *did* know, and that was what it felt like to hurt and, more vaguely, what it was like to be eleven years old.

She felt for the remaining Twinkie in her coat pocket. "Want half?" she asked, pulling it out.

The girl didn't answer, but, without looking at Billie, she took the piece handed her.

"Do you think hiding here will keep Coralee Hutch from coming?" Billie asked as she munched.

"I'm not hiding. You found me." Ronnie gazed at the tiny bite of cake she had left.

"What if I just walked away and didn't tell?"

"Somebody would find me," she said as if Billie were a complete idiot to think otherwise.

"If it won't keep Coralee Hutch from coming, why do it?"

She shrugged. "I don't know."

To drive your father crazy, Billie thought, but she decided pointing that out would be criticizing.

"What's wrong with this Coralee Hutch? Why do you hate her? Has she beaten you, or anything?" Maybe Linc Snow was wrong.

Ronnie shook her head. "No. I'd kick her legs off if she tried to." She peered up with narrowed, angry eyes. "She just doesn't like my mice. One of them got away from me once and before I could catch it, she killed it in a trap. She said it was just an old mouse and dumped it in the trash. She doesn't like animals. And she doesn't like me."

"Oh." It sounded like a good reason not to like the old battle-ax to Billie. "Have you told your father this?"

Again the shrug. "He knew about the mouse. He doesn't care."

And in those few words Billie heard, *"He doesn't love me, either."*

"Your father loves you, Ronnie." The little one needed to hear it, whether or not she was in a mood to believe it.

The child shrugged.

"He called you from his truck when he was bringing me here last night to make sure you were okay."

Ronnie gave her that narrow-eyed look. "He called to see if I was up to something. I do things...I don't mean to, but they seem to come out wrong."

"If he didn't care about you, would he have bothered to fix you the breakfast he did this morning, or to give you vitamins, or to buy you nice clothes and designer tennis shoes?"

She gave that great shrug again but was looking more hopeful.

They sat there a few more silent minutes, Billie on the bed, Ronnie on the floor. Voices, people entering the kitchen reached them through the open door. Ronnie's legs quivered, and she sniffed.

Billie extended her hand. "Want me to go face them with you?"

The girl lifted her face; her eyes were red and watering. "Yeah, if you want," she said as if she didn't care one way or the other. But she took Billie's hand tightly.

"Take a hint from me. Before you say anything, give your father a big hug."

Ronnie's eyes widened. They were a pale green, like her father's. Then she gave a skeptical frown that seemed to mean, *you've got to be kidding*.

As they entered the kitchen, Ronnie shook away Billie's hand. All four male faces turned toward them. Shock and then immense relief swept Linc Snow's face.

"Where in the hell have you been?" His voice was frighteningly low.

Ronnie took a few quick steps forward as if she were about to throw herself into his arms. And for an instant Billie knew by the intense longing on his face that the man wanted to grab his child and hold her.

But in a flash his expression turned dark as storm clouds. Ronnie stopped, and her shoulder got that belligerent slant to it again.

"You owe Miss Ballinger an apology for your behavior. Because of you, I haven't been able to take her to Lubbock—and she's worn herself out looking for you."

"I didn't ask her to."

"Ronnie!" His voice was unbending, unforgiving.

Billie thought they both needed a good smack for not hugging each other. She wondered if the awkward episodes she found herself right in the middle of would ever end.

"I'm sorry, Billie." The girl gave her a quick, apologetic glance, and Billie nodded.

"Now, get on upstairs. Kit will be stayin' here with all of you while I take Miss Ballinger into the city." His voice echoed with fatigue. By the look on his face Billie knew it was the last thing the man wanted to do. "I'll talk to you later, Ronnie," he called after his daughter as she took flight through the hall.

Kit, downcast, moved across the room to slump on the sofa. Toby pressed against his father's leg, and Tommy began to whine, pleading to be allowed to go along.

But Linc Snow extricated himself from Toby's grasp and pushed the boys aside, as if he couldn't stand being touched or hemmed in another moment.

"Go over there with your brother," he said sharply. "Kit . . . put a movie on for them."

Billie watched the boys, Toby, his thumb in his mouth, Tommy wiping his tears, settle close together on the floor in front of the television. Kit, his expression as long as a midwinter day, fiddled with the video machine atop the television. Then she realized Linc Snow was looking at her, waiting. His eyes were dark, his face drawn. Definitely not a man to argue with at that moment. Not a man to say anything to, if you valued your life.

She walked over to the table to get her purse. Her gaze fell to the page of the classifieds sitting right there beside it, and slowly she picked it up.

"Mr. Snow . . ." She turned. "Could I speak to you for a moment before we go?" She glanced at the boys. "Alone?"

His eyebrows rose with surprise, and then that same impatient look that he'd had when she'd first met him swept his face. He rubbed the side of his nose, propped a hand on his belt, then gave a great sigh.

"Why in hell not . . ." He inclined his head. "My study's this way."

She followed him, her heart hammering. An inner voice told her she was really being stupid, but another stronger voice declared the old saw of nothing ventured, nothing gained. She didn't stand a chance of him saying yes. But she wouldn't know unless she asked. And the room was lovely, homey. She didn't have any experience, but how hard could it be? All the old, old dreams—of something stable and solid and complete—surged forward from their private hiding places. *Oh, Lord, could I? Could I have this, just this once?*

He led the way into a small room off the hall at the front of the house. Two windows, oak bookshelves holding a hodgepodge of books and notebooks, a rolltop desk and a computer. The neatest room in the house. Manly, private.

He shut the door, turned and waited with his hand on the knob, an impatient, long-suffering man.

The words clogged in her throat for long seconds.

"I'd like to apply," she said finally.

He frowned, clearly puzzled. "Apply?"

Realizing the newspaper remained in her hand, she held it out and pointed. "For the position of housekeeper."

Chapter Five

"**Y**ou?" Linc, amazed, watched her nod. "You want to be my housekeeper?"

She had to be kidding! This had to be some sort of misunderstanding.

But she said quite clearly, "Yes. I do."

"Why would you want to do that?" Stunned, he glanced from her face down to the blouse he was willing to bet was real silk, over the rhinestone-studded shoulders of that denim coat, and down to her elegant boots. A housekeeper she definitely wasn't.

"I need a job. You need a housekeeper. I like your house and the room you're offering."

He gazed at her, still trying to make heads or tails of what was going on. "What about salary?"

"What is it?"

He named it, and she said it would do.

He remained stumped. That she was a hell of a lot more pleasant to look at than Coralee Hutch flashed through his mind, along with a split second of insane fantasies of what it would be like to have her in his home all the time, as the housekeeper. The kids would like him again.

Get your head on straight, Lincoln Snow. It'd mean trouble and nothing but. And why in the world would a woman like her want to live out here in West Texas?

"What line of work did you say you're in?" he asked. He moved to the swivel chair at his desk and indicated a comfortable leather side chair for her.

She sat on the edge of the chair. "I didn't. I'm not working at present."

For an instant he looked at where her breasts pushed against the fabric of her blouse. He cursed himself for it and hoped she hadn't noticed.

She gazed at him, and he looked back. Then, very deliberately and gracefully, she slid back into the chair, crossed her long legs, and looked him in the eye. She was a good bluffer.

"What do you do when you *are* working?" he asked.

He wasn't going to hire her as a housekeeper. All of Heaven—hell, the entire county—would be wagging their tongues off. In a community like this, everybody knew everybody's business. Besides, a woman like her couldn't handle the job; inside a month, she'd hightail it back to the city lights. He'd be left high and dry, the kids heartbroken. He didn't need any more of that.

She took a deep breath, then slowly let it out. "I don't really have a profession, Mr. Snow." Her gaze fell to the desk. "Until recently it wasn't necessary for me to work. However, in the past year I've suffered financial reverses and now find that I must take a job."

Good Lord! "Are you saying you've never worked?" He'd never known anyone with that kind of money.

"Not for a salary, no." She looked at the floor, as if embarrassed by something that anyone in his right mind would give his left arm for. "My father left me well provided for. Oh, not a fortune," she said softly, "but quite adequate. But I've had . . . reverses, as I said, and I've been seeking employment. I may not have ever had a job, so to speak, but I've done my share of heading charity committees and planning all sorts of parties and affairs." She was almost huffy now, as she'd been last night. "I'm not a lazy, do-nothing sort of person. I've made my way, made a home for myself and my father."

She waited, and Linc thought.

"I don't give many parties or *affairs,* whatever those are. I'm afraid you have no qualifications, Miss Ballinger." He started to rise.

"How do you know?" she insisted, as if she were the Queen of Sheba.

Faced with that, Linc sat back down and considered. He wouldn't let her get the best of him. "All right." He grabbed a sheet of paper and pen and began with the questions he asked of everyone he employed. "Name..."

Her name was Wilhelmina Wallis Ballinger, a real mouthful, he thought. A handful, just like her. Why did he always find blondes so damned attractive? The birth date she quoted made her twenty-eight, which surprised the hell out of him. He'd guessed her younger. But he'd been right about the other stuff—rich, pampered gal.

"Married?"

"No."

"Divorced?"

"Does that matter?"

"It's always on the tax forms," he lied and never batted an eye.

"Never married—no children."

When it came to a home address, she puzzled over it, uncertain at last. Then she smiled. It would be here, of course. She didn't smoke, didn't drink. Nice clean-living gal. He wondered why she'd never married and how many men she'd had affairs with. What had happened to her money—too much spending?

She could talk to his kids. They liked her. Ronnie would probably give up the death wish she had for him. She'd smile again, as a little girl was supposed to do.

"Character references?"

She lifted her chin and gave the smile of a cat who'd gotten the cream. "Marc Thornton, Assistant District Attorney of Washoe County, Nevada, and Patrice and Marc Thornton Sr., former lieutenant governor of the state. All of them can attest to my sound mind and good character. I can provide their telephone numbers—private lines.'' She frowned thoughtfully. ''I can add Lisa Webster, a well-known art gallery owner, and P.J. Montgomery, surgeon at the Mayo Clinic, and—''

Linc tossed down his pen and sat back. ''I believe those references are satisfactory.''

He looked at her, swung the chair around and looked out the window. Having her as the housekeeper instead of Coralee Hutch would be as different as having a playful kitten instead of a saber-toothed tiger. There was no denying that it was a mighty tempting idea.

A woman in the house again, a real woman.

Yeah, and it would be like taking in a kitten with a time bomb tied to its tail.

She wouldn't like it here with them. She wouldn't like the isolation or the mundaneness of it all. The hot winds and the flat land, things he found beautiful but so many women seemed to think ugly. She wouldn't stay long. Not a woman like her.

''The references are more than adequate, Miss Ballinger. But the fact remains that you've never done this kind of work before.''

''That doesn't mean I can't.''

Well said, Linc thought. She waited.

''Can you cook at all? Can you make biscuits?'' That was something Coralee could do.

She nodded. ''Yes, I can.''

''Chicken and dumplings?'' he threw at her.

''Yes.''

He had strong doubts about that. ''Kit and Ronnie have to have breakfast by six-forty-five; they catch the school bus at seven-fifteen. You'd have Tommy and Toby to look after all day. The entire house—twelve rooms plus your own—and the washing is your responsibility. Sometimes the dust is so thick around here that you have to keep the windows closed, but it seeps in anyway and gets over everything. Four kids mean washing clothes every day—and Tommy sometimes still wets the bed.'' He paused for emphasis to let it all sink in.

"Sometimes I don't get in until midnight, and I expect my dinner waiting. I'll try to give you two days off a week, but that's not guaranteed. We work it out as we go along. Sometimes you work seven days straight because I've got to be in the field. Do you think you can handle all that? Do you have anything in your background, Miss Ballinger, that would qualify you to handle that?"

She leaned forward and regarded him with a squared, determined chin and earnest eyes. Beautiful, warm, earnest eyes that had long dark lashes.

"All that work will get done when it gets done. The main thing is that your children would rather eat live frogs than have that Coralee Hutch in the house. *I,* on the other hand, happen to halfway like your kids, and they seem to like me. That's a good start—and aren't they your primary concern?"

"Yes, ma'am, they are. And how do you think they're going to feel in a few weeks when you grow bored of your excursion into this backwoods town and beat it back to the city?"

Her eyes narrowed, searching him. "You have no guarantee that anyone you hire will stay longer than a month or two. If you wish, I will gladly sign a contract to stay a specific amount of time."

"Contracts are worth about as much as the paper they're printed on," Linc shot back. Denise came to mind, and he instinctively averted his eyes. After a moment he looked at her and said quietly, "What do you know about kids, Miss Ballinger?"

"Nothing. Nothing at all. But I do know about being human, Mr. Snow."

And that was a lot more than Coralee Hutch knew, Linc thought, gazing at her. Maybe a lot more than he knew, truth be told.

He leaned forward, gazed into those big blue eyes, then deliberately looked her up and down.

"You're twenty-eight, Miss Ballinger, and a very beautiful woman." There, he'd admitted it, and he saw the understanding in her eyes. "There will be talk, a lot of it in a community like this," he said in warning. But he still didn't tell her no.

"People talk everywhere, Mr. Snow. I've never paid gossip much attention."

A soft bump sounded on the door. Not really a loud enough sound to draw attention, but enough for a father to know immediately what was up. With the swiftness of a cat, Linc crossed the room and jerked open the door. There crouched his brood, four pairs of eyes looking up at him with the fearfulness of whipped pups and making him feel like a fire-breathing ogre. Damn, now they knew about the choice to be made.

When he didn't shout, the fear in those eyes turned to puppy-dog pleading. No one said anything. Anger churned in Linc, along with hope and uncertainty. He glanced at Billie Ballinger and thought of her, instead of Coralee Hutch, in the kitchen. He looked at Ronnie and thought of how she'd probably kiss his feet for this one.

Linc sighed. "Okay. We'll give it a try."

"All riiight!" Kit cheered.

The twins ran forward and threw themselves upon Billie Ballinger's lap. Ronnie gave Linc a hesitant smile. "Thanks, Dad," she said as she wrapped an arm around his middle and pressed her face against his stomach.

A crack a mile wide broke through his heart. He wanted to hold her to him, but a crazy, unexplainable fear gripped him. At last he dared to press his hand to her small back. Felt the warmth of her, his daughter. But the pain, the fear, was too much, and he stepped away.

"Kit, help me get Miss Ballinger's suitcases inside to her room," he said gruffly and headed out the door without looking back.

The kitchen. Beneath the canny gaze of Ronnie Snow, Billie investigated the large room where she was undoubtedly expected to spend most of her time. Linc had gone off to the tractor barn, to do whatever a farmer did in a tractor barn, and had taken Kit with him. The twins were occupied with their collection of miniature cars. Eagle-eyed, smart-mouthed Ronnie had been instructed to show Billie the house, which she'd done—quick peeks into the littered bedrooms, messy baths, and jumbled linen closet, followed by clearly more significant aspects, such as the shiny oak banister, whose sturdiness she demonstrated by sliding down it. There would be little work to keep that banister gleaming, Billie thought; the seat of Ronnie's britches would do that for her.

They'd done little more than glance into the living room and apparently unused formal dining room and then returned, inevitably, to the kitchen.

For her first act as housekeeper, Billie had to make the family supper. Linc himself had done lunch in order to give her time to unpack her things. That had been a reprieve. Now, however, Billie wondered if perhaps she'd unpacked too quickly; the fact was, she had lied to Linc Snow. Baldly lied. Not only could she not make biscuits, she wasn't quite certain what chicken and dumplings were.

Oh, she could cook. Her mother had been thoroughly undomestic and had left to Billie, at an early age, the making of coffee and breakfast. Thus, Billie could boil or scramble eggs and fry bacon on the stove or in a microwave oven. She had cooked sausages but not often. She could make sandwiches and was quite creative in this endeavor. She'd devised her own soup by mixing three different canned varieties together. But most of the time she'd had a cook or housekeeper to put together whole meals. When she hadn't someone to cook for her, she'd eaten out or cooked frozen dinners. But now those restaurants and frozen dinners seemed far away and long ago.

She gazed at the kitchen now, ran her hand along the cool blue tile countertops, opened the oak cabinets and drawers, peeked into the double ovens, and wondered how she was possibly going to pull this off. She would be humiliated if Linc discovered that she couldn't cook. Only small people lied, and she didn't want him to think her smaller than he already did. Oh, no, she didn't want that!

"We have one of those fancy mixers," Ronnie said, opening a cabinet door and revealing a big goose-necked machine. Billie had seen one like it once—in a store. "It will even beat bread dough, but you have to put in the special hooks. But I guess you know that.''

"Oh, yes.''

Their gazes met. Billie saw the suspicion written in the child's eyes. She thought of taking the child into her confidence, but what good would that do? Then Ronnie would be an accessory to the crime, so to speak, and there was little she could do to help, anyway. Billie went back to the pantry and began a more thorough search. Perhaps she could make her soup mixture, claiming it as her specialty. No, there was only tomato and chicken noodle on the shelf.

"We have a big freezer in the laundry room,'' Ronnie said suddenly.

"Oh?'' Billie followed the child and watched her open a chest-type freezer.

"Could you make frozen pizza tonight?'' Ronnie asked. "It's about everybody's favorite. Daddy likes the supreme one best.''

There, right on top, were three large frozen pizzas. Billie lifted them out. "Think all three will do?''

The girl nodded. "We always eat three. The directions are on the back,'' she added casually. "Oh, and there's some cookbooks up there.''

Billie followed the girl's pointing finger. There, beside two old vases, a tea tin, and a shoe box sat a short row of dusty cookbooks.

"They belonged to our mom. One of the housekeepers we had, Pepita, used them some. All she could cook was Mexican food when she came, and Daddy didn't think she did that very well.''

Billie wondered strongly about Mrs. Snow but said instead, "How many housekeepers have you had?''

"You're number five. None of them stays very long. Either they get mad and quit, or Daddy gets mad and fires them. Daddy has a pretty good temper.''

"I see.''

"Daddy's favorite food is chicken and dumplings, and after that it's beef burritos and refried beans. Maybe you could find the recipes in those books.''

"I'm sure I can find the recipes somewhere." Too late she remembered she was supposed to be able to cook chicken and dumplings.

A knowing glint touched the girl's pale green eyes. "Yeah. Well, I guess I could set the table," she said, as if she were doing something above and beyond her duty and turned away.

"Ronnie?"

"Yeah?" The girl peered over her shoulder.

"Do you cook?"

"Not me," the child said with wide eyes, shaking her head as if finding the idea repulsive. "I'm only a kid."

They gazed at each other, and Billie thought perhaps the first thread of friendship had been spun. She was going on instinct, because up until now the child seemed a brat—a trial, as Ronnie had labeled herself.

When she heard Linc and Kit's voices and footsteps on the porch, Billie turned from the sink, eager to see the look on Linc's face when he beheld the table. She was proud of it. She'd found a tablecloth and matching red-checked napkins tucked into the bottom of a drawer. She'd commanded a complaining Ronnie to remove the plates she'd already set and spread the cloth. Then she'd shown the child how to place the napkins, forks and knives in their proper places.

"Seems like a lot of trouble to worry about where the forks and knives go—and we aren't even goin' to use knives," Ronnie had muttered.

"You need to know where to place them."

"Why?"

"Well..." That stumped Billie for a second. "So you can function in polite society. And set a table pleasing to the eye."

"It won't make the food taste any better," Ronnie said.

"Oh, yes it does," Billie replied with a smile. "And here...we'll fold the napkins like crowns." The twins had been fascinated by that, but Ronnie had considered it nonsense. Apparently whimsy didn't come easily for the girl.

Billie had found two large cutting boards and placed them on the table to await the pizzas, which sizzled in the oven according to the package directions. Billie had always sent out for pizza, but she was managing very nicely with these, thank you.

She'd insisted on a water glass at each place, despite Ronnie's skepticism. Two glasses for every person—two glasses apiece for the twins—was evidently the stupidest thing she'd ever heard of. It just meant extra dirty dishes, and she wasn't going to be the one stuck washing them!

Billie, intent on making a good first impression, ignored her. With satisfaction she decided the table looked very much like one in an old-fashioned pizzeria.

"Wow!" Kit said when he came into the kitchen ahead of his father.

Linc Snow was clearly surprised. He stared at the table, then glanced over at Billie. She was pleased at getting some reaction from the taciturn man, even if she wished he'd *like* what she'd done.

But no open approval was forthcoming. He simply said, "Kit, help the boys wash up and we'll eat," then turned and hung his ball cap on the rack on the wall.

Billie was exhausted and glad to retreat to the privacy of her own room that night. It was no wonder, she thought to herself. It had been a very eventful day. And she wasn't accustomed to being in the constant company of so many people. So much of her life had been spent alone.

She glanced around the room and wondered at herself, at what she'd done. Hiring on as a housekeeper! Good grief, what would her father have said? He'd have laughed, Billie decided, and she began to chuckle. It was so...odd.

Feeling a quiet surge of pleasure, she ran a finger down the cherrywood bedpost, then moved to sit in the cozy wingback chair. She'd placed photographs of her father and mother, Marc and Lisa on the dresser. Their antiqued silver frames looked very nice there. Those and her robe lying at the foot of the bed made the room seem hers. As if it had been waiting for her. Perhaps, later, if everything turned out well, she would have Lisa send some of the clothes Billie had stored with her.

Don't go getting ahead of yourself, an inner voice warned. Heart fluttering, she firmly closed the door on speculation or worry. She had a place now—a chance at a place anyway—and that was enough for the moment.

She listened. No sounds penetrated from the house beyond. She knew Ronnie and the twins were upstairs getting baths, and Kit was studying a car repair manual. That afternoon Billie had given him permission to try his hand at repairing the Thunderbird, and the boy had been eager to go at it then and there. But his father had stopped him, said other things must be done first.

Without comment on her pizzeria-style dinner, Linc Snow had shortly afterward shut himself off in his study. To Billie it seemed as if he were hiding, but she knew that could be a snap judgment. She hardly knew the man, after all. Still, he'd barely said two sentences to her. He clearly felt awkward with her in the house.

For the first time, Billie really considered that aspect of the situation—he a very virile man, she a healthy woman. The fact sat there in her mind, as if written in large, bold type. It was a threat to this place she'd found for herself, and she pushed it aside, as if refusing to give it credence would make the threat go away. She'd been associated with men she'd found attractive before; it was a natural situation, something to be accepted, not blown out of proportion.

The telephone rang, and Billie stared at it, wondering if as housekeeper she was supposed to answer it. It rang again. She didn't feel enough a part of the household yet; answering the phone seemed an intrusion into the family's privacy. It cut off in the middle of the third ring, and she let out a long breath. Obviously Linc Snow or one of the children had answered.

She was just unbuttoning her blouse, preparing to take a shower, when a knock sounded on the door. Her fingers were still fumbling with the buttons when she opened the door. Linc Snow stood there, filling the doorway with his lean frame, gazing down at her.

"Telephone's for you," he said tersely, frowning and looking generally irritated. "Marc Thornton callin'."

"Oh. Thank you. I'll pick it up in here," she said foolishly as he turned and strode away.

"Billie! Got your message on the machine. Sorry I was out earlier."

"Don't be silly, Marc. I didn't expect you to sit around waiting for my call."

"Well, what gives, Bill? Where *are* you?" Brotherly protectiveness imbued his tone, and Billie smiled and felt absurdly like crying. It was good to hear his voice, to connect with someone who knew her.

"I'm in Heaven." It was fun to say that.

"Come again?"

"I'm in Heaven. It's a town in Texas. Only I'm not right *in* Heaven—I'm near it."

"Wherever you are, what are you doing there?"

Good question. "Well, I decided to drop down into New Mexico to see Billy the Kid's grave—you've heard of him—"

"Yes." Impatient patience.

"Then I had to drive across into Lubbock, and I got a bit lost, and I came to Heaven ... and, well, I've gotten a job here."

Silence. "A job? What kind of job?"

"As a housekeeper."

Silence again. "You've gotten a job as a housekeeper."

"Yes ... yes, I have."

"Billie, what's going on? Are you okay?" It was his interrogator voice.

"Yes, Marc, I'm fine. And I've decided to try this job instead of going down to your parents' cottage."

"Billie..."

"Marc, everything's okay. Really. Trust me on this." She winced and hurriedly gave him the address of Linc's farm. Cutting off his subsequent protests, she then listened to him tell her that investigators had several leads on Jonathan Bledsoe's whereabouts and that Harry the doorman had said to tell her he and Zoe had become great friends.

"Zoe always did like Harry," she said wistfully. The small collie had been the last of her pets, after a tank of fish, three cats and two hounds, that she'd had to find a home for. She'd been Billie's favorite and for a moment sharp longing for the dog filled her chest.

"Well, guess that's worked out." Marc sighed. "Billie, you could have come to work in my office, you know." He'd made that offer more than once.

And she'd made her explanation more than once. "I know, but how would it look for you to hire someone who can only hunt and peck about five words a minute? Not good for an elected official to hire practically family."

"So... I could have gotten you a job in any of five offices that I know of right here in Reno. You would have been more than welcome." He was talking about the way she looked, implying that she'd make a great office ornament, not realizing it wasn't really a compliment. She pictured him tugging at his tie as he always did when he was agitated.

"Yes, you could have gotten me a job—at something I had little chance of doing well. I got this job myself, and it may be something I have a chance at halfway doing."

"I see." He paused, then said questioningly, "Housekeeper?" as if he couldn't figure out how she could do that, either.

"Yes." She laughed.

"So... this Snow family. Who are they?"

"Linc Snow is a farmer, and he has four children. Two are twins."

"Farmer, four kids. No wife?"

"No. That's why they need a housekeeper."

"Uh... how'd you meet this family?"

"Oh, Marc, that's a long story. I'll write you about it." She didn't want to speak of the car breaking down. "Let me talk to Lisa—is she there?"

"No, she's slipped over to visit her Aunt Jean."

"Well, give her my love."

"Okay." Then he said slowly, "Billie, you'd still have your house if you'd filed bankruptcy. Why didn't you, damn it?"

"Daddy would have died if I'd done that."

"Your father's been dead five years, Billie!"

"I know that, but I'm my father's daughter, and I honor my debts, Marc." They'd been through this argument a number of times, too.

"They were Jonathan's debts. We'll get him, Billie."

"You may get him, but he's probably spent all my money."

"I know, I know..." He was surely pulling at his tie again. "Why'd you do this...take this job as a house-keeper?"

Big question, and Billie didn't know quite how to answer.

Should she tell him about the cozy room and how much a haven she found it? Should she try to explain how low she'd felt at being unable to get a job and having to depend so much on him? Would he think her crazy for taking the job simply because this place was where she happened to end up—a place tucked away from any connection with life as she'd known it? And should she dare reveal how much she'd longed for, for so many years, to be part of a real family?

"Because I need a job, and a place to live, and this one is here," she said at last. "And these children need someone right now, and I'm available. They need me...and I need that right now. I'm twenty-eight years old, Marc, and I don't know who or what I am. I'd like to find out."

She and Marc had shared toothbrushes and T-shirts and first love. Surely he would understand.

"Okay," he said quietly. "I'll keep in touch. Take care of yourself. You need anything, you call."

"I will. I promise." She replaced the receiver and sat staring at the telephone through a blur of tears, feeling lost and scared and hopeful all at the same time.

She'd showered and was dressed in pajamas and robe when a knock again sounded at her door. It was Linc again. She stared at him, and he stared back. His gaze slipped downward, then immediately flicked back up to her face, his eyes nervous, as if he'd been caught doing something he shouldn't.

"Uh...could I talk to you?" He was terse again.

She nodded and stepped back. "Yes, of course. Come in." She was suddenly inordinately conscious of her thin satin pajamas against her skin. But she wore a robe and was perfectly respectable, she told herself, scoffing at her foolishness. Good heavens, she'd worn less at pool parties surrounded by scads of handsome hunks.

"Uh...how about in the kitchen?"

"Oh. All right."

Got it, she thought. Bedroom was off limits. Probably a good idea, especially because of the children. Still, such precautionary measures seemed somewhat outdated to her—men and women could be friends without the slightest thoughts of sex, she silently told Linc Snow's rigid back as she followed him through the laundry room and into the kitchen.

Yet she did experience a warm tingling as she gazed at his broad shoulders.

Perhaps the kitchen was the best place for them to talk.

Chapter Six

Linc was distinctly aware of her following him. He heard the faint sound of her slippers and smelled the fresh-washed womanly fragrance of her. He felt damned awkward with her in her pajamas and robe, all of it gleaming white shiny stuff, not the kind motherly housekeeper-types wore. They covered her fully, but the fact remained that they were bed-clothes—intimate apparel. And even the kitchen suddenly seemed an intimate atmosphere.

He told himself to grow up. He'd seen four housekeepers in their nightclothes plenty of times, and one of them, Pepita, while middle-aged, had been quite attractive. She had been plainly willing, as a matter of fact, but he'd ignored her without a problem.

Then he turned around, glanced at *her* and thought that none of those housekeepers had worn *satin* pajamas. And certainly none had worn *anything* with quite the class that *she* did.

"Kids are all in bed," he said and took up the coffeepot. "Want a cup?" He already had one at his place on the table.

"Yes, thanks."

She took the chair opposite his, where they'd sat earlier. He guessed they'd decided that much.

He brought her coffee, a spoon and the sugar bowl. She proceeded to dump a heaping teaspoon of sugar into her cup. He couldn't imagine how she could stand it. His gaze slipped over her pale hair and down over her shoulders, and an unexpected wanting surged within him. He put a lid on it—fast—picked up his cup and drank deeply.

She sipped her coffee, then raised her eyes to his, waiting. Her lashes were long and dark, her face as smooth as a china plate—nearly as pale, too. Fresh as early morning and patient as a hot summer afternoon. It set him off balance.

"You've had time to reconsider now," he said, making his gaze hard and steady. "I won't hold you to takin' the job."

She looked at him, and stubbornness bloomed on her soft face. "But I hold you to hiring me."

Had he expected her to say that? Not fully. A big part of him had expected her to want to leave now. *He* knew he'd made a mistake. He should tell her she had to go.

But he didn't. He didn't know how he'd tell Ronnie, and he couldn't stand the thought of dealing with all those dirty clothes in the laundry. Fact was, he was a drowning man grasping for a lifesaver, no matter how flimsy.

He took a deep breath. "Okay. If you insist on tryin' this out." He considered it her choice; the outcome would prove to be her fault, too. He reached for a tablet and pencil lying on the nearby counter. "I'll need your social security number and the person to be notified in case of emergency. You'll be paid on Fridays, beginning this week."

While she wrote, he rose, retrieved a set of keys from a drawer, and tossed them in front of her. "These are for the house and the Suburban. The Suburban's yours to use— you'll need it because you'll usually have the kids with you. Charge your gas at Fred's in town. You'll have to drive over to Moorestown or Lubbock to do the grocery shopping. I keep cash for that in the office safe. Just let me know what you think you'll need. Emergency numbers are listed here by the phone. And this is the base radio. Flip this switch to speak into the microphone. Closed channel—ours is channel one. There're radios in all the vehicles and the tractors, so you can get me just about any time. You're base here at the house. I'm unit one. In the car, you'll be unit five.''

She looked up. Her eyes revealed confusion, and he doubted she was following all this. But she nodded anyway, damn fool woman. Linc slipped back into his chair, and she pushed the tablet toward him. He jerked his eyes from hers and focused on the name she'd written—that Marc Thornton who'd called earlier.

''This district attorney fella the first to notify in case of an accident?'' Just how close was she to the guy?

She nodded. ''Yes. He's my attorney and friend.''

''Hmm.''

He set the paper aside and leaned forward on both arms. ''There're a few things about the kids. Kit, he takes care of his own room. Change his sheets, but don't touch anything else. That's his private place, off limits to Ronnie and the twins.'' He sighed. ''Ronnie'll bring home a stray dog or cat or something about once a week, but she isn't allowed to keep it. Ever. No animal is allowed inside the house.''

''Why not?'' Her eyes grew round with amazement, and for a moment she bore a marked resemblance to his daughter.

''Because I'm not runnin' a humane society, Miss Ballinger. If we started keeping every stray animal that came down the pike, word would get out and all those people looking for a home for their unwanted critters would end up dumpin' them at the end of my drive. I don't like animals in the house, never have. Got it?''

''Yes, sir, Mr. Snow.''

Mr. Snow? Oh, yes . . . he'd called her Miss. Still, the formality made him feel foolish, and he resented her for it.

''Tommy's just like he seems, but Toby . . .'' He gazed at the table. ''Well, you know he has a problem with stuttering. He's had some sessions with a therapist but didn't seem to like it much, so I quit takin' him.'' Linc felt helpless and guilty, because he suspected all the mother figures coming and going through the house had contributed to Toby's problem. Even after all the literature he'd read on the problem, he wasn't certain what his son needed. He had been going on instinct but was plenty worried that he could be handling it all wrong.

"Chances are he'll outgrow it."

He glanced up to see her regarding him with a reassuring air that he found immediately annoying. What made her an expert in child-care problems all of a sudden—a woman like her?

"I know the statistics of that happening are good, but Toby isn't a statistic," he said sharply.

She nodded. "I know that, but I'm speaking from experience, not statistical reports. I stuttered, Mr. Snow. Badly as a child of Toby's age, and on up through a good part of the first grade, before the problem gradually slipped away. It's thought that stuttering may be linked to heredity. In my case, my father stuttered as a child, too."

Okay, she'd surprised him. "I see," he said and nodded. "I haven't been able to find out if anyone in my family—or his mother's family—ever stuttered. I don't remember doin' it. I know a lot of people think stress has little to do with it, but Toby does get worse at times, mostly in times of stress." He figured she'd contradict him, as all the experts did, but he knew what he knew.

"I did, too," was all she said. "There's all sorts of theories as to why, but the best way to deal with it boils down to patience. I think it was my parents' attitude that helped me the most. They acted as if stuttering was no big deal. If we all make light of it, never rush Toby to speak and treat him as if he'll grow out of it, he's more apt to believe that, too. Confidence helps."

That she understood amazed him, and that she echoed his own feelings in the matter reassured him, strange as that seemed. He nodded. "It's about all we can do for him right now, anyway." After a moment, he realized that he was staring. He immediately averted his gaze to his cup, picked it up and rose to get more coffee.

"Do you have any questions?" he asked.

"Would it be acceptable for me to call you Linc and you to call me Billie? Or perhaps I should call you Mr. Linc and you should call me Miss Billie."

Linc choked on a sip of coffee. "Just plain Linc will do...Billie," he said at last.

She nodded, her eyes wide and serious. For a split second Linc lost himself in those beautiful eyes. Then he hid his gaze in his cup, murmuring, "Guess that's it. Anything else can be worked out as we go along."

"Okay." She rose and gave a hesitant smile. "Good night, then."

"Good night." He didn't smile.

Her robe made a faint swishing sound as she passed him. He again caught her sweet, warm scent.

"Billie?"

He heard her pause.

"Things may look different to you in the mornin'," he said, staring at the square tiles of the floor. "I'll give you a lift into Lubbock after Kit and Ronnie get off to school, if you want to go."

Silence echoed for several moments. Then he heard her walk away into her room, the door click softly closed.

Linc stood leaning against the counter. He was alone, but somehow he was very conscious of her being only on the other side of that door. In her shiny white pajamas.

He drained his cup and set it aside, thinking as he turned out the light that he couldn't quite figure how he'd come to have a woman like her staying in his house. Shaking off the confusion, he cursed himself for not instructing her about his newspaper. The damn fool woman had worked his crossword puzzle this morning! He paid for that paper— that crossword puzzle was his!

But soon his thoughts wandered again. She was different than he'd first figured her to be. She was classy, sophisticated, but not exactly that, either. She seemed at once innocent and wise. Open to the world. Honest. And all that threw him. Maybe she was simply good at *appearing* honest.

He walked upstairs and down the hall, pausing to look in on his sleeping children. He wondered how long she would stay and cursed the tiny flame of hopefulness. She wasn't going to stay. Matter of weeks and she'd be gone, if not in the morning. He bet she'd have him take her to Lubbock in the morning!

But Ronnie had loved him for his decision, he thought, standing at her door. On impulse, he crossed the room and gazed down at her face. A full moon shone on her freckles. He pulled her spread up over her legs, almost touched her cheek, but stopped. I adore you, his heart cried out.

Some odd emotion compelled him to go over and gaze down at Kit, too. The boy had asked his help with the T-bird. He should have helped him, Linc thought. But it was foolishness, this thing the kid had for fast engines. Why couldn't the boy want to work on the tractor that much? He glanced over and saw a book open on Kit's desk—a car repair manual. The kid should study his lessons so hard. He adjusted the boy's cover even though it didn't need it and thought how this boy, his firstborn, was fast approaching manhood.

Toby had crawled into Tommy's bed, he saw—and stolen the covers. Linc adjusted them as best he could. He gazed down at the twins and gave in to the irresistible urge to touch their hair fleetingly before drawing away.

Billie Ballinger would be here for a few weeks, and maybe for that time the kids would be happy.

Back in his bedroom, he turned on the light and glanced around. He began unbuttoning his shirt, then paused to dig into the bottom of the nightstand drawer. He pulled out a vinyl folder, opened it, and stared at Denise's picture. He'd forgotten about this photograph until tonight, thought little about Denise these days. He hadn't seen her since a brief meeting at the attorney's office ten months ago, and her image in his mind was blurry, indistinct. It didn't seem possible after being married to the woman for fourteen years to forget exactly what she looked like. He guessed it was due to his efforts to forget her. Remembering had been so damn painful during those early months after she'd left. A dream dying.

She stared back at him now. He saw the resemblance to Billie Ballinger. Like Billie, Denise was blond, blue-eyed. She'd been one beautiful woman, was still.

Denise had been a city girl—Linc had met her at a club in Lubbock—and she'd never adapted to life so far out in the country. She'd missed having a lot of neighbors and things like restaurants, nightclubs, theaters, being only five minutes to shopping. She'd hated the winds and the dust and the flatness of the land.

When Kit and Ronnie were small, Linc had encouraged Denise to spend long weekends with her folks. But then Kit had started school, and the twins had come along. Denise had missed those trips to her folks and had resented having more children to care for. Sometimes Linc thought maybe he could have been more of a help to her, but he'd done everything he could.

He'd been all for her going to work, when she said she wanted to a number of times. But Denise hadn't wanted to be a grocery store clerk or a secretary for one of the few small offices in the area, and Lubbock was a long commute. She'd nagged him about giving up the farm and moving into the city, but, hell, Linc might as well rip out his heart as give up being a farmer.

For an instant pain swept across his chest as he recalled asking her to stay. He'd come close to pleading—too damn close. He'd never do that again. It hurt so bad that she'd hated a place he loved so much, that she'd tossed in his face the house he'd built for them and the heritage of the land he offered, that she'd left without a backward glance, from all Linc could tell.

The bitterness was gone now, but sometimes Linc missed it. At least when he'd felt it, he'd known he was alive. Ah, hell, he thought with a deep sigh, none of it mattered. Life went on.

He stuffed the folder back into the drawer, stripped to his shorts and got into bed. He probably should begin wearing pajamas, he thought. At least while *she* was here. Downstairs. In her pajamas. Or did she take them off when she went to bed? For an instant he imagined what she would look like lying naked in bed. Then he thrust the image from his mind.

He wondered if he'd be driving her to Lubbock in the morning.

* * *

When Linc came down in the morning, Billie had coffee made and his paper lying neatly at his place at the table. She'd put on a bit of makeup, pulled her hair back into a ponytail and dressed in sensible, if designer, jeans and a loose cotton blouse. She'd found a blue-flowered apron in the pantry and had taken the liberty of using it. She felt she'd done quite well in assuming her role of housekeeper.

He gave her a quick glance—a scowl actually—and fairly growled "Mornin'" in response to her greeting.

She pushed aside her disappointment, quietly poured herself a cup of coffee and sat at the table, slipping out the comics after he'd chosen his own section of the newspaper.

Linc coughed and slammed down his cup. "Whoever taught you to make coffee?" He slapped the paper to the table.

"I'm . . . I'm sorry you don't like it."

"If I put as much sugar in it as you do, it could be swamp water and it wouldn't matter. But I like it black, and to taste like coffee."

"I followed the directions on the can." Just as she had the previous morning. He hadn't objected then.

"No one follows the directions on the can." He looked at her as if she should know that. "Use two scoops."

"Yes, sir." She rose to throw out the coffee and make fresh. She heard a choking sound behind her and turned to find Linc glaring at her.

"Never, *never* work my crossword puzzle," he said in a voice as sharp as a finely honed knife. "Got that?"

"Yes."

The only reason Billie didn't retreat to her room was that it seemed an awfully childish thing to do. She blinked back tears and told herself that she was an adult, a woman who'd dealt rather admirably with recent setbacks. She was being criticized by her employer, but she could handle that.

She forced herself to be still and tried to read the comics, but her attention remained focused on the man sitting across from her, who kept his gaze riveted to the newspaper. She wondered why he was so angry with her, and she wanted to give his hard cheek a much-needed smack.

When the children came down and he greeted them with similar curtness, she decided that he was angry with the entire world.

"Don't mind Dad," Kit whispered to her as she scrambled eggs. "He's like this sometimes."

And all the children seemed to walk on eggs around him, until he took his plate of toast and cup of coffee and headed for his office. "I'd thought we'd finally get some biscuits around here," he grumbled as he left the room.

"I like this toast," Kit said brightly to her.

She sent him a grateful smile.

"I'd sure like some biscuits," Ronnie said, and Billie saw the child giving her that speculative X-ray look.

"I'll make them tomorrow...after I've found my way around the kitchen," Billie said weakly, a sinking feeling in the pit of her stomach.

Ronnie informed Billie that she was to prepare sack lunches for her because the school food was garbage. While Billie searched the cabinet for peanut butter, which Ronnie said was her favorite, Tommy tipped over his milk. Toby tried to clean it up and tipped over his in the process, then both boys pretended to be cats and lick it up. The phone rang—it was for Kit. Ronnie came out of the laundry room wearing a wrinkled sweatshirt she'd dug out of the dirty clothes. Billie started to protest, but the girl reminded her the sack lunch was needed in five minutes. Toby spilled more milk on the floor so he and Tommy could continue being cats.

When Kit and Ronnie raced out at seven-fifteen, slamming the door behind them, Billie took her first deep breath in forty-five minutes. As she looked around, she realized that the kitchen was at that moment little different from the first time she'd laid eyes on it. And she felt as if she'd been riding down an interstate at eighty miles an hour in a convertible.

She grabbed a dishcloth and approached the boys. "Hey, guys, that's enough being kitties." She tugged on Toby's arm and pulled him up to face her.

Milk circled his mouth and the tip of his nose, making him resemble a miniature clown. He gave a tentative, hopeful smile.

Billie had to grin back. Having had no experience in scolding, she couldn't begin now, to such a timid little face.

Thus encouraged, Toby stuttered. "Me . . . me . . . ow."

Tommy looked up and meowed, too.

And Billie, looking at the milk on their adorable faces began to laugh. The boys followed suit, pushing her onto the floor and themselves into her lap, giggling with glee.

And there she was, wriggling on the floor with two milk-faced boys, when Linc came into the room.

She saw his scuffed brown boots first. Quickly she tried to right herself, the laughter dying in her throat. Her gaze moved up those denim-clad legs and lean hips over a brown-and-white plaid shirt, tanned neck, hard jaw and stern mouth, to his cold green eyes. He filled the room with the taut power of his presence.

The question was there in his eyes, and Billie let him determine the answer for himself from hers.

So be it, Linc thought, relief and anger flashing through him at once. It was out of control. *He* was out of control.

Linc caught a glimpse of soft feminine skin where Billie's neckline dipped, and he saw a pale, slender ankle peeking out from her slim denims. Finally he noticed that three pairs of wide eyes looked up at his, one blue as the sky, two green as spring grass—all apprehensive. What in the hell was he, some ogre?

He reached for his ball cap on the wall hook. "I'll be down at the barn most of the mornin'. I'll have lunch at Fred's. Be back sometime this evenin'. I'll try to give you a time later." He slapped on his hat.

Without a backward glance he left, forcing himself not to slam the door behind him. He headed for the pickup and took surly note of the humid, cloudy morning, but his thoughts remained behind in the kitchen. The three of them, one nearly five-and-a-half feet tall but as much a young'un as the four-year-olds. Laughing, having a high old time. What did they care? They didn't have to put food on the table, keep creditors away, or find a housekeeper who would stay for more than two weeks.

The picture of his boys laughing and rolling on the floor with *her* stayed in his mind as the pickup hurtled down the rutted lane. It'd been a long time since he'd seen the boys laugh like that; he couldn't even recall when.

She had stayed. Even after he'd barked at her. But for two days or two weeks? Two months?

She was beautiful, and she laughed with the boys. And she had legs that wouldn't quit, and she made him feel things he'd thought had faded away a long time ago.

God save him from a beautiful woman.

Linc had already started replacing the carburetor in the tractor by the time Eldon showed up. Eldon had never been one to begin working at the crack of dawn.

"I stopped at the house first," he said, all agog. "Good Lord, Linc! You done gone and hired yourself what I would call one mighty fine housekeeper." He gave a conspiratorial grin.

"Yeah." Linc kept his gaze on the engine.

"Where'd you find her?"

"Her car broke down in town this weekend. She needed a job." He said it as if he was a good Samaritan.

"That her T-bird in your driveway? That's quite a gem. Ain't many of those babies around."

Linc nodded.

"Person with a car like that probably has money." Eldon looked puzzled. "You say she needed a job?"

"Yep."

Eldon was quiet for a minute, as if finally getting the idea Linc wasn't going to offer any information.

Then he gave Linc a playful shove. "Boy, you lucked out, that's for sure. You get to look at that first thing in the mornin' and last thing at night. Sort'a like—"

Linc looked up from the engine, and Eldon stopped, his smile evaporating—just as Linc had intended. "Guess I'd better give you a hand there."

"Get some tools and go have a look at number five well. It didn't come on the other day when I was testin'."

"Okeydoke." Eldon went for the tools. "You finish with the plowin' this weekend like you wanted?"

"Yep."

"Sorry I had to cut out on you."

"Nothin' to be sorry about. Your mother doin' okay?"

"Yeah. My brother's wife'll stay with her awhile." He walked off, whistling on his way.

Ten minutes later Sam Tate showed up to fix the radio in the tractor. Linc had called him two weeks ago, and he picked today to show up. And the first words out of his mouth were, "That's some housekeeper you've gone and gotten yourself, Lincoln, ol' buddy." Sam's eyes were bright with salty speculation.

"She's just a housekeeper, Sam, nothin' more."

"Yeah." Sam chuckled and turned away. "Some guys have all the luck. Their wives leave 'em, so they have to fall back on some old housekeeper. Rough life—if you can get it. Hey, I can probably stretch this job out until lunchtime, if you'd invite me up to the house."

"I'm havin' lunch at Fred's." Linc clamped his jaw. He knew this wasn't the last he was going to hear about *her*.

In the hours after Linc left the house, Billie came to the conclusion that reading was the most important skill one could learn. All day she read—operating instructions for the dishwasher, microwave oven, washer and dryer; directions on a dizzying array of cleaning solutions—heavens, there was something different for tiles, counters, glass, porcelain, wood, you name it; laundering instructions on different garments; warnings on bleach bottles and laundry detergents. She'd never truly appreciated the complexity of her own housekeeper's job.

She probably would have gotten more done, but she kept being distracted by Tommy and Toby. They spilled things, got their zippers stuck, sent the toilet paper unrolling down the hall and stairway—and kept enticing her to join them in play. When she got them interested in their toy logs, it looked like so much fun that she began building, too—until remembering she was supposed to clean house. Then the boys wanted to go outside, and she was uncertain about leaving them alone. So she pushed them in the tree swing, and they pushed her. She played round the mulberry bush and fell in the grass, too, forgetting all about work that needed to be done. She served canned alphabet soup for lunch and made a game of fishing with the spoon for the letters of their names. Afterward she taught them a card game, with the added fun of gambling with spaghetti straws. She decided that while she wasn't much of a housekeeper, she was quite a good child-keeper.

On her way upstairs with a basket of clean clothes, she caught a glimpse of herself in the hall mirror and stopped. Her hair was awry, and her blouse was wrinkled. She looked tired and frazzled, and she was uncertain that she could keep this up day after day. But she didn't want to give up.

After depositing clothes in the children's room, she came to Linc's. She stopped in the doorway, then entered slowly, feeling as if she were trespassing. Snooping. Which she was, she admitted and set the basket onto the floor.

Each of the children's rooms had spoken of its occupant. The twins' room had identical beds with identical spreads and a number of pairs of stuffed animals. There were nursery-rhyme characters on the walls and toys scattered on every available surface. Ronnie's room was a mess, too, more with boy things than girl things—bat, ball and glove, a basketball, sweatshirts, mice in cages, a jar containing something that looked suspiciously like an animal brain, and shelves of books on animals. Kit's room was neater, his floor clear. Large color posters of classic cars and hot rods adorned his walls and the closet door. Books and magazines on cars lined his shelves and were stacked beside his bed.

Linc's room, however, seemed devoid of character. There was an impressive four-poster bed, unmade, with sheets and coverlet trailing onto the floor, nightstands on either side, a matching chest and bureau, and an old wooden trunk. Clothes lay about. A few common prints in common frames, none matching, hung on the walls, haphazardly, as if stuck there simply to get them out of the way. There were no photographs of children or anyone else. No baby pictures, none of grandparents, nor of a wife.

Once again Billie wondered about Mrs. Snow. She'd yet to see evidence of her anywhere in the house. She felt certain the woman must have died and that it was too painful for anyone to mention her.

Billie considered asking the boys about her but decided it was better left alone. She didn't want to upset them, and it wasn't any of her business. Besides she'd be hideously embarrassed if they told their father the housekeeper had been asking after their mother.

She moved to the bed and began to straighten it, catching a faint scent of nice, musky after-shave from the pillows. She worked carefully, doing the best she could despite her lack of experience in making beds.

The sheets were tan, the quilted spread brown and turquoise. Shades of brown and blue predominated in the clothes lying around, too. The colors of the earth and sky. Gradually the room began to echo of the man after all. He was a quiet man, stern and hard, even, but as solid a man as the hardwood of his bed or the earth he plowed each day.

She picked his clothes from the basket, stopping in midstride and gazed down at the underwear in her hands. His jockey shorts. She tossed them to the top of the dresser along with his socks, as if they were forbidden sins, and left the room.

It was with great relief that Billie found a large plastic bowl of stew in the freezer, presumably made from scratch by a former housekeeper. Well, she thought, it now became hers—inherited by right. She had it heating in a large pot on the stove when Kit and Ronnie burst in the door like a good stiff breeze. They headed first to the refrigerator for soft drinks.

"How did it go at school?" Billie asked.

"Same-O, same-O," Ronnie replied while walking past to the television. Kit simply shrugged as he flopped into a chair at the table and shared his soft drink with Toby.

Billie had assumed it would be her role to listen to the children talk about their day, and the children's role to speak of it. She tried again. "What happened at school?"

"We learned," Ronnie quipped.

Kit stepped back to the pantry for raisins and tossed a package each to Toby and Tommy, who'd settled down to watch cartoons, then flopped into his chair again. "Billie?"

"Yes?"

Kit was somber and hesitant. "Could I have a couple of guys over tomorrow after school? We wouldn't make a mess or anything—" he added quickly. "We'd stay outside. The guys'd like to see your car."

"They want to see you, too," Ronnie interjected, grinning wickedly over the back of the couch.

"Shut up, shrimp!" Kit, red-faced, popped up from his chair.

"He told them you're a fox," Ronnie taunted. Kit went for her, but she was up and out the door quicker than a rabbit.

"Kit, you can have anyone over you'd like," Billie told him, masterfully acting as if Ronnie hadn't said a word. "Bring them in for snacks, if you want. Your friends are welcome to your home any time."

"Thanks, Billie." He grinned and about tripped over his feet as he turned toward the hallway.

Billie watched him go and added what she'd just done to the list of the *few* she'd handled correctly all day.

That evening she placed a tureen filled with the stew on the table, along with butter and bread and crackers and sliced tomatoes, carrots and apples. She'd used nice dishes for each and thought the table looked colorfully inviting. As she took her chair, she watched Linc for a reaction. He glanced around with absolutely no expression on his face. Then he filled his bowl and began to eat, while the children sat there, uncertain as to whether or not they should fill their own bowls and risk making a mess on the tablecloth.

Billie motioned to Ronnie. "Fill your bowl."

Ronnie's eyes widened. "Me?" She looked askance at the tablecloth.

Billie stared at Ronnie until she quit the theatrics and filled her bowl; then Billie filled the twins' bowls, and Kit got his own.

When Linc had finished eating, he pushed his plates away, nodded to Billie and retired to his study. He did offer a polite, "Excuse me," as he rose, but other than telling Toby to quit kicking the table leg, those were his only words at dinner.

Billie didn't see Linc again that evening, though she was inordinately aware of his presence in the house. Such an awareness was odd, foolish and most annoying.

After she'd cleaned the kitchen, given the twins their baths and tucked them into bed, and said goodnight to Ronnie and Kit, she retired to the sanctity of her own room. It was barely past nine o'clock, and she'd just survived one of the longest days of her life. A Twinkie awaited her on the nightstand. She hadn't had time for one all day and had promised herself this treat—but now she was too darn tired to eat it!

She stretched out beneath the cool, crisp sheets and thought it heaven, then chuckled at the pun. Her thoughts wandered to Linc's bedroom upstairs, to the big bed with the turquoise and brown spread and tan sheets. Perhaps tomorrow she would wash and hang those sheets out to dry to give them that fresh scent she'd heard mentioned in a television commercial. Perhaps Mr. Snow would be impressed by that.

The telephone rang, and Linc picked it up immediately, hoping it didn't wake anyone—hoping it didn't wake *her*. If she was asleep. In those shiny white pajamas.

It was his brother, Wes. "Ginny tol' me when I come in this evenin' that you've got a new housekeeper, buddy," he said right after the hellos. He still called Linc buddy; Linc hated it and had told him so.

"Yeah." He should have figured the event would rate a phone call; Wes was worse than an old maid about gossip.

"Coralee told Ginny that you'd up and fired her and had hired on this young and mighty pretty little darlin'. Uncle Fred said she came into town in a '55 T-bird. That so?"

Word of his business couldn't have gotten around better if he'd taken a half-page ad in the paper, Linc thought. "I didn't fire Coralee. I just didn't hire her." He ignored the rest of the question.

"Coralee said she was suppose t' start there this week."

"Well, I'd talked to her about it but decided on hiring Miss Ballinger instead."

"Now, Linc. I can understand why ya' might want t' do somethin' like that." Wes chuckled slightly. "Hell, buddy, if I was in your place, I'd be sorely tempted myself. But it don't seem hardly fair to Coralee. You'd told her she was to have the job." Wes assumed his big-brother-knows-best tone.

"And then I told her I'd changed my mind." Linc thought maybe he should feel guilty, but thinking of Coralee's sharp tongue and the hateful way she'd told him he was in danger of going to hell did a lot to erase remorse.

"Now, buddy, don't you think you may have gone and gotten carried away here? Not that I blame you, but maybe you're lookin' more at that little darlin' and not enough at your children. She might be what *you* need but not hardly the type o' woman who should be takin' care of the kids."

Linc swallowed. "The kids like her fine."

"Well, that may be, but it don't sound at all like—"

"I don't care what it *sounds* like, Wes. Billie Ballinger is perfectly respectable. And I hired her to clean house and take care of the kids. That's all."

"Now hold on there, buddy. No need t' get your back up. I'm just concerned. For one thing, Coralee called up here and got Ginny t' cryin'. Ginny had put herself out to get Coralee back for you, you know. And your kids are part of my family, too. That gal may be perfectly respectable, but that ain't goin' t' change how it looks to people. People are going t' talk, and the kids are goin' t' get hurt. Not only that, how's it goin' t' look t' them, their daddy livin' in the same house with some pretty young thing?"

"Wes, you and Ginny should have felt such concern about my kids back when I couldn't find any housekeeper. As I recall, Ginny said she had her own, she didn't need to be carin' for mine and Denise's whelps. I believe that was the term she used. You both said it was my problem and I'd have to deal with it. Well, I am dealin' with it. And it's none of your damn business how."

"If that's the way you feel about it, forget I called."

"I'll try."

"You're gonna regret it, buddy," Wes said, having to have the last word.

Linc let him. He hung up and stared at the telephone. Wes liked to act the part of big brother at the most inopportune times. In reality, he'd never been much of a brother at all. When their father died, Wes had been eighteen, Linc twelve. Wes had taken a good chunk of the life insurance and gone away to college, leaving Linc, a boy learning fast to be a man, to take care of their mother and the family farm. When it'd been Linc's turn at college, he'd had to earn money and go no farther away than Lubbock because Wes had refused to pay or allow him time away from the farm. It was only because of their parents' wills that Linc had managed to get half of the family farm when their mother died. Wes had maintained it should all be his because he was the elder son. At that, he'd kept the family house. The hard truth was that Wes Snow had always resented that Linc worked hard and built his farm, while Wes couldn't ever seem to get ahead.

It hadn't taken long, he thought hotly now, for the telephone wires to be humming with news of the goings-on in his life, and, of course, it was all put into the most tawdry terms.

Well, Linc didn't care what people said. It was his house, his kids and his money, and he'd hire anyone he damn well wanted. And Billie Ballinger was a hundred times better for his kids than Coralee Hutch, or anyone else he'd met. She made them...sort of shine. And he did like looking at her—if that was anybody's business *or* the world's worst sin—and he'd do it as long as he wanted.

Or as long as she stayed.

Chapter Seven

Linc had made it perfectly clear the past two mornings that he considered Billie's presence an intrusion into his private routine. He was a solitary man, and in a house with four children, she could hardly blame him for so jealously guarding his privacy. Billie determined not to push where she wasn't wanted.

With this in mind, the following morning she was in the kitchen by five. Carefully and quietly, because she didn't want anyone to awaken and catch her struggling, she prepared pancake batter according to the package directions. Cracking the eggs proved the hardest thing. Twice she had to fish eggshells out of the bowl, and she feared she didn't get all the pieces.

She made coffee with equal care, hoping Linc liked it this time. She ran down the lane, retrieved his newspaper and ran back to spread it neatly at his place on the table. Last, she set a cup beside the coffeemaker, then glanced around apprehensively. All looked neat and, she dared hope inviting. She so wanted Linc to be suitably impressed with her housekeeping duties.

Recalling his impassive green eyes and the hard, stoic planes of his face, she figured it would take a lot to affect such a man. Perhaps she'd do better to pour his coffee in the nude; maybe that would get a reaction! Grabbing a cookbook for intense study, she took her coffee and herself off into her room, leaving the kitchen entirely for Linc.

When Linc came downstairs he was mildly surprised to find the kitchen empty. The light was on above the sink, coffee made and his cup on the counter. His newspaper, untouched, lay on the table at his place.

He craned his neck and saw a light beneath Billie's door. He recalled how she'd looked in those white pajamas and felt a warm stirring. Well, he figured, he'd be as good as dead if he didn't.

A large, lidded measuring cup sat near the stove. Feeling foolish as if he were spying, he gingerly lifted the lid and found batter. A bottle of syrup sat nearby, and the old iron skillet covered two burners of the stove. Pancakes. He liked them but preferred biscuits.

He poured a cup of coffee, sat at the table, opened the paper and perused the front page, listening for her door to open. Waiting.

The coffee tasted pretty good, he thought approvingly and turned to the crossword puzzle. It was untouched. Which, of course, it would be, since he'd told her to leave it alone. He worked the first easy blocks of the puzzle, then laid his pencil aside.

He wondered where in the world she was. Maybe she'd fallen back to sleep. Maybe he should go knock on her door.

He considered this for ten minutes, in which she still didn't appear.

Well, he wasn't going to do it. She had a job, and she'd just have to do it without prodding from him. Besides, he didn't need her around irritating him.

Leaning sideways, he looked around the end of the cabinet and through the laundry room at her door, and with the act came the image of Wes or Sam or any of the other busybodies catching him heading toward her bedroom. No, he wasn't about to go knocking on that door.

Funny. The kitchen seemed empty. Lonely.

During the following days Billie assumed the role of housekeeper as best she knew how, her guide being what she had expected of her own housekeeper. Every day, she pulled her hair into a ponytail, dressed in sensible pants and blouse, and donned the apron she'd found in the pantry. She liked the apron; it made her feel professional and homey all at once. Pretty, too, for some odd reason.

She could handle the laundry and cleaning, but preparing meals was a problem. Billie had every confidence that she could *learn* to cook well, but not overnight. So she reverted to her youth, buying prepared and frozen items. She selected carefully, though, to preserve the illusion of homemade dinners while she bought herself some time.

That evening after her first shopping trip the kitchen smelled of spicy spaghetti sauce and fresh bread when Linc came in the door. The jar that had contained the sauce and the wrapper of the frozen bread dough were safely hidden in the bottom of the trash. And the coup came the following day, when Billie discovered that Fred made savory chicken and dumplings and melt-in-your-mouth biscuits.

"Well, hi, gal," Fred greeted her that morning, actually giving her a smile that warmed her heart. "I was wondering when you were going to get by."

"Hello, Fred. The boys and I thought we'd been good enough for a soft drink." She grinned and even touched his arm.

"Hi, Uncle Fred." Tommy beamed and waved.

"Been good, huh?" Fred looked solemnly from one boy to the other, while each nodded seriously. "Well, it's on the house then."

Billie and the boys took a booth along the front wall. Immediately the boys began fiddling with the jukebox selector; Billie gave them each two quarters and helped them operate the machine. Then she noticed three older ladies with short permed blue-silver hair in a booth on the far wall.

They were openly studying her and whispering. Self-conscious, she told Tommy and Toby to quiet down, ran a hand over her hair and glanced down at her clothing.

Fred brought Cherry Coca-Colas in the old-fashioned Coke glasses and slipped into the booth beside Billie. While she and Fred made small talk, the women continued their investigation.

"Don't pay them no never mind," Fred said suddenly, and Billie realized her self-consciousness must show.

She gazed into the now-gentle eyes below his bushy eyebrows. "Do I have stuff on my teeth or something else I should know of?"

He chuckled. "You're Linc Snow's new housekeeper and about as pretty as Marilyn Monroe—to show you my age."

"Oh," she said, not certain she really understood. Still, she had more important concerns right now. She handed the twins two more coins and gave them permission to use the selector in the adjoining booth. They scrambled over the back of the seat, thrilled to be allowed to operate the machine alone.

"I see chicken and dumplings on the menu as tonight's special, Fred," Billie said in a hushed voice.

He nodded. "Best in the country."

"Are your biscuits the best, too?"

"Of course." Curiosity touched his eyes.

"Would you sell me enough of both for the family? And not tell anyone?"

His bushy eyebrows drew together.

"Two of Linc's favorite things are chicken and dumplings and biscuits. I told him I could make them . . . but I can't." She held her breath and didn't let it out until, blessedly, a slow grin spread across his craggy face.

"Boys'll know if I send some with you," he said slowly, pulling at his ear. "Linc around this afternoon?"

Billie bit her bottom lip. "I'm not certain. He said something about helping Bob somebody with irrigation ditches. He has a digger?"

Fred nodded. "He has a backhoe—and he'll probably dig ditches at Bob McKinsey's 'til dusk. I'll bring the chicken and dumplin's out to you this afternoon after the lunch rush. I most generally take a break then anyway, and Theo minds the place for me." He winked. "Our secret, gal."

Much prouder than she had a right to be that night, she served chicken and dumplings, hot biscuits, and a gelatin salad concocted as per box instructions. She eagerly waited to hear Linc's approval and was highly annoyed when she didn't. Where were his manners? she thought hotly. And then she somewhat sheepishly reminded herself that the chicken and dumplings hadn't been her own.

She had finally managed to get all the laundry done, sheets included—and had learned that if you added so much detergent to the washing machine that bubbles start coming out the top, you could add softener and the foam calmed down. Ronnie had taught her that in a moment of high emergency. Tucked in between playtime with Tommy and Toby, she had also dusted and vacuumed several of the twelve rooms. Not very well, she admitted, but the place was beginning to look as if someone cared about it.

In a rare moment of talkativeness, Linc told her he'd done much of the building of the house himself.

"We lived in a small cottage way over on the far east section," he said. "We" meaning him and his wife, Billie assumed as he continued. "When the twins were on their way, we had to have something bigger."

"It's so much like a Victorian home," Billie said.

He nodded. "The plans are from an original from that era. We simply made a few modern adjustments—such as two more bathrooms."

His eyes twinkled a moment with fond remembrance and pride. Billie smiled at him, feeling an instant of unity; she had pride in her small contribution of making his home shine.

Then he blinked, and the blanketed expression again covered his face. "I've got things to do...." And he walked away through the hall.

As much in self-defense as anything else, Billie instituted the custom of a daily afternoon nap for the twins. The boys balked at first but were quickly persuaded when Billie announced all naps were begun by eating a Twinkie. Then she read them a story out of *Humpty Dumpty* magazine, and within minutes they were asleep, leaving her free to hop up, regretfully, and get work done.

After finding several more tablecloths, she insisted on either Ronnie or Kit using one when setting the table every evening. There were quite a few moans about both the job and the use of the dining room, which meant it was farther to carry plates. Forks and knives were to be arranged as Billie had taught them, and, yes, water glasses at every place. A beautiful table added pleasure to a meal.

The children were appallingly lacking in social graces. If Linc noticed, he didn't say anything. Actually, he had a few bad habits, too. So, gently, Billie mentioned things: elbows didn't belong on the table, napkins should be spread in laps; a fork rested between the fingers, not poised like a spear to stab food; chewing was done with the mouth shut; and burps were kept small, not loud enough to wake the dead. Further, telephones should be answered politely with "Hello" or "Snow residence," and doors should be closed, not slammed. Please and thank you were very important.

Ronnie, of course, balked. "Who cares about all this stuff?" she said, rolling her eyes.

"You will someday, perhaps when you're asked to a friend's house. You don't want to embarrass yourself."

"All my friends eat like I do." She deliberately stabbed a piece of meat.

"Then maybe you could show them up for the slobs they are," Kit put in.

At an age where he wanted to appear a man, a suave man, Kit was eager to learn about social things. He was also sensitive and gentle—unlike his cold, hard father and Billie adored him for it.

Ronnie, the crackerjack rascal, was a tomboy through and through. She wore only jeans and shirts, without frills of any kind, and enjoyed boasting that she could beat up all the boys in her class. She made out to be tough, but Billie saw the crack in her armor. Every morning before she left for school Ronnie said "See you later" and waited for Billie to reply in kind before going out the door. After several days Billie realized that the girl was worried about her leaving.

Tommy wore his heart on his sleeve, cried and laughed easily and was given to singing with gusto. Toby was more somber. A wound to his body would not make him cry, but a wound to his esteem would send him hiding in his bedroom closet. Billie found him there one day, crying because Kit had not heard what he had to say. "Be-bec-cause I c-can't t-talk r-right!" he wailed.

Near tears herself, Billie sat down amid the toys and told him about her own stuttering at his age. He was skeptical at first, but he listened. Then Billie took the gamble of promising Toby that he would not be stuttering by the age of nine.

Later, stuttering but proud, Toby declared to his family that Billie had stuttered and now didn't—and had told him that he wouldn't be stuttering by the time he was nine.

Alone with her in the kitchen that evening, Linc scowled. "You aren't the one who'll have to deal with the boy's disappointment if he doesn't stop stuttering like you promised him. What do you think that will do to him?"

"I've given him hope—what he needs most right now." Did the man have to see the dark side of everything? "It's as practical to imagine how wonderful he will feel at nine when he has quit stuttering as to believe the other way."

He frowned, turned and headed for his office, as was his evening habit.

Frowning appeared to be the natural state of Linc Snow's face—which Billie thought was such a shame, because he was a handsome man. Or he was when his expression softened just a bit. She knew he could smile, but he didn't seem to like people to catch him at it.

It hurt and confused her that Linc didn't like her. She realized she liked *him,* strange as that seemed. He certainly hadn't given her any encouragement. In fact, he was the most standoffish man she'd ever met. But he was also fair— she saw the way he settled arguments between his children. He was a hard-working man, modest about his accomplishments and straightforward about his failures. His reverence for nature was obvious; he watched the sun rise each new day, and he kept feeders for the birds, which he often paused to watch. For those reasons, and for a dozen others she couldn't give name to, Billie Ballinger liked and respected Linc Snow.

As the days went by, Linc found the image he'd first formed of Billie Ballinger being stretched all out of shape. She wasn't quite as city-slick as he'd thought, nor as scatterbrained as she often appeared. She seemed at times, almost secretly, a deep thinker. And earthy, picturesque words crept into her precise speech. Words like *plumb*—plumb worn out, plumb baffled, plumb full up—and *hogwash*. She liked early mornings and didn't seem to mind mud tracked in onto the floor.

She just didn't fit any mold he tried to place her in, and this proved highly unsettling.

Every evening when he'd near home, his heart would pump a tad faster, his gaze racing ahead in search of the red car, wondering if Billie Ballinger would still be at his house. Which was a hell of a thing to wonder, since her car still didn't run.

When he reached the kitchen door, his ears were already listening for her laughter—she laughed easily and often. In fact, she seemed one of the happiest people Linc had ever met, as well as the most openly expressive. Whatever the woman felt, be it anger, amusement, annoyance, hurt or affection, was immediately evident on her face. This as much as anything caused him a great deal of irritation—and fascination.

He did absolutely nothing to encourage it, but every time he turned around, there she was, being friendly. And laughing, or giving her opinion. And he didn't know how to react.

Yet, though he would have died before admitting it to a soul, he was glad for the aura she'd brought to his home.

Each night they all sat down to a real meal—and here Linc overlooked some nagging suspicions—at a fine table, complete with cloth and formal place settings. A foolish extravagance, maybe, but a good lesson for the kids, Linc told himself.

His dresser drawers now contained clean underwear, and fresh shirts hung in his closet, a little wrinkled here and there—the woman wasn't the best at ironing—but clean. One night his sheets smelled of sweet, fresh air from being hung on the line—Lord, it'd been years since he'd savored that pleasure.

Maybe she wasn't the best of housekeepers—she spent more time playing with the boys than straightening up—but still, within two days the house was taking on a tended look. Damp towels disappeared from the baths, and fluffy clean ones took their place. Cut flowers appeared in vases not only in the dining room but in the kitchen and hallway. Their scents mingled with that of fresh, strong coffee and savory food and feminine perfume.

Kit brought home the first friends in months; Ronnie's sarcastic mouth slowed some; Toby talked more; Tommy sang even louder than usual.

There was a woman in the house again. A real woman.

She'd been the housekeeper for five days—and five nights—when Linc brought home the fuel pump for her T-bird and proposed he and Kit work on it.

"You don't have to do this, Linc," Billie said when Kit, as eager as a hound for his first bird, ran outside to begin assembling the tools. "I'm sure Larry is about recovered from his measles. I can call him." .

She had that tone that said she thought he was doing her a great favor, and he didn't like her thinking that.

"Tomorrow's your day off. You'll want the car for going into Lubbock—or whatever you might want to do. Besides, I already told the boy we could, and there's no stopping him." He kept his eyes on the pump as he removed it from the box. "You owe me thirty dollars."

"Please take it out of my pay."

"Okay." He headed for the door.

"How long would you like me to wait dinner?" she asked.

"'Bout an hour, if we don't run into trouble." He turned and looked at her then, something drawing him.

Her eyes were blue as the sky, warm as summer sunlight, and focused on his. They beckoned him—to what, he wasn't exactly certain, but he felt it was something powerfully pleasurable.

He opened the door and got out of her sight as fast as he could and cursed himself for being stupid. Once her car was fixed, she'd probably light out, and he'd be stuck with the laundry and cooking again.

The first time Linc gunned the engine, the woman burst out the door. She stood there staring at the car as if she'd just been given a kingdom. And then she started thanking Kit and him, spewing as much gratitude as if they'd given her a diamond necklace.

Linc, knowing he wasn't deserving of such high praise, couldn't look at her and tried to suppress the foolish swelling of pleasure in his chest. When she got carried away and hugged Kit, Linc panicked, thinking she might throw her arms around him, too! And he thought . . .

Their eyes held for an instant, hers as shiny as sapphires. Then she looked away and stayed where she was, saying, "Oh, thank you both so much!"

Sharp, unexpected disappointment sliced through Linc, and he cursed himself a fool for it.

Nothing would do but that everyone had to take a ride. Linc wanted to eat, but seeing how excited Billie and the kids were, he figured he'd be smarter to let them work some of it out before having to sit down at the same table with them.

First she took Kit and went for a spin down the road.

"Oh!" she said when she returned. "I'm the Good Queen of the World again!" She clasped her hands together and did a little dance.

Linc had to chuckle at that, and at the pure, unadulterated joy on her face. Never had he met such a woman.

"She says that's how she feels in the car," Kit explained, standing beside him.

"Yeah, I gathered that."

She took the twins and Ronnie at once, the three of them jammed in the second seat and wrapped in one seat belt. "I promise I won't go fast or far," Billie said earnestly. She ended up taking a short spin down the highway and then around the yard.

Then it was Linc's turn, and he'd already determined he wasn't going down the road with her. It was all foolishness.

But instead of offering to drive him, she insisted *he* drive and take Kit again, while she went in and put dinner on the table. That touched the boy in Linc, and, besides, he rationalized, Kit was about to skyrocket out of his shoes for a second ride.

Taking care to hide his childish enthusiasm, Linc folded himself into the seat behind the wheel of the lollipop-red car. The fragrance he'd come to associate with Billie enfolded him as he positioned himself on the white leather seat and fastened the seat belt. Every bit of red enamel and silvery chrome on the dash glimmered; the engine purred as gently as if brand new.

Billie leaned on the open window. Strands of her silky hair fell around her face, and her creamy neck disappeared into the slightly gaping neckline of her blouse.

"You can adjust the seat here." When her arm snaked down between the door and the seat and brushed against his leg, Linc almost jumped out of his skin.

He found the lever and busied himself fiddling with the seat, getting it into position for his longer legs.

"You might want to adjust the mirrors, too," she said, her arm again poking through the window.

At last she stepped away. "Take as long as you like, you two." Linc felt self-conscious under her gaze as he turned the Thunderbird and headed down the driveway. A strange elation tried to ease into his veins, but he pushed it away as nonsense.

As he pulled out onto the blacktop, he glanced over to see Kit with a mile-wide grin on his face. "You sure made Billie happy, Dad."

"No big deal. Besides, you did most of the work."

"We did good together, didn't we?" His son was so thrilled with the small, insignificant endeavor.

Ah, hell, Linc was pleased with their work, too. "We did well, son." The elation returned.

"Dad, could you drive past John's house and maybe blow the horn?"

Linc started to protest that John's house was five miles away. Then he cut his eyes to the boy, remembering being fifteen. "Yeah, guess we could do that." Seized by the long-abandoned foolishness of youth, Linc pressed the accelerator. "Let's see how this baby cruises, shall we?"

Kit laughed aloud and lowered his window, allowing the air to buffet their hair. It seemed that twenty years rolled off Linc's shoulders—and he felt closer to Kit than he could ever remember.

The air was uncommonly still, the day's burning heat fading, when Linc and Kit strolled out between the rows of thick cotton plants in the field bordering the yard. Linc no longer took his tractor into the fields; now was a time of waiting for what he'd sowed to mature. At the moment he savored both the dry soil crunching beneath his feet and the presence of his son. It was the first time he could remember Kit walking the fields with him.

"Billie should be comin' soon," Kit said.

Linc had been thinking the same thing, glancing often toward the road.

"You know, Dad, Billie wasn't always rich. She said her dad went broke three times. She said a couple of times she and her dad lived in one motel room for months at a time."

He hoarded the information that brought Billie into slightly sharper focus.

"Her dad was real crazy, too," Kit went on.

Was that where Billie inherited her eccentricities? Linc wondered.

"He did stuff like rent elephants for her birthday and let her ride one in a parade down the main street of Las Vegas. And once he wanted to see this tycoon on Wall Street but couldn't get an appointment, so he shipped himself to the guy's office in a box."

It was plain Kit was impressed by such romantic tales, and Linc experienced a fleeting jealousy. He himself wasn't the stuff of legendary tales. He was just a guy trying the best he knew how to cope with life and raise his children to be *their* best.

Kit kicked at the dirt. "Sometimes I wonder what places like that look like. Las Vegas, New York. Billie says Reno's lots different than here."

Linc's heart tightened. "You'll get to see those places if you set your mind to it, son." He gazed into Kit's eager eyes and wished the boy would be content here.

"Well, I mean to see them, but I'll always come home. Billie says that travelin's nice but comin' home's even better."

"She does, huh?" He peered at Kit. "You kinda' like Billie, don't you?"

"Aw, Dad, just as a friend. I know she's older than me and everything." He looked away, blushing, then back at Linc. "Billie likes us a lot, too. She likes it here."

"I hope so, son." He thought that maybe she did—for now.

"Well, she does. She said so."

Kit decided to head back for the house, but Linc lingered in the field. He looked down the road in the direction of Lubbock. A blue pickup whizzed past.

Resting his hands on the belt at his hips, he surveyed the seemingly never-ending field lying beneath the rays of a golden evening sun. The cotton flowers were dainty pale dots against the thick, loden-green leaves, and bolls were already prevalent. His heart swelled with wonder and pride. All of this from tiny seeds.

It promised to be a bumper crop this year. He prayed no hail or flood or windstorm came up to change that. He intended, by God, to prove wrong all the naysayers who said he'd been too late with half his planting.

He lifted his eyes again to the road, looking, anticipating Billie's return. *If* she returned. Which was a pretty stupid concern on his part. Hell, her clothes and personal things remained in her room. And Kit had just said she liked being here. He wondered about that. People said a lot of things that turned out not quite so. And he knew that for now, having only been with them a week, maybe she found it a nice diversion. But he couldn't imagine a city woman liking this place for long.

Still, though he tried not to, he watched for her, and a strange tightness clutched at his gut. He knew it was foolish, impractical and dangerous. He knew full well the temptation rising within him was apt to bring full, monster-size trouble.

No, there would be no trouble; he wouldn't allow it.

It was just after six when Billie arrived. Linc allowed himself to come as far as the hallway door, while the kids eagerly ran forward to greet her. As if one day without her had been unbearable.

Feeling pretty stupid watching such a display, Linc started to retreat into his office, but something compelled him to stay. To cover his interest, he walked across the kitchen to pour a cup of coffee and remained leaning against the counter, watching.

It appeared by the number of shopping bags Kit helped bring from the car that Billie had spent her day shopping—exactly what he'd expect from a woman like her, Linc thought dryly. Minutes later he was amazed to discover she'd done some shopping all right—she'd bought gifts for the kids! There were giant candy suckers, complete with bows on the sticks, for each. Then for Tommy there was a harmonica—small, but the real thing. Toby got a tape recorder with child-sized, reporter-style microphone. Ronnie's surprise was an elaborate mouse cage—mouse condo was more like it. Kit received a full-color book on race cars.

And, oh man, were the kids agog. Ronnie sat there, gazing at everything. "It's not our birthday or Christmas or anything," she said in that fresh-kid way she had. What kind of father was he to let her talk like that? Worse, she made it seem as if he never bought them anything. Well, it wasn't all that good for kids to be given so much, he reasoned. Then they didn't appreciate it. The woman was spoiling them, buying them off, that's what.

Then he realized that the house had been singularly lifeless without her presence. In the space of six short days she'd come to know his children well enough to give something special to each. And Linc couldn't decide who was the more eager: the kids to get the gifts or Billie to give them. His heart constricted as he gazed at her and then at each of his children. He'd been trying. So damn hard he'd been trying, but he couldn't seem to get past the concrete wall that had gone up inside him when Denise left. He couldn't be all his children needed, because he no longer had it in him.

They needed, he thought, a woman's touch. They needed, as all kids, a mother. And for the space of a heartbeat a very old, deeply buried, painful longing rose within him. For that moment he became again the youth who wanted the lavish love of a mother and father and who vowed to have the sort of family he'd missed out on.

"Didn't you get anything for yourself?" Ronnie asked, bringing Linc back to the present.

"Well, of course." With a flourish, she pulled something colorful—pale yellows, browns, and blues—from a sack. "How do you like it?" Doing a graceful pirouette on those long legs, she held an apron to her breasts. Laughing like a child, looking like a woman. Linc couldn't stop staring at her.

"An apron?" Ronnie said, her voice reflecting Linc's incredulity.

"It was what I wanted," Billie said simply.

"W-what d-did y-y-you g-get our d-daddy?"

Toby looked from her to Linc, and a cold chill of embarrassment shot across Linc's shoulders. The glance Billie exchanged with him was as nervous as his own. He checked his urge to flee the room but kept all emotion from his face.

"For your father..."

She'd bought something for him! His heart beating overtime, he watched her pull a box from one of the shopping sacks. She walked forward; a tentative smile curved her lips, and two bright pink blotches appeared on her cheeks. His gaze dropped to the box she extended toward him and then to her hands, white, long-fingered, feminine. He swallowed and reached for the box. It was a boxed set of crossword puzzle books. It'd been years since he'd received a genuine gift for no reason. A gift. From her to him.

"They're for advanced puzzle workers," she said.

Looking into her eyes, he found them hopeful, warm. Openly offering friendship. It scared the hell out of him— mostly because he was afraid he wanted it.

Chapter Eight

The house was quiet at midnight when Linc came into the kitchen. He stood there in the dark, holding one of the crossword books *she'd* given him. He'd been working a puzzle in it—or trying to. He peered through the laundry room for long minutes at *her* door. A sliver of light shone beneath. He thought of her silky hair. He heard no sounds other than the beating of his own pulse in his ears. Either she was awake or she'd fallen asleep with the light on.

He had the crazy, totally insane urge to go knock on her door. The kids were asleep; no one would know. He had a good excuse—to thank her again for the crossword books. For everything she'd given them the past week.

Thrusting the urge aside, he moved to the counter, flipped on the light and reached into the cabinet for the coffee tin. He slammed the door closed and wondered if she heard it. He thought of what her perfume did to him. He began to whistle. Loudly. He wondered if she could hear, if she might come out.

He quit whistling. He had to stop thinking like that. He didn't want her to come out.

But he did; he knew he did. He wanted to talk to her, to find out why she'd never married, if she'd ever been involved with someone. Hell, she'd no doubt had a string of lovers—and it wasn't any of his business!

But he knew he wanted to know. And he not only wanted to talk to her, but he wanted to touch her. His mind filled with the image of her naked form, and he fantasized stroking the inside of her thighs....

No! He didn't want complications. He *wouldn't* want her.

Then, as he replaced the coffee tin in the cupboard and allowed the door to bang closed again, he wondered why human beings were drawn to wanting things they shouldn't.

Billie laid aside the book she'd been reading and listened. Someone was in the kitchen. Linc. She thought she heard his whistling, and warmth rushed across her chest and down her limbs. Sometimes, not often, Linc whistled, always the same tune.

She couldn't be certain. Then she heard a thud—a cabinet door banging maybe? Wasn't that water running?

Was it simply that her thoughts were so focused on Linc Snow that she strongly sensed he was in the kitchen beyond her door?

She could go and see.

She could...talk to him? Simply see him. How she'd like to touch his thick hair.

Wilhelmina, really! Slipping from the bed, she turned out the lamp and moved quietly to the window. Involuntarily she listened but heard nothing more from the room beyond. She wanted to go in there, could pretend she wanted...what? No doubt, if it were Linc, he wouldn't welcome her presence.

She leaned on the sill and gazed out through the screen. The bare breath of a breeze caressed her cheeks and neck. The night whispered of approaching fall; the stars were as diamonds scattered on black velvet, the moon full, magically lighting the earth with its silvery glow.

There was a lot of beauty here, she thought. She just hadn't been in the frame of mind to see it that evening when the Thunderbird broke down. So much had happened since then. Her father and mother would both have gotten much amusement over it all. Over what she'd done. And thinking of it, she shook her head and hid a smile of wonder behind her hand.

How wonderful had been her greeting when she'd returned that afternoon! She held it close in her heart. She'd been so frightened at what she'd taken on, so afraid that she couldn't do even half of it. Even now her self-doubt was about the size of Mount Everest. She truly wasn't very good at keeping a house, but she had managed for a week. And today when she'd come home, it had almost been as if they were her own family. They like you, Wilhelmina! They really like you. And Linc...

Her heart fluttered, and a chill shivered down her spine. She recalled the look in Linc Snow's green eyes when she'd handed him his gift. It'd been the first friendly, warm look he'd ever given her. And for an instant she'd seen a glimmer of childish wonder there on his harsh, manly face, telling her much pain was hidden in this tough man. He was indeed very human.

She'd pleased him, she thought. She'd seen the proof in his eyes. Had seen that...and more. And she'd felt more than simple joy at giving a gift.

Looking out at the night, she thought of Linc's rich mahogany-colored hair and imagined the feel of it against her skin.

Threatened by the stirring inside her, Billie pushed from the window and crawled back into bed, settling the covers as firmly as she rebuked her wayward desires.

Billie had been attracted to many men in her twenty-eight years, had truly loved two. She recalled for bittersweet minutes the things that once experienced were never forgotten—the feeling of her hand snuggled within that of the man she loved. The rough tenderness of a male hand on her breast. The aching pleasure that rose in her throat with a flaming kiss. The delicious throbbing of her love's body against hers. She recalled the dear pleasures with deep, great longing. And she recognized the seductiveness of the sweet desire stirring between herself and Linc as surely as she recognized the signs of a gathering storm.

But she must not think of it. Such desire was a threat to her staying in the Snow home.

Yet, as she closed her eyes, she thought of the man whose bed was only rooms away, in the same house, beneath the same roof.

Billie faced another week. She learned to close windows when the wind rose, that weather reports were more important than dinner, and how *not* to make biscuits. Tommy and Toby each gave her their first true hug and said very easily, "I love you, Billie." "M-me, t-too, Bil-lie." And on her second Friday night as housekeeper, she met Wes and Ginny Snow.

The house was already full of visitors: two of Kit's friends had come for supper and had brought Fred for a rare time away from the café. Fred had insisted on providing dinner—ostensibly to give Billie a break—so she hadn't had to worry about her cooking abilities. And Ronnie had insisted on seeing to the table setting and drinks for everyone. Thus pampered, Billie sat and delighted in the conversation and laughter around the dining room table.

Covertly she watched Linc. He smiled a number of times, several times at her. Those times she glanced away quickly, lest he or anyone see her feelings on her face. Feelings she couldn't give name to, understand or trust.

Things had changed between her and Linc in the past several days. Not visibly, but in a way Billie could feel so strongly she knew it was true. There was a different look on Linc's face, a welcoming look. He spoke more often without a frown or growl and appeared in a much better humor toward everyone, not so quick to jump down throats. Tonight he allowed Toby up into his lap and, as if hesitant but unable to help himself, stroked the boy's hair. He was the most relaxed that Billie had ever seen him. Until the unexpected arrival of his brother's family.

Within the first five minutes Billie came to several conclusions. There was definitely little brotherly love between Linc and Wes. While Linc was cordial, he was far from warm. Wes Snow, wearing an orange-and-red shirt as bright

as casino lights, was a bag of pompous hot air. Ginny Snow
was about as brash as the bright blue shadow on her eyes
and as brittle as her overpermed hair. They had one teen-
ager, a bashful boy Billie liked on sight, and two whiny girls,
aged ten and six. It wasn't too hard to conclude they'd all
come to inspect Billie. They surveyed her as if debating
whether she dyed her hair or if her blood was as red as
theirs.

"So this here's the lady we hear's been teachin' our little
niece and nephews to gamble?" Wes boomed out. Ginny's
expression was clearly critical, either of Billie or the poker
or both. Linc raised an eyebrow, but his lips twitched.

Billie withdrew from the big man's handshake. "Yes, I
guess I'm the one. We play go fish and use spaghetti straws
for money."

"Know a lot of gamblin', do ya?" Wes ogled her.

"Some," Billie admitted.

"Well, why don't you play with her, Wes," Fred drawled,
"and find out? You play poker once a month up at Bob
McKinsey's, don't ya?"

Ginny frowned, and Wes mumbled, "Sometimes. Guess
we could all sit down, huh?"

In an effort to lower the din and to ease Linc, who seemed
to be contemplating escaping through the window, Billie
shooed the children upstairs. Slipping into her best humble
housekeeper mode, she gathered dirty plates and politely
announced she would bring cake and coffee.

"I'll help you, darlin'," Fred said, rising.

"You're a guest, Fred. I can do this." Billie saw Ginny's
eyes, sharp as an eagle's, watching her.

"Aw...I feel out of place *not* doin' it." The older man
gave a dismissing wave and reached for glasses. Easily
bringing half of all the dishes, he followed her into the
kitchen. "Now, gal," he said in a low voice, "why would I
stay in the room with that big ass and old biddy when I can
be in here with you?"

Billie laughed. "That's your nephew and his wife you're
speaking of."

He nodded as he set his load on the counter. "And Wes
is just too much like his daddy to suit me. And me and

Harley got on about like Wes and Linc, too. I always thought the good Lord got things mixed up and Linc should have been my boy. We look alike, don'cha' think?'' He exhibited his hawkish profile.

"Yes, you do." He did, though she would have agreed even if he hadn't. "Do you have children, Fred?"

He shook his head. "Missed out on that. Was married twice. First gal died early, and the second one decided Hollywood was a lot more promisin' than a café in Heaven." He motioned for the scrub brush. "I'll rinse, you go ahead and get them the cake. Better cut half of it for Wes."

Thinking of Fred and his wives and Linc and his father, Billie got out dessert plates. "Linc's father was like Wes?" she asked, trying to picture what that must have been like for Linc.

Fred raised a bushy eyebrow. "Harley? Yeah, pretty much...mostly in his smallness of feelin' for others and his inflated opinion of himself. He worked a hell of a lot harder than Wes, and he expected those boys to work hard, too. Harley never had any use for fun. He was a cold sort. Lord, he was a hard man." He gazed ahead, his eyes filled with sad memories.

Billie thought that perhaps that was why Linc had such trouble expressing his tenderness, for he wasn't as hard as he appeared. Stubborn maybe, but not half so hard.

"Fred . . . what happened to Linc's wife?" she asked suddenly, regretting the question almost as soon as it came out. She had no right to pry.

"Denise?" Fred looked at her. "He hasn't said?"

Billie shook her head, averting her eyes. "It really isn't any of my business."

"Sure it is. You're takin' care of his kids—you need to know everything that affects them. He should have told you, but Linc's a pretty proud man, and to flat out admit that your wife left you is a mighty hard thing for a man to say."

"She left him—and the children?" Billie had not expected that at all. Cancer, an accident, something like that, but not . . .

Fred nodded. "One day Denise just up and told Linc she was leavin', that she couldn't stand this back-road place anymore. She didn't want the kids, either."

Billie's eyes burned as she thought of the children. And the man. How could any woman not want her own children?

"You know this visit is an examination of you, gal? Wes and Ginny'll have to report back to all the other busybodies wantin' to know more about the pretty gal livin' here with Linc."

Billie took a breath. "I guess I'm flattered to be of such importance."

Fred winked. "Well, you sure are a sight and more for these busybodies around here, little darlin'."

"I try hard." And they chuckled together.

"Well, you two are certainly having a good time in here." Billie looked around to see Ginny Snow surveying them sharply. "What are we all missin' out on?" Her voice was syrupy, her expression avidly curious.

"Nothin' much, Ginny gal." Fred slapped an arm around Billie's shoulder. "Billie here was just givin' me the recipe for this scrumptious chocolate cake of hers." He nodded toward the elaborate cake Billie had purchased that day at a bakery on the outskirts of Lubbock—and Fred knew that darn well. "Secret recipe she got from her grandmother, and she don't give it out to just anybody, so I feel very honored." He beamed down at Billie, and she gave him a grand smile.

You should be ashamed of yourself, Wilhelmina! But she wasn't—she was too taken up with enjoying the moment between herself and this rare man. And minutes later in the dining room, when Fred made a big deal of how Billie had made the cake herself from scratch, she felt only a tiny twinge of guilt at the growing lie. Her gaze locked onto Linc's. His eyes twinkled with merriment, and she quickly looked away, feeling the embarrassing heat rise to her cheeks. Did he know? It would serve you right, Wilhelmina!

She concentrated on efficiently serving the cake and coffee, as a good housekeeper should, she thought primly, pulling fresh cloth napkins from the sideboard for each person. The table was neat and lovely, the coffee fresh, every cup had a saucer. Give these people something to think about, anyway. Maybe she couldn't cook, but she knew a thing or two about the amenities in taking care of guests. She noted that Wes was looking at her with admiration—and that his wife had noticed and didn't like it.

When she turned to leave, Linc's arm snapped out, and his hand closed around her wrist, giving her a gentle tug. "Aren't you going to enjoy some of your delicious cake?"

A mischievous grin tugged at his lips. Between her shoulder blades, she felt the weight of Wes's and Ginny's gluttonous curiosity.

"I'd thought I'd begin cleaning up," she said, irritated that he continued to grip her wrist in front of prying eyes. It was the first time he'd ever deliberately touched her.

"That can wait—the kids'll help you later. We'd like the pleasure of your company."

It was more a command as he nodded to the chair on his right, where Kit had sat earlier. He didn't let go of her wrist until she moved to sit. Fred cut her a piece of cake, and, surprisingly, Linc poured her a cup of coffee, both of them serving her while Wes and Ginny watched, their eyes bright as new pennies.

Wes praised her cake; Ginny said it was a bit too chocolaty for her taste. Wes eyed her and said he understood she was from Reno, Nevada. "What did you do there?" Ginny asked. "I'm sure you weren't a housekeeper." Left unsaid, but plainly written in the woman's eyes, was the accusation that Billie had surely worked in a casino or perhaps a house of pleasure.

Billie almost told her that she had indeed been a housekeeper, then bit back the lie. She was in danger of becoming a compulsive prevaricator, she thought, inwardly amused.

"No, I wasn't a housekeeper," she said and leisurely raised her coffee cup to her lips.

After thirty seconds of uncomfortable silence, Wes asked Linc about how his cotton was doing. As if disappointed when Linc told him fine, Wes shook his head and predicted problems in the future because of the lateness of Linc's planting. Their conversation turned heated. Billie heard about frost dates of days past and learned that one good hailstorm or an early frost could completely destroy a cotton crop. She saw that Wes was not a man to take chances and that he highly resented Linc for being one *to* take chances.

Listening and watching Linc's expression, Billie saw the great importance of the cotton crop to him. It was his livelihood, she realized, but more, growing cotton was what he did with his life. To be good at it, to be among the best, was a driving force within him.

The conversation turned to a number of other things—Wes's gallbladder, Coralee Hutch taking a plum job with a rich lawyer up in Clovis, one Tom Canby who'd lost his place for nonpayment to the land bank, and lastly to the children. Repeatedly Ginny slung little barbs at Linc's children: "Kit better watch out who he hangs around with, Linc, or you're goin' to have trouble with that boy," and "Ronnie needs to study harder and keep her mouth shut," and "Toby should be tested. He's rather backward for his age."

When Wes and Ginny finally gathered their children and left, the house, though still full of people, seemed oddly quiet. Peaceful. Discord came with those people like a plague, Billie thought as she began clearing the table. Her mind replayed some of the obnoxious things the two had said.

Seeing Linc's hand close around a cup, she looked up, surprised to see him helping clear. His eyes rested on her for a long second.

"That Wes has a head as big as his belly," Fred commented.

Billie bit her lip, then just had to say, "I wanted to push Ginny's face into the cake when she suggested Toby wasn't very bright—just because he stutters." Recalling the woman's comments made her anger grow. She glared at Linc. "Why didn't you say something back to her?"

"Like what?" He was clearly taken aback by her fervor.

"Stand up for your son and tell her she's the one who needs testing."

"Would it have helped? Would it change her mind?"

"Maybe not," Billie conceded reluctantly. "But it would have been better than appearing to agree with her."

"I don't agree with her, and I didn't appear to."

"Well, you should have told her so." Then Billie realized that Fred was watching them closely—and she thought that she'd overstepped her bounds as an employee. It wasn't for her to criticize the father or give her opinions on the son. "I'll see if I can squeeze these into the dishwasher," she said and left.

Her hands shook as she stacked the dishes. She was simply tired, she told herself. And confused.

Her neck prickled and her back tingled when Linc came up behind her, leaning over to place plates on the counter. She felt foolishly angry with him. No, she thought. She was angry at something but not at him.

His wife had left him. Oh, Lord, what a horrible thing. What had Denise been like? Had he loved her deeply? He'd had four kids with her; he'd had to feel something for her. And he was still hurting, she thought, recalling his reactions to so many things. He was afraid to get close, even to his children. But this was intolerable! He was their father, an adult, and they needed his love. He had no right to close himself off from them. From everyone.

Even from her, Billie thought hotly, feeling immensely foolish for it.

The following morning Linc made certain to rise before Billie and was sitting on the tailgate of his pickup at first light when she came outside to get the newspaper. It was her day off, but he'd counted on her following her usual pattern. Each day, even those she had off, she prepared the coffee and got the newspaper for him before disappearing into her room. Well, he was getting pretty tired of having his coffee alone—and he needed to speak with her. For some unknown reason she'd seemed angry with him last night, and he didn't like it. He wanted . . . oh, hell, he didn't know what he wanted, but whatever it was, he probably shouldn't!

"Hi," he said.

"Hi." Her hair was mussed, her cheeks aglow from sleep. She wore a loose blue velvet top that fell to her thighs and hid her shape, skintight black pants and slippers. She glanced around as if uncertain what to do. "I was just going to get the paper. . . ."

"Just waiting for the sunrise," he said, looking her in the eyes. "Want to join me?"

She hesitated, then gave him a smile that made his heart skip a beat. "It won't come up for another thirty minutes." She sauntered over to join him, though.

"Close enough," he said. He returned his eyes to the east and felt the pickup give as she slipped onto the tailgate beside him. He caught a faint whiff of her scent. They sat there in silence, and Linc was as aware of her as if she were in his lap.

Billie tried to see the view with his eyes. The beautiful glow of a new beginning, one more day of sunshine for those miles of cotton plants that grew out there by his hand. Those plants were the future for him and the children; they held his hopes and dreams and pride. All that in something as lowly as a cotton plant.

She looked at Linc's profile. "Fred says a farmer is as much a gambler as a man playing the tables in Vegas."

He nodded, keeping his eyes on the field. "I'd guess that's close to truth. We'll have us a good crop this year—if we don't get a windstorm or hailstorm that knocks the blooms off or an early killing frost. All of it's beyond our control."

"Maybe all three will happen," Billie said dryly.

He turned his head toward her and looked down from his taller height. "Maybe." His voice came soft and low, and a bare smile curved his lips, softening his harsh features.

"You are a most pessimistic man."

"I think of myself as cautious with my expectations."

"Oh."

"You and Fred seem pretty close." He crossed his arms, tucked his hands beneath his armpits and peered at her. "You two seein' a lot of each other?"

Billie looked away at the field as the image of Fred lugging pans into the kitchen appeared in her mind. "I've taken the boys to the café for soft drinks a couple of times."

"Just drinks? Too bad. Fred makes great chicken and dumplings."

She swung her head around.

He returned his gaze to the field. "He can't make chocolate cake like you can, though. For that we used to have to go to the bakery."

How long had he known? Billie took a deep breath. "You haven't said anything. Why?"

"You were gettin' the job of feeding us done. How you did it was your problem."

"I apologize for lying." She looked at the gravel drive. "I knew you'd say no to giving me a chance if I told you I couldn't cook."

"Hell, yes. Cooking is the main part of a housekeeper's job."

"Then why didn't you fire me when you found out I couldn't?" She peered up at him, trying to read his expression.

"Now how could I have done that with the kids so enchanted with you? I'd have been the biggest monster of all time. Besides, your meals, however you were providin' them, weren't half bad—and I didn't have to cook them."

"I'll learn to cook."

He sighed deeply. "I hope so. The way you're doin' things is pretty expensive." He chuckled.

Oh, so rare a sound from him! He really and truly was amused.

His expression sobered, grew intense as he gazed at her, searching for what she wasn't quite certain. Yet she was searching, too. And drawing close to him within her soul.

"You don't know how to cook, and you don't strike me as the type who's had a lot of domestic-type experience. Why do you do this?" His brow creased. "Why put yourself out here in nowhere-land, trying to cook, ruining your fingernails cleanin' and wipin' up after kids?"

He still couldn't believe she *wanted* to be there, she saw. A most skeptical man was Linc Snow. She smiled. "I needed a job. It's hard to get one when you don't have previous experience or training.''

Linc ran his eyes over her elegant features. He thought of the personal references she'd given him. ''You have influential friends. Seems like you could have gotten a better job in a city with one of them.''

She nodded, and her silky eyelashes fluttered downward. ''Yes...I have several who would have given me a job.'' She paused, then looked back up at him. ''But I find it embarrassing to accept charity. Something happens to the friendship then. And really, I wasn't certain *what* I was going to do. My immediate plans were to spend some time alone down at the cottage and figure that out. I probably would have gone back and taken any position I could get. But I happened onto your family and this job, and, well, this opportunity seemed a better choice. My father always told me to be quick to answer when opportunity knocks.'' She smiled softly. ''And I like the room.''

''You like the room?''

''It's a lovely room.''

He couldn't look at her smiling face without smiling in return. She liked the room he'd made. And only *she* would make a choice based on such unorthodox reasoning.

''I *have* taken care of someone before,'' she said, lifting her chin. ''My father. My mother died in a car wreck when I was nine. She'd never been a homemaker sort—she was always busy with her charities. I don't remember her clearly, except that she laughed a lot and liked to kiss me.'' Her features softened with pleasurable memories.

''Daddy missed her so much, and he was helpless around the house. Couldn't cook and even had trouble with something as simple as a vacuum cleaner. We sent all our clothes to the laundry, even in the years we had to pawn something to get enough cash.

''Daddy, like you, was a gambler of sorts—not at the tables but with all kinds of business propositions. An entrepreneur, he called himself. He grew up poor and determined to be rich. He made and lost more than one fortune, and there were a number of lean times. At six, even before my mother died, I was putting frozen dinners on the table.

Daddy always raved over the way I heated those dinners. I had a rare life having such a father. Everything I did was right, and he tried to make every day a holiday. He considered life one big blessing to be enjoyed."

Linc thought fleetingly of his own father, a stern, forbidding man, and his mother, who'd been a bare shadow of her husband. "What happened to the money your father left you?" he dared to ask.

She sighed. "My accountant ran off with it."

He stared at her. She didn't speak with bitterness so much as resignation—and a hint of incomprehensible amusement.

"Your accountant just up and stole it?" How in the hell could the woman take it so lightly?

She nodded. "My daddy made a fairy-tale world for his Princess. He picked out a personal friend to be my accountant—to handle all my finances and even a great deal of my life. And I accepted it all because it was the easiest thing to do. I charged everything and had the bills sent to Jonathan—something many, many people do, I might add. It was so easy to skate through life, leaving the details to someone else."

She looked off at the horizon. "Jonathan was able to move things into his name, liquidate, and vanish—with a number of his other clients' money, too. In settling the mess I lost my house and most of its contents and two cars and most of my jewelry."

A whisper of sadness touched her then, making anger flash in Linc's chest at the one who'd hurt her. "A lot of people go broke. They simply file bankruptcy and save most everything." But not her, he thought even before she shook her head. This woman would never do the normal, the practical.

"I had the means to pay the debts. I couldn't place my failure onto the people who'd given me credit in good faith." Her eyes took on a faraway look. "I guess that was the first decision I made on my own and for myself, ever." She cut her eyes to him. "You know, I am angry at Jonathan for what he did...but I can't help thinking that maybe he did me a favor. There's a lot I've been missing out on in my fairy-tale world, and I wouldn't have breached the walls to go and see on my own. I was too comfortable for that.''

Linc gazed into her eyes and thought how amazingly clear they were. "How is it you never married?" There had to have been a number of men in love with her.

She shrugged and looked at her toes. "I was almost— twice. The first love faded with youth. The second . . . well, it just didn't work out.''

Billie thought fleetingly of Marc, who'd been the first, and then of Parrish. Parrish had wanted children, and she couldn't give them to him.

But it'd been more than that, she could see that now. Recalling both loves in that moment, she understood herself more clearly than ever before. She'd devoted herself to her father and the wonderful world Michael Ballinger had created for her. For years her father had been both parents as well as the child she couldn't have. She'd loved him so thoroughly that she'd been unable to leave him for anyone, even a husband. And then he'd left her in that lovely, lonely kingdom, not knowing who she was or of what she was capable.

She glanced up to see Linc gazing out at the field of cotton.

"Fred said that your wife left you. How long ago was that?''

His eyes swept around to her. Slowly he twisted and leaned against the side of the truck bed, bent his knee. "Almost a year and a half ago.''

"You two must have been married a long time—Kit's fifteen?''

He nodded, his green eyes very dark, not looking at her. "I met Denise when I was in college—she was in her last year of high school. She got pregnant with Kit in the back seat of my car. An old story. She was from the city, over in Lubbock, didn't know anything about livin' in the country and never knew much what it was like not to be married to me. Guess it was natural for her to want to find out. She just got tired of being married and livin' out here.''

His eyes rose slowly to meet hers. Billie ached for him, for it seemed that the pain, the bitterness, remained within him.

She knew he'd loved his wife, maybe still did. The possibility made her sad.

She looked to her feet. "She left her children."

"Yep, she did."

"They never mention her. Does she speak with them, see them?"

"She sends a card now and then."

She told herself it was foolish to judge someone she didn't even know, but the woman had hurt the children, and it was as if she'd hurt *Billie's* children.

"I think she was a fool," she said, slowly lifting her eyes to his. "She tossed away so much love."

His expression turned hard, cynical. "Love. Lots of songs written about that, but who knows what it really is? I guess it's somebody wantin' something from somebody else."

"Maybe," she conceded. "But I think it's more what someone gives to someone else, and it's the person giving who gets filled up inside." This she'd gotten from her father, worth far more than the money and something never to be stolen—love and the ability to give it.

They sat there staring at each other.

Billie felt her body pressing toward him, though she didn't move at all. The muscles of his jaw clenched while his gaze swept up to her hair and down over her face, as much a caress as if done by his hand. Her breath choked in her throat as longing rushed through her veins.

Damn! Linc wanted to grab her to him. He wanted . . . he wanted a lot of things at once, but he had to tell her at least one thing or he'd burst.

"You're good for the kids," he ground out. "You're the best thing that's happened around here in a long time . . . and I'm glad you took the job as housekeeper."

Housekeeper.

He knew it, and she knew it—they'd have to keep things cool between them if she was to stay. And he wanted her to stay. Which was why he'd forced himself to open up enough to say that much.

A tender smile touched her lips. "Thanks for telling me that, Linc."

"Yeah . . . sure." Uncomfortable as if he'd stripped buck naked in front of her, he looked away and pushed himself to the ground. "Did you make coffee?" He caught her smile out of the corner of his eye.

"Yes."

"Let's go have some."

He took her arm to help her from the pickup. She felt so fragile, so feminine within his grasp. He let go as soon as her toes touched the ground.

In the kitchen she poured the coffee, and he brought the sugar bowl to the table. When she remained standing while stirring sugar into her cup, he reached into a cabinet, drew out a couple of packaged Twinkie snack cakes and tossed them onto the table. Her eyes flew up to his.

"Share a before-breakfast snack with you."

She finally sat down at the table with him. They listened to the weather forecast on the radio and chatted, and Linc realized it didn't seem quite so hard to talk to her now that he'd spilled his guts about Denise leaving him.

He wondered how long she would stay and decided he'd have to be careful not to do anything to drive her away. He'd put off the inevitable as long as possible. And then he wondered which was more inevitable—that she would simply grow tired of life at the farm and leave, or that she'd be forced away because he couldn't keep his hands off her.

That morning, as they talked and shared coffee, Billie sensed she and Linc had established a sort of truce. Over the following weeks they came closer, but only so far and no farther. By tacit agreement they each ignored what lay between them. They didn't speak of it or acknowledge it in any way. Though, if pressed, Billie would have had to admit to times she felt Linc's gaze upon her, to moments they shared in silent wanting.

Ignoring the wanting seemed the best course, in the hope it would simply go away. It didn't. As if feeding on secrecy, on forbiddenness, their desire grew. It took additional nourishment from the hundreds of daily situations and common concerns that brought them together.

They lived in the same house. They shared meals and responsibility for the children. Their lives brushed and bumped, rubbed and smacked, against each other. They saw each other first thing in the morning and last thing at night.

Most of the time Billie told herself they were both adults and in control of themselves. But sometimes...

Sometimes they'd brush against each other when together in the kitchen or meeting on the stairs. "Excuse me," Linc would invariably say, and Billie would immediately avert her eyes.

Once he took her and the twins into the field for a minilesson on cotton. "Here—I'll help you," he said, quickly taking her hand to help her cross an irrigation ditch. Then she was standing beside him, and his hand, hot and rough, was still on hers. They each pulled away.

Another time she took a picnic lunch to him out in the tractor barn, telling herself with every footstep that it was perfectly innocent; the twins needed to share a whimsy time with him. She sat on the pickup tailgate beside him while the twins wandered down the lane, tossing rocks.

"This is good fried chicken," he said, but his eyes revealed he wasn't thinking about fried chicken.

"Mrs. Smith's frozen." And she wasn't thinking about chicken, either.

"You microwaved it well." His gaze lingered on her lips.

"Thank you." Her gaze lingered on his lips. When she forced herself to look away, she squirmed so hard she thought she'd get blisters on her behind—and she knew she'd deserve them.

And still another time she'd tossed caution to the winds, left Kit in charge of the kids and gone with Linc to see the farm. He stopped at the pond, and they both got out and walked beneath the shady cottonwoods.

"There's good fishin' in this pond." He stopped suddenly and turned, his face a scant distance from hers. "Do you like to fish?"

Billie gazed into his eyes and swallowed. "I've never fished."

"Never?" His eyes held hers.

She shook her head. "Never."

They'd almost kissed then—and Billie had felt desire burn in every cell of her body.

Sometimes he'd pull a package of *Twinkies* out of the cabinet and toss it to her to open and share. Sometimes, as she spread clean sheets on his bed, she'd picture him lying on them at night. Sometimes when she bid him goodnight, his spring-green eyes would linger on hers, and she'd detect a hint of heat there. Quickly she would look away, unable to conceal her own wanting. Sometimes she would lie in bed and think of him and remember how it felt to curve her backside up against a warm male front side and sleep... or other things.

Billie came to know Linc Snow as a man of strong principles; he was honest, hardworking to a fault, scrupulously fair, and at rare times generous. But a bitterness ate at his soul, put there, Billie guessed, when his wife abandoned him. As a result, he trusted neither life nor people and had become one of the most temperamental, cantankerous men she'd ever had the misfortune to meet. Along with the times he shared *Twinkies* and coffee and conversation with her, came the times he complained that her coffee tasted like dishwater, that the stray cat she and Ronnie wanted absolutely had to go, that Kit had to help him in the field instead of going to some nonsense school dance, and that Tommy had better stop singing, by damn!

Sometimes when he snapped and barked at her, she wondered how in the world she could continue to care for him. Pity? she wondered. Surely one had to have pity for a man so sharp he could cut himself rolling over.

Yet it was far more than pity that she felt for Linc Snow. Day followed day, and just as surely as the fluffy cotton fiber ripened, unseen within the hard boll of those plants out in the field, so did Billie's sensual attraction to Linc ripen deep within the secret places of her being.

Day after day, pulling nerves tighter than an overwound watch spring.

Chapter Nine

Day followed day and turned into weeks. Soon Billie had been the Snow's housekeeper for nearly two months. Both cotton-picking time and Kit's birthday loomed.

The cotton harvest promised to be the best in a decade. As morning after morning the killing frost held off, a number of farmers sprayed defoliant on their fields, anxious to go ahead and pick the crops that had reached maturity. Left behind in those fields were stark black stalks and dark earth dotted with white. Bits of cotton fiber drifted in the constant fall wind, caught on the dry grass and weeds edging the roads and looked for all the world like a dusting of snow.

The Heavener Gin began operation, as did gins all over West Texas, and Heaven became quite different from the sleepy spot in the road Billie had first seen. People came and went from the feed and grain store; trucks brought packed cotton modules and trailer baskets heaped with cotton into the gin yard and left empty.

Whenever Billie and the twins went for an afternoon drive and a cherry Coke at Fred's café—which they did with some regularity—they could see the waste fiber from the gin filling the air like a blizzard spewing from the fierce mouth of Old Man Winter. Cotton caught on house shingles and in tree branches, coated fenceposts and windowsills.

Over the weeks, Billie watched Linc avidly consult weather forecasts. He was as edgy as a cat walking a tightwire, waiting, wondering, worrying, as if any of that would ensure he brought in a good crop.

She tried to point that out to him. "It's planted and growing, fertilized and sprayed. You can't stop rain or hail or an early frost, so why wear yourself out fretting about it?"

"That's mighty easy for you to say, I guess," he'd replied, his eyes like cold hard jade, "bein' as it isn't your crop or your farm—your kids that have to be fed and clothed. Ah, hell, it's not something you'd understand."

But Billie *had* understood as she'd watched his lean back disappear out the door. For one thing, his pride was at stake. He wanted to harvest not only the most cotton per acre but for his cotton to be of the best quality, too. And she understood that all his fretting was part of being a farmer, part of being Linc Snow. In essence, she'd criticized Linc for who he was. That had been unthinking and callous.

And she understood, too, that another problem plagued Linc, just as it did her. She knew that he was having an awfully hard time living in the house with her—just as she was with him.

When Linc balked at the idea of holding a birthday party for Kit at the house, Billie went to Fred. Together they planned a party at the café, and Fred not only gave over the entire café for a private party on Friday night but insisted on making the cake for the occasion. With enthusiastic help from the twins and Ronnie, Billie threw herself happily into party preparations. If there was one thing she was certain of, it was her ability to give a bang-up party. She determined that this party be a wonderful memory for *her* Kit. For that was how she'd begun to think of the children—as her kids.

She was starkly reminded that they indeed were not, however, when Kit's birthday arrived and brought with it not only the first heavy morning frost but four cards from Denise Snow as well.

Billie didn't find out about the cards until she arrived home in the late afternoon. She and the twins had been to Lubbock to pick up decorations and Kit's birthday present—a deluxe set of tools and tool box with his name engraved on it.

"You can't look...can't look!" Tommy cried, pushing Kit.

"Hey, squirt. Can't look at what?" Kit held both brothers at arm's length by a hand to each forehead.

"It's okay, guys. I've got the bag closed." She carried only a small sack of groceries for the home, had left the gift and decorations in the Suburban to take later to the café. She acted as if her one sack was Kit's gift, though, because she wanted him to continue to think they were having a small, family celebration at home that evening. Kit's friend, John, was joining them for dinner and had the job of getting Kit to the café later that night.

Setting the sack on the counter, Billie told the twins to go upstairs and prepare for a bath. She picked up the stack of mail lying on the counter, intending to sort out the junk from the important and take it to Linc's desk. Just as she came to two identical envelopes, she became aware of Kit standing and staring at her.

"Got a birthday card from Mom." He waved the card slightly. His gaze met hers then skittered away. He was trying so hard to be unaffected. "She sent me a check for a hundred dollars."

Billie swallowed. "That's awfully nice." Don't you dare feel jealous, Wilhelmina! Think of the boy. She searched his face.

"Yeah." He averted his eyes to the card. "There's two cards there for the squirts. Don't know if they got money, though. Ronnie took hers upstairs."

"Yes...here are the ones for the boys." She held them gingerly by the edges. "I think I'll give them to your father. He might rather see them first."

Kit nodded, gazing down again at his card. Billie went to him, put her arm around his shoulders. She said nothing, just stood there with him.

"I'm okay," he said, his voice tight.

Billie squeezed him, pressed her cheek to his shoulder.
The two bright splotches on his cheeks showed in stark
contrast to his pasty white face. His eyes remained on the
card as if glued there; his jaw muscle worked. Slowly he
looked at her, and the pain and concern in his eyes shot clear
through her heart.

"I don't know about Ronnie, though. I wouldn't have
given her the card but she saw it before I could hide it." He
inclined his head toward the stairs. "She's been up there
with her door closed ever since. I would have kept it from
her if I could," he repeated with a desperate air.

"It's not your fault," she assured him, touching his
cheek. "And don't worry about her—she's strong. You
know that. Now, I'll go up and speak with her, just to make
sure, and you get a shower for tonight. You're sixteen today, and I don't want to be having to remind you to take
showers anymore."

He gave a lopsided grin. "Okay."

"Kit..." He turned. "I think you're awfully special."

He grinned, almost. "Later, dude." With a mock salute,
he was off up the stairs.

Billie listened to the rare quiet coming from Ronnie's
room, then knocked. Ronnie's answering voice was unusu-
ally subdued. Billie opened the door and peeked in. The girl
sat at her desk, her chin propped upon her hands, staring at
the mice in their elaborate cages. Billie crossed the room and
sat nearby on the edge of the bed. She saw a card lying
facedown beside Ronnie's hands—and a small photograph
frame, too.

"I got everything we need for tonight. And the engrav-
ing turned out beautifully on his tool box."

"What time are we leavin'?"

"Fred wants us there around six-thirty to start decorating. I told John we'd have pizza at five."

Ronnie cut sarcastic eyes her way. "You didn't get those
disgusting pizzas in the green boxes did you?"

"No, I didn't. I went to the pizza place and had them
make me up two larges, barely cooking them, so they'll be
fresh made. Whitie there looks like he's getting a little fat."

Billie indicated the mouse nibbling on food in the corner of his cage-condo.

"He likes to eat. Not much else for him to do." Silence for long seconds. "I got a spankin' at school today."

Billie sucked in a deep breath as thoughts of marching to that school and telling those people a thing or two flashed across her mind. She didn't approve of spanking.

"Don't go gettin' all bent out of shape," Ronnie said, as if reading Billie's mind. "I guess I deserved it, and Mr. Lee doesn't hit hard enough to kill a mosquito anyway. It's the principle of the thing, he says."

"What did you do?"

"I squished a cupcake in my sweet little cousin Meggie's face." Her sweet lips curved. "Real good, too."

"So you deserved the spanking. Did Meggie deserve the cupcake?"

"Yes. She was sayin'…things." She stared at the cage in front of her.

"What things?"

Ronnie shrugged. "Oh, just things."

"Ronnie…" Billie said in her best threatening voice.

"She was just makin' remarks about all of us."

"About me living here?" Billie guessed, knowing immediately that she'd hit her mark by the expression on Ronnie's face.

"That and Toby being stupid."

Billie thought that Meggie did deserve a squished cupcake in the face. They sat for long seconds in silence. Ronnie stared at the mice. Billie gazed at the back of the photo frame.

"Kit told you about us gettin' cards from Mom, didn't he?"

"Yes. I set Tommy's and Toby's aside for your father to see first."

Ronnie sat up and looked at Billie, her young freckled face stoic—so like Linc's. She lifted the picture frame, looked at it, then extended it to Billie and moved to sit beside her on the bed. "This is my mother."

Billie held the frame and stared down into a three-by-five photograph of Denise Snow.

"Daddy put all the pictures of her away. Oh, he doesn't keep us from the albums, but he'd just as soon nobody looked at them when he's around." Ronnie leaned against Billie's arm and pointed. "They don't show real clear, but her eyes are blue—just like yours."

Billie met Ronnie's gaze, then looked again at the picture. It appeared to have been taken outside, close up. The woman had blond hair about the same length as Billie's, the same cut except with thick, full bangs. Her face was square, perfectly formed, her nose a perfect slope. A vibrant, saucy smile. She was easily beautiful.

"She looks a lot like you," Ronnie said softly.

Billie was thinking the same surprising thing. Images of those first searching looks she'd received from Linc, Kit and especially Ronnie flashed through her mind. They made sense now.

"She's very pretty. And you look a lot like her, too."

Ronnie's sober eyes studied hers. "Do I?" She wrinkled her nose. "My hair is a mousy brown, and my eyes aren't blue."

"Your hair is like dark honey and your eyes like jade. You're just as pretty as your mother."

A sadness swept Ronnie's face, and Billie thought perhaps she'd said the wrong thing. The girl reached for the card, opened it and stared at it. She pointed with her fingers, then looked up. Emotion, at last, seemed to fill her face and run over down her shoulders.

"She signed it, 'Love, Mom.' But she left me. She *left!* How can she still say she loves me?"

The bewilderment and pain in the girl's features and voice cut right through Billie, becoming her own. She shook her head and wrapped an arm around the child. Ronnie buried her face in Billie's shoulder and cried, quietly, which seemed to make it all the more painful.

Billie prayed for the right words. "You have a right to your mother, Ronnie. She should be here with you. To take care of you—watch your mice and make you hot chocolate. But she...had problems and desires that made her unable to do that."

Billie rocked back and forth, wanting so to take the pain from this special child. "Darling, your mother does love you—she sent you this card to say that. She could not give birth to you and not have a special place for you in her heart. No mother can." Her voice came husky past the enormous lump in her throat. "Why her reasons for leaving were stronger than that love, I don't know. I only know that you had nothing to do with her leaving."

She moved to cup Ronnie's cheeks between her hands and stared into her tearful green eyes. "I know, too, that your father loves you deeply, so do your brothers and Uncle Fred." She blinked away tears. "And so do I."

Sitting on the edge of the bed, they held tight to each other. Billie cried, too, and gave thanks for being allowed to comfort his child-woman, who wasn't her daughter, but who had been lent to her at a time when she so obviously needed someone.

"You won't go away, Billie?" Ronnie sobbed into Billie's breast. "Not for a long time?"

"I will always be here for you, darling. Always."

The two hugging on the edge of the bed didn't see him, and Linc quietly closed the door. He stood for a moment with his hands on the knob, the feelings of frustration and anger building within him like the hot pressure in a volcano.

Damn Denise! Damn her, damn her. He strode down the hall to his room, shutting the door behind him. He tossed his hat to the bed and moved about restlessly, as if a dog nipped at his heels.

Wasn't it enough that the woman had left the kids, without bringing more pain into their lives by sending occasional cards and notes? Never a full letter. Only three damn phone calls in all this time. She'd stepped out of their lives by her own choice. Why couldn't she just stay out?

And now Billie had just promised Ronnie to always be there. Oh God, what lies people told each other! He looked through the window, tracing the gravel drive to the black-top with his gaze.

Billie shouldn't have said that to Ronnie, shouldn't have promised the girl what would never be. She'd leave, and there'd be ol' Linc, stuck with brokenhearted kids again. Alone again . . .

But she'd been trying to help, he thought, the fierce energy suddenly draining away. Billie really and truly cared for his kids, and they for her. She'd been there for Ronnie and had no doubt done a hell of a lot better than he would have. His heart ached for his kids, and he wished he could take all their hurts upon himself. He wished he could be a better father. He wished he could have been a better husband so that Denise wouldn't have gone and left the kids motherless.

With the sun setting low, Linc left the refuge of his room for the familiar activity going on in the rest of the house. Rock music sounded through Kit's bedroom door; Ronnie was talking to her mice.

He stopped in the kitchen doorway and watched Billie flitting happily about the room. Her hair was extra curly, and she wore a soft-flowing skirt and colorful sweater belted at the waist. Dressed for partying. The sweater had a scooped kind of neck, revealing lots of skin. She looked soft and feminine, and he would have liked to look at her a long time. She and the twins were doing their rendition of "Zip-a-Dee-Doo-Dah," Billie humming, Tommy singing the words and Toby supplying the birdie's tweet-tweet at the appropriate time.

The silly ditty had become "their" song. They liked to sing it, Tommy had told him, when they rode in the Thunderbird—Billie was the Good Queen of the World then and they were the Princes, he'd said. Billie and the boys were now a common sight cruising down the road in that lollipop-red machine.

Guys would say to Linc, "Saw Billie and the boys zippin' along today." And they'd give him a wise grin, as if they knew things were going on at this house. But it no longer bothered Linc what people thought. His kids were happy, and he guessed he'd have to admit to feeling adolescent pride that Billie was considered his.

Passing by the boys, Billie kissed each of their heads, which were bent over paper and colors on the table. She spotted Linc as she whirled around toward the refrigerator. She paused, and a familiar look of uncertainty crossed her face.

Electricity shot across the room.

He averted his eyes to the coffeemaker and headed for it, thinking that things *were* going on in this house, if only in his own mind. There was enough in his thoughts to get him arrested.

"I saw the truck outside," she said.

He nodded. "Yeah. The module builder was havin' trouble so Con's shuttin' down at dusk tonight."

"Oh . . . will you be going to the party with us then?" she asked in a hushed, eager whisper.

He shook his head. "I'll come later. I've got to go over to help Con with the repairs." And I'll be damned if I'll feel guilty over being a little late for a party I wasn't wild about in the first place, he added silently.

"Oh. Well, we're going to eat in about ten minutes." She lowered her voice. "Did you see the cards addressed to the boys?"

He nodded. "Yeah. Thanks. I'll take care of it later."

Then she nodded, saying, "Will you take these plates into the dining room?"

"Sure."

Without looking at her, he took the plates from her hands. He caught her scent, and the soft, feminine smell raised the same pulse beat within him that it always did. Damn her! Damn him! He'd worked hard all day, and he'd work hard until bed so he could fall asleep without having to lie there thinking of her and the empty hole within him that kept getting wider.

When he got to the dining room, he had to smile. She'd created her replica of a pizza parlor again, this time with candles that she'd no doubt light—clumsy little boys at the table or not. He'd better have the fire extinguisher handy.

He thought of the red envelopes sitting on his desk, the cards for the boys. He wondered what in the world he would say to Tommy and Toby. Eighteen months was a long time in their young lives; their mother was gone, no longer a part of their world. How would they understand what she was and wasn't to them?

Kit came into the room, interrupting his thoughts. "Need some help, Dad?"

"Appreciate it."

They grinned at each other, and Linc was filled with thankfulness—even with everything that troubled him.

Linc's present for Kit was his first pair of genuine snakeskin boots, handmade by one of the best boot makers in the West, soft and supple from the start. They'd cost over three hundred dollars, but Linc had reasoned that the boy's feet were about done growing. And at sixteen, it was time the boy had fine dress boots.

"For impressing the girls," he told Kit and shared a wink with the boy—young man, he silently corrected himself.

Kit was appreciative and tickled to death to have the boots, Linc could see, but when the kid saw the tool kit, his eyes lit up with fireworks on the Fourth of July.

"A whole set of sockets, too!" Kit leaped out of his chair to give Billie a hug, while she explained that she and Fred and Ronnie and the twins had all gone in together on the gift. When Kit and John prepared to leave, Billie gave John the keys to her Thunderbird for the evening.

"No hot rodding," she told them.

What in the hell did she think two boys were going to do in a car like that? Linc thought. She didn't know the kids as she thought she did—not by a long shot!

Then he told himself that the jealousy squirming around inside him was stupid childish stuff. And he took himself off to work, where he belonged.

Heaven was an oasis of light in the darkness when Linc drove in to town. The gin was going. Stray cotton puffs drifting in the breeze reflected in the glow cast from the tall yard lamps. Pale yellow beams streamed from the café windows; it looked as if every light was on inside. Heads and shoulders moved around, and the driving beat of a Hank Williams Jr. tune could easily be heard.

Linc sat in the pickup and watched for a minute. He'd driven over to Con's but had turned right around and gone back home to shower. It was Kit's sixteenth birthday. That it was cotton harvest, that he hated to be amongst a crowd and that he both anticipated and sweated being in a social atmosphere with Billie, should all be put aside. He was Kit's dad. That meant more.

He got out of the truck, touched the unaccustomed ribbon tie at his throat and polished the toes of his best boots on the backs of his starched and creased jeans. Then he caught a glimpse of Billie through the window.

"Hey, Linc!" Joel Heavener was across the street, flashing a wave as he walked over to his Caddy. "You pickin' yet?"

"Helpin' Con Hawthorne. Start on mine in a few days." He felt self-conscious—as if he'd been caught peeking at a woman undressing.

"Hell of a good year!"

"Yeah!" Linc waved and headed around the rear of the café to slip in the back door.

Billie was behind the counter serving soft drinks when she caught sight of Linc. He had an arm around Kit; they slapped each other's backs. She looked from Kit's delighted face to Linc's. His eyes met hers. Pleasure sliced across her chest and blossomed in her belly. She averted her eyes to the glass in her hand and stuck it beneath the spigot of the soft drink machine.

He'd come early. Oh, Kit was probably literally in heaven. Had that truly been admiration on his face when he'd looked at her? No...mustn't think of such things...

A Billy Joel song reverberated through the room. In the space cleared for dancing, five couples gyrated around. Fred yelled from back at the video machine, where he and Ronnie were having a hot game with two teenage boys. A girl squealed, someone called out for Kit. Billie lined up clean glasses and began filling them with ice, tapping her feet to the music. Tommy and Toby ran past, giggling, bumping into her legs.

"No playing behind the counter!" It was hard to see with the lights turned down as they were.

"We're cowboys in a shoot-out," Tommy said, sprawling on the floor and peeking around the end of the counter.

"Well, okay..." She smiled. One of these days she would have to learn to be more firm with those two.

"Four vanilla floats, please, ma'am." Turning, Billie saw John grinning across the counter.

"After these six Cokes." Billie laughed. "I only have two hands, John."

He assumed an exaggerated frown. "Gee, my mom has four."

Suddenly a body was next to her. It all came to her at once: long, lanky legs, familiar crisp white shirt—that she'd ironed—Chaps cologne. Linc.

His green eyes sparkled at her then skittered away. "How about an assistant, boss?" His crisp shirt sleeve stretched toward the tulip-shaped glasses on the top shelf while his other hand took up the ice-cream scoop.

"You can make ice-cream floats?" She watched in amazement as he deftly flipped up the freezer compartment door and reached inside.

"Yes, ma'am. There's a lot of things I can do that you don't know about."

Suddenly he was looking at her, his twinkling eyes intense. A lock of his hair fell across his forehead, and a shadow of a smile touched his lips. *He was flirting!*

Billie quickly looked away. Yet mischief led her to say saucily, "I'll bet that's so."

He shot her an enigmatic grin and focused on the glasses before him.

They worked together behind the counter. Their arms brushed, and they collided front to front, back to back, side to side.

"Oops, sorry."

"Me, too."

"Need more ice."

"Got it."

"Rag, rag! Gotta spill!"

"Catch!"

Then suddenly Linc grabbed her hand. "It's time we got a dance in before this thing breaks up."

Billie held back, but he tugged her along. Around her, youthful faces laughed, then chuckling herself, she followed, with only a bare thought to reputations or practicality.

"Make room! Gramps on the floor," someone called out.

The banjos and guitars played gaily, and Linc whirled Billie loosely into his arms.

"Can a woman from up there in the big city do the West Texas two-step?" Linc's expression was daring as he guided her across the small area.

"This woman can follow *any* man dancing." His thighs whispered against hers, and she stepped back quickly.

They danced with the younger couples to the tune of "Rocky Top Tennessee," and kept their bodies a perfectly respectable one foot apart. But Linc gazed down at her, and she gazed up at him, feeling not quite innocent. His eyes spoke of intimate thoughts, his hand was warm upon her back. And Billie felt gloriously alive.

A single light burned above the sink when Linc entered the kitchen. Ronnie and the twins, exhausted from the party, had fallen asleep as soon as their heads hit the pillow. Kit was still out somewhere in the Thunderbird, having been given permission to stay out until one. Probably neckin' with that sweet young Julie Pratt, Linc thought with a hint of a worry. He wouldn't be able to go to sleep until the boy came in.

For long seconds he stood gazing at the sliver of light beneath Billie's door. She'd been beautiful that night. He just hadn't been able to resist flirting with her, being around her, dancing with her. Damn it all to hell, something had come over him and pushed his good sense almost into oblivion!

He wanted her, and bad.

He went to the cabinet, opened it and took out the coffee tin, then let the door slam. He whistled then broke off and cursed himself a fool. Then he opened the cabinet door again, replaced the coffee, and let the door slam once more. Again he began to whistle and again stopped. He leaned against the counter and listened for sounds from her bed-room. He heard nothing.

When the coffeemaker finished, he took his cup of cof-fee and stepped outside, stared up at the stars and tried to train his thoughts on finding Orion or the dippers.

Suddenly the hairs on the back of his neck pricked, his ears picking up a slight sound. Behind him the door creaked softly. Expectantly, he turned and watched Billie join him on the porch. Her face was hidden by the deep shadow. In a swift glance he saw she wore a dark, oversized sweater and leg-hugging pants. He sensed her hesitant smile, though he couldn't see it. He inhaled her faint scent, and his groin swelled.

"Waiting for Kit?" Billie asked.

"Yeah."

Nervous, she held up the cup in her hand. "Thought I'd have a cup of your coffee before bed."

He said nothing. She stood beside him and gazed through the screen, her eyes adjusting to the dark. Stars glittered like jewels; the air was sharp. She rubbed her arms against the chill.

"We'll have frost again," Linc said.

"When will you start picking your own fields?"

"Next week."

"Thanksgiving is Thursday."

"Only the weather holds up pickin'."

Silence stretched while they each drank coffee.

"I'm awfully glad you came to the party tonight. It meant so much to Kit."

"I know." He lifted his cup, drank. "I don't imagine I'd be too far wrong to guess you're waitin' up for him, too."

"Oh...I was awake anyway." She felt silly, self-conscious. She told herself she would go in in a minute.

"Kit was over the moon with the tools you gave him," he said. His voice held a curious vibration.

"They weren't just from me. Fred, Ronnie, even the twins donated to the cause."

"But you chose them."

"Well, we all agreed."

He looked downward, and she heard the scrape of his boot on the porch floor and his deep sigh. "I've always hoped Kit would be a farmer, would join me in the operation here. We could expand. But all he can think about these days is fast cars."

"He's young yet," she offered.

"Huh." He shook his head, raised a hand to prop against the porch post, rubbed his nose with the thumb of his other hand. "As far back as I can remember, all I wanted to be was a farmer. I knew that when I was Kit's age."

"And what if he wants to be a racing mechanic? Would that be so terrible?"

"Has he told you that?"

"He's talked of it."

She thought she saw him nod.

"It's Ronnie who would be your farmer," she said softly. "If you'd let her."

"Ronnie..." He turned his head to her. "I heard what you told her today—about always being here for her. Always *here?*" His tone was sharp, sarcastic. "You plannin' to grow old and gray as our housekeeper, Billie?"

"I...I'm not planning anything. I probably won't grow old here, no," she said, feeling foolishly defensive. "But I don't have to be physically in this house with her to be available to her. There are telephones, letters. I meant what I told her—I will always be there to help her."

She peered at him, searching features she couldn't truly see, feeling his observation. His energy.

He took a step toward her. "How long are we goin' to be able to pussyfoot around what's between us?"

"What's..." She swallowed, not knowing if she should deny any knowledge of what he'd asked. Or if she wanted to deny it. "I don't know." Her voice came out a bare whisper. Longing flooded her chest so painfully it brought tears to her eyes.

"How long do you think we can go on like this?" he demanded again.

"I don't know...I don't know." She shook her head powerlessly.

His arm shot out, and his hand closed roughly over her upper arm. He jerked her against him.

"You're drivin' me crazy, damn you!" He growled the words and shook her. "You're—"

Then his lips were on hers, his arms wrapping around her, crushing her against him.

They kissed, a long, hot, greedy kiss. The delicious warmth of desire flowed over Billie like a beam of hot Texas sunshine. She pushed her arms up and around his neck and clung to him, savored the taste and smell and feel of him. When the air was gone from her lungs, her pulse pounding in her ears, their lips broke apart. She breathed rapidly. Her heart beat so loudly she thought surely he could hear it, too. His neck was hot and damp beneath her fingers.

Oh, Lord, she wanted... No, she thought, trembling. *Oh, Lord, she couldn't think.*

They remained with their arms around each other, their bellies, groins, and thighs pulsing. Neither moved, as if the floor would fall out from beneath them or a thousand sirens would go off if they did.

Billie struggled for control against her will. She wanted him to pull her to him again. To kiss her again.

Lights of a vehicle—the Thunderbird—flashed across the porch, and Linc thrust her from him, as if discarding something repugnant. Dazed, Billie moved for the door, groped, found the knob and fled inside to her room.

Chapter Ten

The next day, Saturday, was usually Billie's day off, but she and Linc hadn't discussed it that week. She knew he'd be heading out for Con Hawthorne's field, but she also knew Kit was available to watch the younger children. So by six o'clock she was dressed and reaching for her coat.

With relief, she found the kitchen empty, dark. She set a note she'd already scribbled on the table, then hurried out the door, for the first time not making the morning coffee. Minutes later she was driving east along the blacktopped highway.

The frost had been heavy, and in the glow of early morning Billie saw the blackening cotton plants on either side of the road. Since she'd come to the area the grass had been brown, and now the few trees had no leaves. Such a stark world, she thought. Oh, but she'd been so happy here, and she'd come to find great beauty in the painted evening sky, the deep gray to rosy dirt, the flat land that went on forever, the trees whose branches bent to the north because of constant south winds.

The memory of Linc's kiss and then his shoving her away festered in her mind like a gaping wound.

Would he ask her to leave now? Would she choose to leave because she simply couldn't trust herself, because staying hurt too much?

Have an affair with him? No. There were the children to consider, and she'd feel somehow as if she were letting them down. And herself, too. She wanted the type of love not found in a sneaking-around type of affair—and that's what it would end up being.

She thought of the picture of Denise Snow, and pain shot through her chest. Did she remind him of Denise—is that all this was? He wanted her body. But she thoroughly doubted he wanted her heart.

And still, she wanted him. And his heart, too.

Linc watched from his bedroom window as the bright red Thunderbird disappeared down the highway. A vise squeezed his gut. Hardly realizing his own steps, he went downstairs. In the kitchen he stared for long seconds at the white paper lying on the table. He could hardly breathe. Slowly he reached for the note and gazed at Billie's handwriting.

Gone for the day. Back in time to fix supper. Billie.

He read it again. Gripping the paper, he strode through the laundry room. The door to her room was ajar. He pushed it open, and her scent hit him full in the face. He skimmed the room, saw her photos still on the dresser, her robe tossed across the end of the bed.

He let out a breath he hadn't known he'd been holding. She'd be back. But for how long?

Slowly he returned to the kitchen, wondering what he was going to do about this thing growing between him and the woman who was his housekeeper. Could they just pretend that what had happened last night never was? Seemed a plausible course, yet Linc heard the echo of derisive laughter in his mind.

He didn't know anything for certain except that for just a little while longer he wanted her to stay.

* * *

Well before sundown Linc told Con he needed to head for home. He had to show the boys their cards from Denise, and he knew he was anxiously waiting for Billie. Knew it was stupid, too.

He soon discovered his worries over the boys and explaining about their mama were all for nothing. They both listened as he told them their mother had sent them cards and showed them their names on the front. They were excited that they recognized their names—Billie had taught them.

Linc read the cards to them, and together they studied the pictures on them, one of a boy cowboy, the other a boy spaceman. They all agreed the colors were pretty. Then Tommy asked if they could go now and play miniature cars.

So that was that, Linc thought, left sitting there alone in his chair. He felt dazed, as if he'd narrowly missed falling off a cliff.

He was still in his office when he heard the Thunderbird pull up the drive. He'd just stepped into the kitchen when Billie walked through the door. Her hair was windblown, she wore her colorfully beaded denim coat, and she carried a box of fried chicken. She looked too fragile in that moment to be the Good Queen of the World.

She shut the door behind her and stood with her hand on the knob, as if ready to turn back around and leave. She eyed him tentatively and Linc felt pressed to say something.

"We waited dinner," he said. "Hoped you might bring something."

The pleasure, hope, relief that he felt inside flooded her face. She held out the box of fried chicken. "I got both—regular for you, extra crispy for the rest of us."

There he was again, he thought with wry amusement, the odd man out. But that didn't seem so important right then.

"Kids!" he called. "Billie's home!"

He'd meant to say "dinner!" but somehow the other had come out. He quickly averted his face and strode away to the cabinets, busying himself with getting the plates.

* * *

The children were out of school the following week for the Thanksgiving holiday, so Kit was able to join his father and the other men—hired hands Eldon and Joe, as well as Con Hawthorne, who'd finished with his fields, and Carlos Ramey, who needed Linc's help in the weeks to come—in the work of picking cotton. Billie suspected that Linc had held off harvesting for this week so that Kit could be included.

The dry weather continued, and the only problems the men had to contend with were the brisk winds and breakdowns of the machinery. It seemed to Billie that as much time was spent repairing all the machines as operating them.

Eager to see the picking and to have the children a part of it, Billie took Ronnie and the twins to the fields each day. With Ronnie's help she would distribute cold drinks and snacks to the men in their trucks and tractor cabs. Eldon was the funniest, dearest man. He turned blood-red the minute he laid eyes on Billie, and would bob his head, repeatedly thanking her for the things she'd brought.

She and the children took upon themselves the job of raking up spilled cotton around the boll buggy and module builder. The children had great fun climbing up into the buggy, crawling and bouncing on the soft cotton, helping to compact it as well as having one devil of a good time. Billie joined them a number of times when they crawled into the tub of the big module builder, which was like a giant trash compactor, compressing the cotton into a huge rectangle equal to about twelve bales of cotton. Each module was later hauled by truck to the Heavener Co-op and stored there in the yard to await ginning.

Once when Billie was in a module, Linc drove a buggy over and emptied the cotton it contained right on top of her. She came up sputtering.

"You all right?" he asked, his green eyes twinkling wickedly.

"You did that on purpose."

He expressed grand innocence. "I was only putting the cotton where it belongs."

For a brief moment his eyes softened, and she smiled foolishly at him. Then he looked away to the tractor levers. Billie concentrated on pulling tiny bits of twigs and cotton from her hair.

They had, since that moment of Billie's return on Saturday, settled into a fragile relationship, one that made Billie feel like a cat stepping across a table setting of fine crystal. What lay between them seemed to sizzle in the air whenever they looked at each other. They each drew back from it, yet not very far.

For the days of harvest, this delicate balance could continue. The cotton was coming in, a bumper crop, and all Linc or anyone seemed to be able to think or talk about was cotton, cotton, cotton! Billie went along with the tide, content to share the exciting days and grateful for the reprieve from dealing with what must inevitably be dealt with. Yet Billie knew this time was short, that what vibrated between her and Linc would have to be faced. Now they'd each had a taste of what could be, there was no escaping it.

Denise called Wednesday night. It was the first time since their final divorce business that Linc had spoken with her. He was immediately glad one of the kids hadn't gotten the phone. It'd been Billie who'd answered, and Linc suspected she'd guessed the identity of the caller when she'd so quietly informed him of the call. He changed to his office phone and shut the door, feeling as if he was cheating on someone—only he couldn't figure out who.

"Was that your housekeeper?" Denise asked. He'd always liked her husky voice. A blurry image of her face popped into his mind.

"Yes."

"Oh." Pause. "How are you, Linc?"

"Can't complain." He didn't feel pressed to say more.

"Did the kids get my cards? I sent Kit birthday money."

"Yes—and Kit got your check, too."

"Did he have a nice birthday?"

"He had a fine time. Had a birthday bash at Fred's café."

"I'm . . . I'm glad. I wish I could have been there."

For an instant he thought of the fun he'd had with Billie and was glad Denise *hadn't* been there.

"What do you want Denise? Didn't you get your last settlement check?" He didn't know what dance she had in mind, but he knew he didn't want to follow the steps. That she might have gone through the settlement money from the divorce and was wanting more flashed through his mind. But to go through that much money seemed highly improbable.

"Yes, dear. The check was prompt as always, and I thank you. You've always been good to me, Linc." Her husky voice dropped a notch. "I simply wanted to wish you a happy Thanksgiving and thought it might be nice to talk. I wanted to hear how things are doing. I understand the cotton harvest is great this year."

"It's been eight months since we talked, and you just now want to know about how things are?"

"I'm getting myself together, Linc. I wanted you to know that. I'm doing well with the telephone company—I got another promotion last month."

"That's nice."

Seconds ticked by.

"Could I talk with the kids?"

Linc had to think about that. There were a thousand reasons to say no. But she was their mother, and there was no getting around it. "I'll see," he said at last.

Linc let Kit speak to his mother in private. Whatever they said didn't take more than five minutes. Tommy told his mother about playing video games and sang a verse of "Zip-a-Dee-Doo-Dah" for her; Toby listened at the receiver but said nothing. Ronnie refused to come to the phone.

"What have you said to her?" Denise demanded.

"I told her you wanted to talk to her."

"Don't keep her from speaking to me, Linc. That's not fair."

"I'm not keeping her from doing anything. She doesn't want to talk to you. Damn it all to hell, Denise, you left here a year and a half ago!"

"I've called, sent cards. I'm still her mother, and I want her to know that."

"You've called three times and sent what—four notes since you left? You weren't the one gettin' up with her when she had nightmares after you'd gone or holdin' her head when she was puking her guts out with the flu. A mother stays around and takes care of her kids, Denise.''

''Oh, go ahead and point the finger, Mr. Perfect. You never even tried to understand!''

It was the beginning of a big fight, and suddenly that seemed pointless. His anger drained away. ''Is there anything else, Denise?''

''No,'' she said after a long pause. ''It was good hearin' your voice, Linc.''

''Yeah.'' He said goodbye and hung up. *Oh, hell, when did life get so crazy!*

Billie saw Linc stepping from his office just as she was coming down the stairs. His face was drawn, and he rubbed his eyes. He glanced at her, raising an eyebrow.

''You speak to Ronnie?''

She nodded. ''She's fine. She showed me a picture of a new outfit in a young teen magazine that she'd like.''

''Ronnie?''

''Yes.'' She smiled at his surprise, and tenderness swamped her. ''It is a sweatshirt, but with a lace collar.''

He nodded, eyes taking on a thoughtful look. ''Get it for her.''

''I will.''

Their eyes met and held, his revealing nothing, searching.

''Think I'll just walk outside awhile,'' he said, poking his thumb toward the front door.

''Good night.'' She walked away toward her own room, resisting the impulse to join him. He wanted to be alone. Her heart squeezed as she thought of how the telephone call must have stirred up memories of Denise, the life he'd shared with her. Had it reminded him of loving her? Did he still love her?

Fred invited them to Thanksgiving dinner at the café. Billie had wanted to fix the dinner but was voted down immediately.

"We don't want to take a chance on Thanksgiving," Ronnie had baldly stated.

Billie took the poke against her cooking ability good-naturedly. She truly was a long way from being a good cook—about a lifetime away, actually. Besides, she'd be foolish to complain about having to do nothing more than sit and eat.

Linc insisted on going into the field on Thanksgiving for a morning's work. A storm was coming out of southern New Mexico, and he wanted to get as much cotton out of the field as he could before it arrived. He and Kit went together and worked until eleven.

By twelve o'clock, when they drove into Heaven, the wind was like nothing Billie had ever seen. It gusted between fifty and sixty miles an hour out of the southwest. Dust from the dirt roads and picked fields cast a gray-pink haze over the blue sky. Pieces of cotton blew past like snowflakes, along with tree branches and grass. Billie was glad Linc had insisted on putting the Thunderbird in the garage.

"Will it blow the cotton off the plants?" she asked, looking over to Linc behind the wheel of the Suburban.

He frowned. "It can—we'll go back to picking right after dinner." And he searched the sky. Then he looked at her, and his eyes warmed for a second of lingering before he again stared out the windshield.

Billie gazed at him a few moments longer, noting the slicked-back hair above his ears and the crisp collar poking above his jacket. It was the first time since that night he'd brought her to his house that they'd ridden together, sitting a mere two feet apart. He seemed to be warming toward her, as amazing as that seemed. Could it truly be? Her heartbeat seemed to skim across her chest at the thought, and she turned her mind to other things.

The Heavener Gin was shut down for the holiday, and Heaven was as desolate looking as it had been that long ago evening when Billie had walked into it—even more so today because of the dust and bits of cotton blowing across the blacktop, giving the place a ghost-town aura.

Fred had asked Gracie Hendricks to join them for dinner. Gracie was older than dirt, as Ronnie described her, and quite a bitter old woman, but today she appeared content as long as she got to sit beside Fred. The children remained on the opposite side of the table, and Billie was both amazed and proud to see the polite graciousness they displayed toward the old woman.

Fred had formed one long table out of three small ones in the middle of the café and covered it elegantly with a white cloth. He served all the standards: golden turkey, savory cornbread dressing and gravy, sweet potatoes, cranberry sauce, a vegetable for every taste and three types of pie. The dinner was a noisy family affair, so different from the Thanksgiving dinners in Billie's past. She'd had quiet ones with her father, both staid and rowdy ones with her father's adult friends, pleasant ones and uncomfortable ones with her own friends, and lonely ones alone. But this, this was as if she were a part of the family, and she thought she would remember it for a long time.

Linc was enjoying his second piece of pie and felt as expansive as that turkey Fred had served when he saw the first gray wisps float by the front windows. Curious, he watched and saw what appeared to be gray clouds catch in the wind and disappear. Apprehension creeping up his back, he laid his napkin beside his plate and rose to take a better look.

"What is it?" Billie asked as he passed her chair.

Intent on the buildings across the road, he simply shook his head and peered intently out the large, plate glass windows.

Fresh puffs appeared above the tall gin building, then swept down in the wind. They darkened. *Smoke. Oh, God, it was smoke!* A cold blast of alarm flashed down his back as he bolted for the front door.

"Get Joel Heavener on the phone. There's a fire at the gin!"

He opened the café door, and the wind jerked it out of his hand, slamming it back against the wall. He left it open and ducked his head against the wind, gasping as it took his breath. Trying to run across the road was like trying to swim upstream in a raging river. The wind roared in his ears and the cold cut through his shirt. He smelled the smoke and knew in his gut it was burning cotton.

Billie was struggling to shut the front door as Kit came racing past. "Where are you going?" She grabbed his arm.

"With Dad. He may need me," he added when she continued to hold him back.

Reluctantly she released his arm. "Okay...but don't stay away long. Wait! Your coat—and take your father's." As she spoke she ran over to gather their coats from the booth.

Kit grabbed them from her, racing away even as he struggled to put his on. Ronnie came flying behind, tugging on her own coat.

Leaning against the door to push it shut, Billie emphatically shook her head. "I can't have you all scattered everywhere." Angry, Ronnie flounced away.

Hearing the glass rattle in the door, Billie made the children get out of the booths that were right against the big windows and move onto the stools at the counter. She stood beside Ronnie, watching. She'd seen Linc disappear around the tall round gin building and believed Kit had followed him. The yard was back there, where dozens, Lord, maybe more than a hundred cotton modules were stored. *Maybe she shouldn't have let Kit go.*

As she watched, two pickups flew past on the highway and careened south on the dirt road that bordered the cotton storage yard. At least more men were coming to help Linc and Kit, she thought, though with small comfort.

A loud siren pierced the air and made her skin crawl. "That's from the gin," Ronnie informed her. "Daddy probably set it off."

The gray wisps of smoke grew darker, thicker. They appeared to roll over the roofs of the gin buildings, slip down the northeast side and fan out over the roof of the Feed and Seed and straight across to the café. The burning was easy to smell now. When Billie saw the first fiery embers blowing in the wind her blood chilled. The siren continued.

"Got Joel." Fred came to stand beside her. His breathing was heavy. "He'll be in directly. Called the Moorestown Fire Department, too—and the Webster's over here." He inclined his head in the direction of the houses to the east of the café. "They'd seen it, but the Morenos and Ledford boys hadn't."

"Does Heaven have some sort of fire department?" Billie asked without taking her gaze from the window.

"An old fire truck we keep parked in a shed out back of the gin, with volunteers to run it. That's Rick Moreno now. He's fire chief this year." A battered blue pickup zipped past. "The gin has a number of hydrants and hoses. There's Joel."

A silver Cadillac coming from the west turned south as all the other vehicles had.

The smoke darkened. Within the blink of an eye it had blanketed the gin buildings, almost hiding them. Against the smoke, burning bits of cotton could be seen. Billie's heart leaped to her throat.

"Ph-ewy," Toby said, waving his hand in front of his nose.

"I'm goin' home," Gracie Hendricks announced.

"No ye'r' not!" Fred countered as he stepped quickly back to the telephone. "Grab her, Billie."

Instinctively Billie did as she was told, then called the children again away from the front windows. "Sit here, Gracie—Ronnie, sit with her."

"I ain't a'gonna stay. I got a dog in my house." Gracie pushed up from the table.

"I'll help you get your dog," Ronnie said.

"Don't you dare, Ronnie! Gracie, I'll get the dog in a minute." Billie heard Fred speaking to someone. He hung up and dialed again. Billie brought drinks for everyone. More vehicles passed and more smoke rolled down upon them, growing thicker by the second. Billie glanced at her watch and guessed somewhere near twenty-five minutes had passed since Linc had left.

"Billie! Bil-lie!" Tommy and Toby called, jumping up and down and pointing.

She saw flames burst through the smoke that was wrapping around them like the dark velvet of a coffin. One of the gin buildings had caught fire. Smoke was seeping into the café, and she knew cotton bits were probably raining down upon the roof right this minute.

"Fred—we've got to get out of here!"

The smoke was so thick only the ground at their feet could be seen as they fled the café. They held cloth napkins over their faces, and Billie wondered if it were possible to die of smoke inhalation outdoors in a fifty-mile-an-hour wind. Tommy and Toby clung to either side of her coat and Ronnie and Gracie were in front of her. She caught a glimpse of Ronnie's purple tennis shoes right before she bumped into them. Then they all bumped into the Suburban, at last.

Oh, God, what about Linc and Kit?

Billie edged the Suburban around to the back of the café and promised Gracie she would stop and get her dog. She got out and groped her way to the back door, calling for Fred. The roof of the café was on fire!

"Fred! The roof's caught fire! You've got to come!"

"I've been here fifty years. I lost a wife 'cause I wouldn't leave this place. I ain't leavin' now!"

"Damn you, old man! Get the hell out!"

"Get out of my way!"

Water splashed Billie in the face as Fred hauled a hose from the shabby enclosed porch and passed her on his way out the screened door. He refused to come with her, and he was too big for her to wrestle to the ground. Terrified for him and terrified of the smoke killing the children right in the car, Billie had to make a choice. She got back in the Suburban. *She hoped Linc didn't come looking for them and find the café on fire!*

She made her way past Gracie's house. The old woman was screaming in her ear about her Bootsie, and everybody was coughing. Tears streamed from Billie's eyes. Tall grass flamed here and there so that Billie couldn't tell where one fire ended and the next began.

Suddenly they broke out of the smoke. They were almost in a ditch. It wasn't too deep so Billie went across it and into a bumpy field, heading for the highway. They rolled down the windows to gasp fresh air. Gracie kept screaming and the twins were crying. Ronnie pointed to all the activity going on at the southwest side of the gin.

Her heart leaped to her throat at the sight of hundreds of tarp-covered cotton modules lined in rows close together beyond the gin buildings. How many burned, she couldn't count—but there were a lot. Flames shot into the air and were snatched away by the wind. Two fire trucks were there—men everywhere, some beating shovels at flames, some directing hoses of spraying water. Two trucks were moving modules away.

Not wanting to get in the way, she chose to head west on the highway, into the wind and away from the danger.

She turned down a gravel drive that led to a small tin barn. "Belongs to the Parsons," Ronnie told her. She deposited everyone there, out of the wind and where the fire could be clearly seen.

"Stay put and mind Ronnie." She shook her finger in the twins' faces. "Can you handle it, Ronnie? I need to go back for Fred."

"We'll be okay." She looked straight into Billie's eyes, then turned to comfort a wailing Gracie.

Linc felt helpless against the raging wind. A thousand times faster than he could put out fires, the wind ripped burning pieces of cotton from the modules and scattered them like dancing devils to start more. It was hard to stand in the wind, much less fight a fire in it. There wasn't enough water, enough hoses, enough sand or shovels or enough men to fight the inferno. Still, he pressed on, knowing no other choice.

And then suddenly the module behind him—an area they thought was safe from fire—burst into flame with a loud roaring *whoosh,* sending pieces of tarp and cotton flying. Instinctively, he turned. Joel Heavener had been behind him, helping with the hose. Too stunned to move, Joel stood completely still, and Linc saw sparks in his hair. He leaped and pushed Joel to the ground, rubbing the man's head roughly to put out any fire. He faintly heard Kit calling his name and answered.

"Get going!" he yelled at Joel, gesturing.

Crouching low, Joel ran from between the modules, and Linc followed, coughing and gasping in the fresh wind beyond.

"Dad?" Kit, his eyes anxious, stood in front of him.

"I'm okay."

"Oh Lord, Linc."

Linc glanced over at Joel and followed the man's gaze to see the roof of one of the gin buildings burst into flame. And more modules were burning.

A sudden terror gripped him. He thought of the café, where he'd left Billie and his children and Fred. "I've got to check on the café," he called to Joel and grabbed Kit by the collar, practically dragging him across the ground away from the fire.

"You stay back here!" he yelled above the wind and crackling fire. "I'm going to get Billie and the kids."

"I'm going with you." And Kit came behind him.

When Rick Moreno called to him, he waved him away and headed on. Rounding the gin buildings, he saw all of Heaven engulfed in black smoke forced close to the ground by the wind. Flashes of flames shot upward, cutting through the smoke. Some of those flames came from where the café stood. A sparse line of people, gripping their coats against the wind, stared at the sight. Linc urgently scanned the familiar faces, but none of them belonged to his family. He heard a familiar voice call his name and turned hopefully. But it was just Ginny.

"Have you seen Billie, Fred or the kids?"

"No. I—"

But he was already turning away.

"Last I saw Fred, he was trainin' his garden hose on the café roof," rummy Al Ledford hollered.

At the far side of the highway Linc turned on Kit, grabbing him by the arms. "You stay here and keep an eye out for Billie and the kids. I'm going to check the café."

"You don't think they're still there?" Kit asked, his voice hitting a high pitch.

"No. Billie has enough sense to get out, but I've got to be sure. Now, do as I say."

He was close to the café before he could see enough to know that the roof and west wall were a mass of flames. Moorestown's second fire truck had just pulled up, and firemen were unrolling their hoses. When he headed for the front door, a fireman called to him, but Linc ignored the warning.

Coughing and blinking, straining to see through blurred vision, he peered into the interior. It appeared empty. He called out and got no answer. He pivoted and ran around to the other side of the building. The Suburban was gone.

Relief washed over him, only to be followed by an intense urgency. He had to know his family was safe. He had to hold them in his arms, he thought as sharp coughs racked his chest.

Minutes later he came upon Billie at Gracie Hendrick's house, where the smoke was thinner. She was leaning over the open door of the Suburban, throwing up. Fred was patting her back—and for some unfathomable reason, she was clutching Gracie's black-and-white dog.

Speculation was rife as to how the fire had started. Whether by spontaneous combustion, a carelessly thrown cigarette, stray cotton catching in the catalytic converter of some passing vehicle and coming out again carrying fire, no one was likely to ever know. Sitting there in the precious comfort of his kitchen, Linc thought that knowing how it had started wouldn't change what had happened. He looked down at his hands and thought about his children upstairs, safely in their beds.

By some miracle no one had been killed, though very few buildings in Heaven remained standing. Thanks to Joel Heavener's new steel storage building that housed the fertilizer well away from everything else, they hadn't all been blown to kingdom come. The main part of the gin was relatively unscathed as well, most of it being steel, and it remained operational.

But the Heavener Feed and Seed was gone, blown up by chemicals, and one of the older storage buildings housing five thousand bales of ginned cotton was lost, too. Gracie Hendrick'2 house alone had walls standing. The Morenos' and Ledfords' trailers were gone, and so was the Carters' rental house, garage, and all their little outbuildings, and Fred's little one-bedroom place.

Of course Fred's house would have blown away in a good wind, like the one today, so it wasn't such a loss. But Fred's café, the dearest part of the old man's life and the hub of the community had been turned to ashes.

If it hadn't been for Billie, they might have lost Fred, too. When she'd gone back for him, she'd almost run over a fireman who tried to stop her from going back into the smoke. Then she'd fought with Fred and finally rescued him by turning the garden hose on him full blast.

Linc started to chuckle, thinking of it. Fred said Billie had been one mad woman, and Linc could just imagine her wielding that hose. The Suburban seat was soaked, so she must have just about sprayed the old man into it. Then after all that, she stopped to get that mean old woman's stupid dog.

The chuckles shook Linc's body, and before he realized what was happening his eyes started watering and wouldn't stop. He took a deep breath and looked up at the dimly lit ceiling, blinking and trying to swallow the lump in his throat. He thought about how since he could remember he'd eaten at Snow's Café, bought seed from Heavener's and taken wheat there in the spring, cotton in the winter.

He thought that forevermore he would attend town meetings just so he would never again be named mayor. All during the fire and afterward he'd felt so responsible for everybody—had everybody asking him everything! He'd been the one to have to make certain the fire was indeed left only smoldering, that everyone was accounted for, that everyone left homeless had somewhere to go, that all questions to the news people were answered.

He thought about all that had been lost, about the fears and reliefs he'd suffered through in the space of several hours, and he blinked and sniffed and swallowed painfully. Oh, God, he couldn't remember the last time he'd cried— when he'd been a snot-nosed kid, he guessed.

Hearing Billie's footsteps on the stairs, he quickly stood and moved to the counter, wiping his eyes with the back of his hand. He caught the faint smell of smoke on his skin, though he'd showered and scrubbed.

"Fred's all set in your room," Billie said, coming into the kitchen.

He turned, leaning back against the counter and watched her carry blankets and a pillow over to the couch in the den. She wore an oversized pink satin shirt and leotard-like black pants. Her hair was still damp from her shower.

"The children..." she paused and smiled softly "...and Kit are asleep already."

He nodded, not trusting himself to speak yet.

She walked tiredly forward into the full circle of the kitchen light, raking her hair from her face. "I'm awfully glad Wes and Ginny volunteered to have Gracie stay with them." Wonder echoed in her soft voice.

Linc grinned wryly. "It's been widely speculated for years that Gracie has a considerable amount of money stashed away."

"I sincerely hope she does. Insurance at least."

He beckoned her into a chair. "I made fresh coffee." He sensed her searching eyes as he focused on pouring her a cup. He set the steaming cup on the table in front of her and still didn't look her in the face.

"How much cotton was lost?" she asked as she reached for the sugar.

Linc massaged his neck. "No clear count yet. Maybe up to a hundred and fifty modules."

"Good heavens! I didn't know there were that many in the storage yard."

"There were over four hundred modules out there." He sighed. "Wes, Joe Silva, some other guys, tryin' to save their own cotton and to just cut down on the fire, moved modules that didn't look like they were burning. Only they were burning, smolderin' inside. When these broke into full flame somewhere else, they just spread the fire."

"Were any of the modules yours?" she asked quietly.

He nodded, recalling how he and Con had spent half of the previous day toting modules to the yard. If they'd just held off...

"How many?"

"I don't know yet. Not too many—not as many as Con."
He met her gaze then. "And I've got insurance. It's really
not so bad."

He really didn't know how bad it would prove to be. It
would take weeks to sort it all out. Damn, he was tired. So
damn tired. And he shook inside.

The next instant she was standing in front of him, her eyes
searching his. He opened his arms, and she put hers around
him and pressed close.

"I'm so sorry, Linc."

He held on to her and experienced something long forgotten—the warm comfort of being held. Eyes closed tight,
he nuzzled his cheek against her silky, sweet smelling hair
and inhaled deeply. Her body beneath his hands was fragile
and strong at the same time.

"Kit worked right beside me," he mumbled into her hair.
"He had a hose out by the time I got back from setting off
the alarm. God, I worried about him with all that burning
cotton flyin' around. But he did well, never lost his head."
He tightened his arms around her.

"He's had a good teacher."

"I was scared when I saw the café burning," he said
hoarsely.

"I was scared when I saw all the modules burning and
knew you and Kit were down there."

She rubbed her cheek against his shoulder. Her back beneath the satiny shirt was warm beneath his hands. For long
seconds they stood together, quietly giving and taking so-
lace.

And then, as naturally as breathing, Linc moved his
hands up and down her spine, savoring the feel of her feminine body close to his. Her warmth came through the satin
shirt that was the only barrier between his hands and her
skin. Gradually he became aware of that warmth seeping
into him, growing in his vitals and spiraling upward.

Slowly, hesitantly, he put two fingers beneath her chin and
tilted her face upward. The desire shimmering in her blue
eyes ignited a fire within him wilder than the one he'd fought
that day.

Chapter Eleven

Staring into those wondrous eyes, Linc slowly lowered his head to kiss her. Her lips were soft and moist. And eager. He drew back and fought for air, for some shred of sanity. He pressed his cheek against hers and squeezed his eyes closed. Her scent filled his nostrils.

She felt so good, smelled so good. Giving. He'd seen that in her eyes, felt that in her body. It seemed that no woman had ever given him so much. He ached all over, thought fleetingly of the people upstairs. Sleeping. He was alone with her.

The next instant she was drawing away. She took a step backward. His gaze fell to her breasts, so visible now through the thin satin shirt. He jerked his gaze up and looked straight into her eyes. They were hot and wanting.

And as ripe cotton bursts from the hard shell burr, the hidden, long-denied passion burst up from his most inward parts.

She held out her hand. He took it. She turned and walked toward her room. And he followed.

She released his hand to switch on the bedside lamp.

He closed the door and turned the lock.

She began stripping out of those tight black pants.

He concentrated on her shiny blond hair falling across her cheek as he removed his shirt. He sat in the chair opposite the bed to take off his boots. That he could get her pregnant crossed his mind, but when he looked up and his gaze lit on her pale shapely legs, sensible thought faded.

His pulse pounding, he followed those creamy legs up to where the loose satin shirt stopped at the juncture of her thighs. His eyes lingered on the shadowy part. The wanting swelled inside. His gaze riveted upon her, he rose and unbuckled his belt.

When her fingers moved to the top button of that satiny shirt, the blood pounded in his ears. Her lips parted, her eyes locked on to his as she unfastened the button. They glimmered hungrily, making him feel like one hell of a man. He just stood there, staring at her.

If he had to give a color to desire, he'd say blue—like Billie's eyes.

Her fingers moved to the second button, and she turned her back. Watching her, he hurriedly stripped out of the rest of his clothes. She didn't remove that pink, shiny shirt, but let it drape off her shoulders while she bent to pull down the bed sheets.

He reached over and jerked her into his arms, pressing her bare breasts against his chest, her groin against his.

He found her lips again, and he kissed her, sampled her sweet lips and came back for more. He raked his fingers into her hair, savored her warm, enticing, feminine scent, tasted the inside of her mouth, shared her breath. He demanded and received contact. He felt himself slipping away and into her and didn't care. He only knew the wonderful, sweet aching of coming alive with new, ripe life.

While his lips held her captive, Linc's hands roughly pushed the shirt from Billie's shoulders and to the floor, then moved to her breasts. His hands stilled. Then hands shaking slightly, as if trying to control himself, he massaged her tender skin, bringing a moan of pleasure from her lips.

She felt as if she were growing, opening toward him as a plant blossoms in the warm sunshine. Wilder and wilder she spun inside. His hair was so soft, so luxurious beneath her fingers. He smelled of Chaps after-shave, faint smoke, and his own seductively male scent.

She sighed luxuriously and melted against him. At last she was in his arms. He was holding her, kissing her. *She was holding him.*

He pressed her against his swollen organ, and she thought she would shatter into a million pieces. Her legs gave way, and he grasped her tight against him. His stomach, his groin, his thighs, all pressing and throbbing against hers. His kiss took her energy and gave it back again. The next instant his arms lifted her and deposited her on the bed, gently laying her back onto the pillow. His eyes shimmered like morning dew on the grass, and the sharp intent written there set her on fire.

Her head reeled as his hands moved everywhere, seemingly at once—on her thighs, on her breast, on her neck and into her hair. His hands fondled and massaged, his mouth kissed and licked. She tasted his skin at his neck and buried her nose in his shoulder, inhaling his drugging scent.

Faster and faster her breath came. His hand slipped fully between her legs and cupped her pubescence and caressed. She pushed against him, throbbing, seeking what she had to have, moaning in spite of herself. And then his fingers found her tender hub and set her spinning off into the exquisite world of hot, sweet pleasure.

Released from restraint at last, their passion came to full fruition. Their mating was hard and fast, grasping and giving. It was more than Billie had ever experienced, ever dreamed of. Linc took her to the sky and held her there with him. When she felt herself floating to earth, he took her up to the peak again, his breath hot in her ear, his body moving so wonderfully against her and in her. Three times he sent her flying into that world of sweet, mindless bliss, before they at last descended together.

And somewhere in that splendid time, the words "I love you," reached her lips but remained unspoken, fear holding them back.

He held her to him as he rolled to his side. The sweat of their bodies mingled; their heartbeats pounded in rhythm. His hand played over her hair, lightly, tenderly. Oh, so lovingly. And knowing this brought great gratitude at being allowed this in her life.

"Are you all right?" he whispered.

They were the first words either of them had spoken since they'd stood in the kitchen, and they sounded odd to her, mingled as they were with the beating of his heart in her ear.

"Umm," she managed, letting her body speak for her.

His thumb wiped across her cheek, and she realized she was crying. She opened her eyes and gazed at the smooth skin of his muscled arm, warmed in the yellow glow of the lamp. She stroked it with her finger and rubbed her cheek on his breast. Emotion filled her that seemed just too much for any heart to bear. This, she knew, was love. Was as close to heaven on earth as she could ever be. And she would stay here for all of her life, if only she could.

Her tears wet his chest, though she made no sound. Swallowing the lump in his throat, Linc held her to him and savored gazing at her pale, shining hair and creamy skin. Great satisfaction and wonder mingled with shame at the way he'd almost mindlessly taken her. She'd been tight, not a woman who'd had a man recently—or much at all, he thought with a bit of wonder and a lot of male pride.

He'd tried to hold back, but once started, nothing short of an atomic bomb could have stopped him. Oh, God, she felt so good in his arms. So good.

He pulled back and forced her to look at him, seeking to know that she was all right, that it'd been good for her, too. Their gazes locked. The intimate satisfied light in her blue eyes made his heart trip over itself.

Oh, man...oh, damn! The way he felt! The next second he knew he was smiling at her in a way he'd never smiled at any woman after sex. *No...hell, no. He'd never felt like this before.*

And if he had to give a color to love, he'd say blue—like Billie's eyes.

All those fancy words written by poets and sung on the radio clogged in his throat until he thought he'd burst. But he'd never been good with words, and the fear of making a fool of himself kept him silent as he continued to gaze at her.

Then, to his amazement, the burning started again within him. He rubbed his hand down her velvety hip and felt a little foolish, averting his eyes.

"I'm sorry...about getting so carried away before," he whispered hoarsely, self-consciously, as he nuzzled her ear—a way to avoid her seeing into him and as an excuse for what he was wanting to do again. *But, damn, he'd been kept from this for so long. Had it dangling in front of him like a damn carrot!* And now the deed was done, he intended to savor it.

He'd push repenting time away a little longer, he thought as he almost surreptitiously slipped his hand across her sleek thigh. His heart leaped when she gave a low chuckle and entwined her leg with his.

As in no other time in his life, for the following hours Linc strove to give to this woman as much as she'd given him. He gave shelter to her and accepted it greedily. He loved her as best he knew how and reveled in the way she moved and kissed and loved him in return.

The fear and losses of that day faded into distant memory. And the uncertainties of tomorrow seemed far away.

Billie awoke when Linc moved away. She watched him stand and reach for his pants. His muscles were taut over his ribs and shoulder blades. The pleasurable memory of his body against hers flashed across her mind.

He turned, and she quickly closed her eyes. She didn't want to see any regrets or worries in his eyes. She didn't want them to be caught up in explanations. Not now.

As the bedroom door softly closed behind him, tears seeped beneath her lashes, and she allowed herself a deep sniff.

"I love you, Linc Snow," she whispered at last.

Did he love her? Even a small bit? Or was it simply that he'd needed the comfort of a woman—and she was a close facsimile of his ex-wife? Denise's picture filled her mind.

A helpless desperation washing over her, she pulled the pillow where his head had rested into her arms and held it tightly, burying her face into the remnants of his scent.

It was barely eight o'clock the following morning and Linc doing his best to deal with rowdy children, Fred, who had to have the television volume at ear-blasting level, and the fiery memory of his forbidden night with Billie, when Denise telephoned again.

Kit spoke to her briefly, then called Linc to the telephone.

"I just heard about Heaven yesterday," she said. "Oh, Linc, are you and the kids all right? The news said no one was hurt."

"No, no one was hurt." He kept his eye on Billie's door through the laundry room, wondering why she was so late in coming out. She probably didn't want to see him. He wasn't keen on facing her, either—and couldn't wait to see her at the same time.

These were the thoughts running through his mind the entire time he talked to Denise.

The smell of frying sausage was strong before Billie gathered enough fortitude to go out and face everyone, face Linc, and act as if the previous night had never occurred. And as fate would have it, Linc was the first person she laid eyes on.

"Hi." He looked at her from where he stood in front of the stove. There was a hesitancy in his eyes, just as she knew must be in hers.

"Hi." Knowing she blushed violently made her all the more embarrassed. Memories of last night sprung so vividly to her mind, they seemed to shout loud enough for all to hear. There was much she wanted to say, but the words were all tangled inside. And they couldn't be spoken here. She averted her eyes and walked toward the coffeepot.

But he took a quick step toward it, too, and grabbed it to fill a cup. His gaze caught and held hers. There was something there—a warmth. Shared memory. He held the cup out to her, rubbed the side of his nose and smiled self-consciously.

"You go on and sit down. I'll have us some breakfast pretty quick."

"I'm supposed to be the housekeeper."

"Yeah, well, I'm the boss giving you breakfast off. I'd like to have eggs without those crusty edges this morning."

Oh, Lord . . . the way he was looking at her. He cared, surely he cared.

"Bil-lie! Hey, Tom-my, B-Bil-lie's a-wake!" Toby came rushing across the kitchen at her. She knelt and scooped him up in her arms, taking refuge in the distraction.

"Oh, Billie, I lost Whitie somewhere." Ronnie came through the door. "Will you help me find him? Maybe he'll come to you."

And so the day went, taken up with people and matters having nothing to do with the two of them.

All day, while she cleaned house, washed clothes, wiped noses, found runaway mice and answered how-come questions, Billie wondered what would happen now between herself and Linc.

What did he think? What did he want now?

A cold dread engulfed her when she wondered if he'd decided he could now come into her bed and arms at will. Oh, she wanted him again—but not like that. Last night had been special. To continue, having to hide it from the children and everyone, would turn it into something tawdry.

Billie was helplessly in love with Linc Snow. Experiencing an emotion more consuming than she'd ever felt for anyone.

Every time she entertained even the slightest prospect that she would have to live without Linc's love, an overwhelming, frightening desperation gripped her. She felt quite literally that she would either fly to pieces or simply drop dead. She *needed* Linc to love her as much as she needed air to breathe, food to eat.

And, as it'd been since the beginning of time, therein lay the problem. She did not know, had no reason to believe, that Linc loved her in return. And, oh Lord, the painful suspicion that she was simply a substitute for his ex-wife was growing by frightful proportions.

As much as Linc hated being mayor, the responsibility now provided a blessed opportunity to block all thought of Billie and their night together from his mind. When he left the house, he turned his full attention to figuring out his own and everyone else's loss in cotton and property. That a rainstorm had blown in made the job all the more difficult.

Joel Heavener had found a portable building and set up temporary offices, his own having gone up with the feed and grain store, when Linc, Kit, and Fred arrived in Heaven—or what was left of Heaven. Linc joined Joel and others in consultations with various insurance adjusters, fire investigators, and government men who descended upon the scene. He personally made calls to every man who'd been treated for smoke inhalation and made certain the needs of those who'd lost their homes and belongings were being met.

He took Fred into Lubbock to buy new clothes, find a portable building to serve as the café, and check out mobile homes; Fred didn't like the idea of staying long at Linc's house. When they returned, with help from Fred and Kit, he organized volunteers to begin clearing out the burned rubble and contacted a number of builders he knew about rebuilding costs.

For those long hours, he didn't have to deal with himself or what remained between him and Billie. But when he stepped into the house and met her gaze, he was overwhelmed by the powerful memory of what she'd felt like in his arms. He had the urge to open his arms and enfold her again, to take the sweet warmth and ease which she offered. The eager light that flickered in her blue eyes didn't help at all.

There in the house, practically rubbing shoulders with her at every turn, emotions assaulted him that he condemned at once as foolish and weak. He knew the facts of life—that love was a fairy tale, fleeting. He had no excuse forgetting all that happened last night, for acting like an adolescent and letting his hormones get the better of his head. He had it all under control now, and he wasn't going to get off track again.

And there was something else he'd had no excuse forgetting, either, especially since he'd fathered four kids. What if he'd gotten her pregnant? Damn! He should have had more sense. And the possibility ought to have been as effective on him as a cold shower—but instead he was wanting to go back for more. And he was feeling way too much for Billie Ballinger than was wise.

With Fred and the kids in the house, there wasn't any time for them to speak alone, and Linc kept telling himself that there wasn't anything that needed to be said between them, anyway. Still, when Fred and the kids had gone to bed, Linc stood in front of Billie's bedroom door, having a long argument with himself. At last he rapped lightly.

Almost immediately the door flew open. Billie stood there, gazing up at him. She wore that blue velvet shirt that covered her from her neck to thigh and baggy velvet pants, all concealing her shape—but he had a good memory. Her eyes were wide; a smile played at the corners of her mouth.

"Could we talk?" he asked. His heart pounded and the damn sensuous swelling took hold of his loins.

"Yes . . . of course."

Her voice was warm, welcoming. She nodded, backed up to let him inside.

He closed the door and leaned against it, not trusting himself to go any farther into the room. She stood at the foot of the bed and rested her hand on the post, as if she, too, wanted to keep a safe distance between them. He glanced at the neatly made bed, then back at her. He started to throb.

"About last night . . ." he began, searching for the right words to express his feelings without sounding like a jerk, without revealing himself too much. "I didn't mean to get carried away."

"It wasn't totally your doing." Her voice was gently amused.

"No. It wasn't." He gazed at her, then reminded himself. "But I should have done my part in using birth control."

Billie felt her stomach tighten. His words were as effective as a dunking in cold water.

"There's no need for you to worry for that." She consciously made her voice light. "I'm infertile. I had a bad kidney infection when I was a child—almost died, in fact. It affected everything. I barely menstruate, and the doctors have said I could never have children."

For an instant he looked as if she'd hit him in the face with a snowball. Then relief replaced his surprise, and a crack opened in her heart.

He raked a hand through his thick hair. "That's good...I mean, because of last night. Not good that you can't have children."

She nodded. She wanted him to go. She wanted him to hold her.

He wet his lips and rubbed the side of his nose. "I don't want you to think I take last night for granted. I..." He looked straight at her. "It was a rare experience, Billie."

"Yes...yes it was."

They gazed at each other, mutual memories filling the air.

"But if it's worryin' you that I'll step over the line again, I want you to know I won't. If you're thinking that you should be leavin' because of it."

"I wasn't thinking that." He'd said nothing about love. Oh, Lord, don't let him ask to stay or move toward her. She couldn't be held responsible if he did—and she'd despise both him and herself.

They gazed at each other, then looked away. She wanted to tell him how she really felt but knew he'd hate to hear it. Then she wanted to slap him.

"Good night," she said and turned her back.

"Good night." He opened the door and closed it softly behind him.

She slowly lowered herself onto the bed. She listened for another knock, for him to return. She wanted him to and didn't want him to.

It had taken a lot for him to come speak to her, she thought, her foolish anger draining away as she recalled his nervous expression. How worried he must have been about her getting pregnant. It was something she'd never had to bear so she never thought of it. She should have told him earlier.

She thought she should probably leave. But what about the children? She loved them, and they needed her. *They needed her,* and that was too wonderful to turn her back on. And so was what she felt for Linc.

That night she lay awake, too numb to cry, thinking of him upstairs in his bed with the brown-and-blue cover. Remembering the sheen of his skin in the light from her lamp.

It rained enough in the following days to keep tractors out of the fields, but not enough to stop the clean-up effort in Heaven. Linc left the house early, returned late, and took care to stay out of Billie's sight as much as possible. He spent hours clearing away rubble, then more time helping to set up several portable buildings and mobile homes. He kept his mind on work and refused to think about the emotions tugging at him.

Every once in a while the big question nagged at him: When would Billie leave? But he allowed the thought to do nothing more than flit through his mind. And when the memory of the time spent in her bed tried to sneak in during the late-night hours, he willed it away. He only once considered, and just for a few seconds, going down and knocking on her door.

Sunday the gin began running again, and by Monday morning Fred was serving coffee to bus passengers in the portable building that was the temporary café. By Monday night, Fred went home to his new mobile home, leaving Linc feeling vaguely abandoned in the house with Billie. Abandoned with his own foolish self was a better description.

It didn't help his mood when he arrived home and discovered Denise had sent notes again to each of the kids—and one to him this time. He gazed at the envelopes and considered throwing them away. But still, she was their mother. So he gave Kit and Ronnie their envelopes, read the twins theirs and got the same unconcerned reactions. Finally he opened his own. It was one of those cute thinking-of-you cards. *Just remembering old times—Denise.* He laid the card and envelope aside with all the other papers he wasn't quite certain what to do with.

He spent the evening ensconced in his office, forcing his mind to concentrate on accounts. But when he heard Billie's voice in the hallway outside his door, his concentration shattered like a broken light bulb. He tossed his pencil to the desk and sat back, listening.

She and the boys were singing as they went up the stairs—not "Zip-a-Dee-Doo-Dah" for a change, but "The Twelve Days of Christmas." They were taking one step for each day, Linc finally figured out.

"On the fo-fourth day of C-Christ-mas . . ." Toby sang, and nobody butted in to help him with the line. His stuttering was improving, Linc thought. And it was due mainly to Billie's patient, repeated efforts with him.

He looked at the calendar and wondered where the time had gone. Christmas was barely four weeks away. He sighed as he thought of it all—the presents to be chosen, then bought and wrapped. Billie would no doubt be decorating to the hilt, planning parties and special dinners; that woman loved to celebrate. Ronnie would bug him for a big tree, and this year she'd have Billie to back her up.

Billie. All the emotion he'd been trying to push away came rushing back. He was feeling for her what he damn well knew was stupid. What he shouldn't. What he'd promised himself he'd never feel for another woman, ever. What in hell was he going to do?

He could fire her.

But the thought of the house without her opened a wide, desperate hole within him.

The telephone rang, nearly sending Linc rocketing out of his chair.

"This is Marc Thornton," came the voice across the line. "I'd like to speak to Billie." The guy sounded like a preppie stuffed shirt accustomed to people jumping at his command.

"Yeah. Just a minute," Linc answered. He poked his head out of his office, saw Billie on the landing upstairs and called, "Telephone's for you." He waited for her. Her eyes rested hesitantly on him. "You can get it in here."

He remained in the doorway, forcing her to slip past, brushing against him as she did. When he saw her blush, he told himself to grow up.

"Hello, Marc!" Her voice was thick with pleasure.

Linc pulled the door closed. He was walking toward the kitchen when he heard loud voices from the upstairs hallway—Ronnie and Kit arguing about something. He changed direction to go settle it. He faintly heard Billie's voice, but not distinctly enough to tell what she said.

Billie was on the phone to her old friend Marc Thornton for a long time. Linc settled the dispute between Ronnie and Kit, sang a chorus of "Jingle Bells" with Toby and Tommy and tucked them into bed. He heard Billie's light laughter when he passed by his office on his way to get a cup of coffee in the kitchen. He was watching the weather report on television when she finally came out.

"Did you have a nice talk?"

Linc's voice startled her. Billie saw him sitting in his big chair in the family area. The only light came from the television.

"Yes. I'm sorry I took so long in your office. I didn't realize the time." This was probably the first direct conversation they'd had since . . .

"No problem. I was about done anyway."

"It was Marc on the phone," she said, wondering why in the world she should tell him. It was just that she had news and wanted to share it with him. To bring him closer to her by sharing, foolish thought that probably was. "He wanted to tell me that they've found Jonathan Bledsoe—my accountant."

"That's good news I take it." He rose and rounded the sofa.

She nodded. "For me it doesn't matter that they've found Jonathan. Marc's prosecuting him, but I don't plan to personally file charges. But Marc says they've found some of my money, too."

"I guess that would be good news. Very much of it?"

"It could be. Marc's not certain yet—it's all still so complicated. But he's meeting me on Sunday and will have more information then. I hope you don't mind, but I told him I'd have that day off."

"That's fine."

"I'm supposed to meet him in Lubbock. He's stopping there on his way down to Mexico City. That's where they found Jonathan—Mexico."

"There's no problem. I may be in the fields, but Kit can watch the kids." He gestured toward the television. "Good news for here, too. The rain's done. It'll probably be dry enough for us to start picking again tomorrow afternoon."

"That is good." How in the world was she supposed to behave? she asked herself for the hundredth time. If she behaved exactly as she felt, she'd go over and wrap her arms around him. That was open communication—but she didn't think it would be the appropriate action.

She started toward the kitchen to do the final tidying before bed. A part of her hoped Linc would follow. Her heart leaped when he did.

He leaned his backside against the counter and tossed down a folded section of the paper. "I didn't work the crossword puzzle today. I thought maybe you might want to."

"Thank you," she said after a moment's surprise. "Maybe I will tonight."

She placed the children's ice-cream bowls in the dishwasher while Linc remained standing there. She thought of him reaching out for her.

"I've decided to get Kit a car for Christmas," he said.

"Oh, I think that's a wonderful idea! He'll love it."

He rubbed the side of his nose, looked away from her, folding his arms across his chest. "Well, I thought I'd go into Lubbock this week and check around, see what's available. Thursday evening, maybe, if the pickin' goes good." Pause. "Would you go with me? You seem to have a better idea of what he'd like than I do. Kit could watch the kids. And we could get dinner. I know a nice Mexican restaurant—if you like Mexican food."

For long seconds Billie could only stare at him, amazed at the suggestion and the anxious, uncomfortable expression on his normally stoic face.

"I like Mexican food. I'd love to go."

"Well, good." He almost smiled, then said, "It all depends on the pickin', don't forget."

"Oh, yes. I know."

Thursday afternoon Billie had already showered and curled her hair when Linc radioed from the field to say he'd be coming in and would be ready to leave when Kit and Ronnie returned from school. With help from the twins, she chose a dark blue wool skirt and black sweater, with a silver concho belt that hung around her hips. Not too date-ish, she decided. Because technically, she wasn't certain this was a date. But if it were a date, her clothes would be appropriate, too.

But when Ronnie widened her eyes and gave a low whistle, Billie feared she'd gone too far. Perhaps she shouldn't have curled her hair, or worn the flashy earrings, or sprayed on the Chanel. *Oh, everyone was going to know—see right into her heart!* Linc would probably run the other way, and no telling how the children would react.

However, at the approving light in both Ronnie's and Kit's eyes, her fear subsided some. Then it turned to total joy when appreciation flickered quickly but plainly across Linc's face. And when he helped her into her coat, she knew they were going on a date.

They decided to take the Thunderbird, and Billie had Linc drive.

"Does this mean I'm the Good King of the World?" he asked.

"Yes," she told him, laughing, her heart rocketing to the skies.

They toured several car lots, talked with salesmen and made comparison notes. They stopped to get soft drinks and perused the auto listings in the classified ads. While driving to several private addresses to look over possibilities, they passed a giant toy store, and Billie insisted they stop—only to look. But they came out with enough presents to fill the trunk of the Thunderbird. And then they had to stop and purchase Ronnie not just one but two of those sweatshirts with the fancy lace collars.

They laughed and teased and argued. Linc wanted a modern, sporty economy import for Kit, while Billie leaned toward old classics. He wanted dark blue and green sweatshirts for Ronnie; Billie wanted pink and violet. He wanted practical on everything, while she wanted sparkling fun and beauty.

He laughed more than she'd ever seen him. She felt, there in the midst of the city, alone with him and free to express her feelings and knew he felt this, too. They brushed shoulders and clasped hands. With every glance and touch, the heat vibrated between them. And Billie accepted the agonizing tension this wrought inside so she could experience the sweet bliss that accompanied it.

The restaurant Linc took her to was a favorite of his, and one in which they weren't likely to run into anyone he knew. The main reason he took her there was for the good food, he defended to the accusing voice in his mind. But he had to admit he was enjoying the time alone with her. Time in which he'd felt more himself than he had in the months she'd been in his house.

It was only the third time he'd taken out a woman since he and Denise had separated. It was the first time he could honestly say he was enjoying himself. It scared him to admit it, but not enough to keep him from doing it just the same.

True to form, he ordered all the red-hot spicy foods while Billie ordered everything mild, dumped heaps of sugar into her iced tea and drizzled probably half a pound of honey on her sopaipillas.

Through a couple of remarks, Linc learned that Billie had known Marc Thornton since school days, and he guessed this Thornton must have been one of the men Billie had almost married. He could tell her attachment to the guy remained and found himself absurdly jealous.

Their conversation wound around to the kids and Christmas and what their childhoods were like. Billie fondly recalled her father dressing up as Santa even until she was sixteen years old.

"Well, you're a pretty good Santa yourself," Linc told her dryly. "Never have I seen anyone buy presents with more gusto than you. It's a wonder there's anything left on the shelf in that toy store." He patted his breast pockets. "And you spend everybody's money, too. I'm just a poor ol' farmer—not one of those rich guys from up there in Reno."

"If I excel, I have my father to thank," she said haughtily, taking it all as a compliment. "He was a wonderful teacher at spending money. He and I used to buy gifts for each other all the time. It was a game to see who could surprise the other the most."

In that instant Linc had an inkling what it must be like for her to have lost a man she clearly idolized, and not to have any children of her own, not be able to. He wondered if her gift-buying habit was an effort to fill that gap in her life. And if maybe her lack of children was why she retained so much of the child within herself.

He realized he was just sitting there, staring at her, when she reached out and laid her hand atop his. He looked at their hands. He moved his thumb to clasp her fingers, continued gazing at them while pleasant but suspect feelings whirled around inside him.

They were about to walk out the door when Sam Tate and his wife walked in. Seventy miles from home, in a city of two hundred thousand people, and they had to run into a neighbor.

"Well, hi, buddy! Thought that T-bird out there was familiar. You all are sure a long ways from home." Sam's eyes were ripe as fallen peaches as he smiled and glanced from Linc to Billie. "Hello, Billie. Linc finally gettin' you out of the kitchen? Honey," he gestured to his wife, "this here's Billie Ballinger. This's my wife, Jeannie."

Billie and Jeannie exchanged polite hellos, and they all commented on the recent burning of Heaven, as everyone was now calling it. Soon as he could, Linc hustled Billie out the door into the cool night.

He reached out and took her hand as they walked across the parking lot.

"You didn't want anyone to see us," she said quietly.

Hurt echoed in her voice, and he felt like two cents. But then he halted beneath the pole lamp, shaking his head, rejecting the false guilt.

"No. It wasn't that I didn't want anyone to see us, or wanted to hide being with you. It wasn't that at all." He rested his hand on his belt and took a breath. "I just liked being *unobserved* for today. I wanted to be alone with you without feeling like someone's looking over my shoulder. *I* didn't want to *see* other people. I just wanted time alone—and not with all the complications of a damn bedroom."

Damn! He hadn't meant that last part to blurt out.

But he saw the understanding written in her eyes. And suddenly it was there again—the fire, the wanting, the memory that charged it. It remained there between them like a living thing, both a blessing and a curse at this point. If he didn't know what he knew now about sleeping with her, he wouldn't be having such confusion inside. His mind kept turning in directions it shouldn't have at this stage of their relationship.

Relationship? *Yes, God help him, a relationship.* Somewhere in the past days Linc had come to realize he'd fallen in love—though he wasn't at all certain love even existed. But if it did, it would be with Billie. And maybe he just had to find out.

She slipped her arm through his and pressed close. "I had a very nice time. Thank you."

He felt like a man with pockets full of gold, although he told himself feelings weren't to be trusted, ever.

Chapter Twelve

"**Y**ou look great."

"You said that already." Billie laughed at Marc.

"Well, it bears repeating. You're practically blooming." His gaze was sharply questioning until he glanced away. "Here—this way."

Gesturing with his suitcase, Marc headed through the airport like the seasoned traveler he was, moving and talking rapidly as usual. He always seemed to be trying to crowd two days' worth of events into one.

"I can't believe Lisa didn't come with you," she said, panting in her effort to keep up with him.

He shook his head. "She's in the middle of a show at the gallery—oh, she sends her love. Besides, she wants to go to Mexico City for our honeymoon and says that to go now would spoil it. I'm only hopping down there for a couple of days, anyway."

"Honeymoon? Oh, Marc!" She threw her arms around his neck. "When?"

"January 20th at St. Michael's. You'll be there won't you? Ah—" He tugged her hand. "Over here."

Billie looked at the sign for car rentals and hung back. "I brought the Thunderbird."

"I know, but I've arranged to rent a car. I want to get a look at this Heaven of yours."

"You want..." She halted, forcing him to stop. "I thought you only had a few hours' layover in which you were going to explain more about Jonathan and my money."

"We have to talk about taxes, too. I have enough time to get out there and see where you're hiding yourself and meet this Linc Snow, who needs lessons in basic civilities, I might add."

"You want to check up on me."

"Right. Now come on, I'll follow you. We can talk about your money when we get to Heaven." And away he strode, long coat billowing out behind him, tugging Billie by the hand.

"If I'd known you were renting a car I wouldn't have driven in to meet you, Marc."

"Oh, yes, you would have."

When Linc saw Kit stop the farm truck in the road and not bring it into the field, he silently commended the boy. A chance of fire was the last thing they needed at this point. Modules dotted the field where he, Con, and Eldon had harvested the past two days. This afternoon they would finish up this field. Linc was both tired and eager.

Seeing two figures get out of the pickup, he idled the tractor, jumped down and walked across to meet them—Billie, and that friend of hers, Marc Thornton.

Linc was surprised and suspicious. Billie hadn't said anything about bringing Thornton out from Lubbock. Had plans changed? Was she going to be leaving with this guy? The questions made his skin crawl, and he steeled himself against answers he might not like.

Billie made the introductions. Linc stuck out his hand to take Thornton's, examining the man the same way he was being examined. He knew it would be polite to take off his sunglasses, but he left them on.

Thornton was young, younger than Linc, anyway, by the lack of lines in the face. Dashing stud, was the description that came to mind, fancily dressed in a pale shirt, pleated slacks, and a trench coat—all of which not only yelled money, but wouldn't dare wrinkle on the guy. His hands were callous-free, clean as a surgeon's, but his shake was strong and firm. His gaze was steady, and his expression said clearly that he considered Billie his business.

Seeing Billie's expression, Linc relaxed some. Her eyes were still warm for him. But then they were awfully warm for Thornton, too.

"This soil isn't too good on shoes," Linc said, nodding at Thornton's dust-coated leather loafers. "Sorry you had to walk out, but we risk fire by bringin' vehicles into the field."

"So your son and Billie explained. Sounds like you've had enough of that around here recently." Thornton looked around. "So this is where my underwear comes from. Guess I owe you my thanks."

Linc hadn't expected to start liking the guy. "Accepted. Though I can't lay true claim to your underwear, I'm afraid." Slowly he removed his sunglasses. They kept looking each other over, squinting in the sun, with the stiff breeze smacking their ears.

"It looks like you're getting close to finishing," Billie said, glancing beyond him to where Con was working. She, too, in her pale wool coat and elegant sweater dress, was attired more appropriately for a high-class restaurant or one of those "affairs" she'd once mentioned than for standing there in his cotton field.

"We have the rest of this and that area Con's working in now," Linc said. "Then I have that eighty acres bordering Wes's land. Couple more days ought to have it."

"Then what do you do?" Thornton asked.

"Prepare for next year."

Thornton nodded, gave him one final piercing look and appeared suddenly satisfied with whatever he'd come to see. "Well, my time is short. Hope you don't mind, but I'm stealing Billie away again for a while. She and I have a few things to talk over."

"Her day's her own."

Thornton again stuck out his hand. "I'm glad to have met you, Linc."

"Same," Linc replied shortly but honestly. He shifted his gaze to Kit, waved, and then turned and headed back toward the tractor. He refused to acknowledge the fears tugging at him—he had work to finish.

Billie sat across from Marc in Fred's temporary café. They'd chosen a booth next to one of the small sliding windows. The portable building was much smaller and, while modern, lacked the nostalgia of the old clapboard building.

She had to chuckle at Marc's disbelieving expression and the way he kept looking at the bits of cotton fiber blowing in the wind. "This is Heaven?" he asked for the fourth time.

"It's not much after the fire."

"Don't let her kid you." Fred set their coffee and a Twinkie cake for Billie on the table. "It wasn't much before the fire." Then he walked away.

"That guy always so amicable?"

"Always just like that. He's Linc's uncle."

"The family resemblance is striking."

Billie smiled. She looked around and saw Larry, Theo, and several other familiar faces casting curious glances her way, as usual.

"I definitely feel like the round peg in a square hole," Marc muttered and sipped his coffee. He studied her. "Well, Bill, you finally have your kids."

"Funny, but I never really knew I wanted them."

"I always knew you should have kids. As long as you had your dad, though, you had a kid. And all your animals."

"I guess that's true."

He sighed. "I just wanted to make certain you were okay."

"I'm okay." She laid her hand over his.

"You're in love with this guy."

"Yes. I am."

"He seems one cold hombre, Billie." His expression was clearly doubtful.

"I know he seems that way. But he's not inside."

"Well, he surely isn't like any of the guys you've dated before. He's..."

"Exactly," she said, looking him in the eye.

He raised an eyebrow. "Does he love you? I should have been able to tell that, but I couldn't. I couldn't even tell if he has the hots for you—and that's saying something about the man's expressions. Every man who looks at you gets the hots for you."

"Oh, Marc."

"It's true."

"I think Linc loves me." She could have told him that Linc had the hots for her, too, but she kept that bit of information to herself. "Right now he needs time to decide that. He's cautious and has reason to be. His wife left him about a year and a half ago, Marc."

"Oh." He nodded, played with his cup. "Do you really want to settle down here..." he glanced out the small window "...in this place? Good grief, Billie, after all the places you've visited, you want to hide yourself away here?"

"I like here. And it wouldn't be hiding."

"You don't fit here."

"I do. Just like I am, I fit—because I want to."

He looked skeptical. "I just don't want you hurt, Bill. If anyone on this earth deserves the best, you do."

"You spoil me."

"And you love it."

They both chuckled.

"So, did you find out anything more about Jonathan? Is he all right?"

Marc nodded. "Appears fit as a fiddle is the word from Mexico City. Why in hell he went there, I'm not certain. He was easy to find there, compared to a million other places where he lived safely. Fellow who picked him up says he thinks Jonathan wanted to be caught. It seems Jonathan just went a little crazy, playing with other people's money all those years. He just had to experience having it all for himself. He'd always dreamed of going around the world—so he went.''

"I'm glad he got to go."

"Oh, shi—, Billie. He stole from you."

"And I got to come to Heaven," she said lightly, laughing at his irritation. "Now, what's this about taxes? How could I possibly have to pay more taxes? And with what?"

"You don't," Marc said, brightening again. "It appears the IRS owes you."

When Kit found him, Linc was in the tractor barn, fiddling with this and that. Procrastinating going up to the house. At last glance, Billie's T-bird had still been gone from the drive, the brown sedan sitting in its place. He didn't much want to return with her gone. He didn't much want to watch that Thornton guy and Billie together, either, if they happened to show up. It was one of those times he needed the comfort of something familiar, something he thoroughly understood. A place where he was totally himself.

"Billie wants to know if you're coming up for supper," Kit said, stepping into the barn.

"She's back?" A foolish relief flooded him.

"Yeah, few minutes ago."

"Is Thornton still here?" He immediately wished he'd bit his tongue on that question.

"No. He had to catch a plane. Are you comin'?"

"That depends. What frozen meal is she cooking up?"

"She brought chicken and dumplings from Uncle Fred. Biscuits, too."

"Then I'm comin' directly." They shared knowing grins.

Kit stepped in to help Linc put away tools. "Do you know what I heard that guy, Marc, and Billie talkin' about, Dad?" His eyes grew wide. "That Billie might be getting over two hundred thousand dollars. Somethin' about them finding some guy that had stolen from her. How much do you suppose she had in the first place—before it was stolen?"

"I don't know, son. Enough for her to live well, I guess." So she'd be getting a large chunk of money, which meant...

"She probably won't need to be workin' as a house-keeper anymore," Kit said.

Linc shut the tool box and reached for a rag. "No, probably not."

"Dad . . . she'd stay if you asked her to marry you."

Linc's hands stilled on the rag. He lifted his gaze to his son. "Why do you think that?"

"Because she would. I know she would."

Linc said nothing, tossed the rag aside and moved toward the door. "Let's go get supper."

But Kit didn't move. "I've seen the way you guys look at each other, Dad. I'm not a kid anymore. I'm old enough to see what's happening between you and her."

Linc sighed. "Okay. Billie and I look at each other. She's a beautiful woman, and I'm certainly not blind. But what you see, or what you *think* you see, between Billie and me doesn't mean either of us are up for gettin' married. You should know that, if you're all that grown-up as you think. And I'd do an awful lot for you kids, Kit, but marrying just so we can have a housekeeper isn't one of them. And I don't think Billie would appreciate the idea, either." He opened the door and headed out.

Kit came behind, muttering, "Doesn't seem like it'd be too hard to be married to Billie . . ."

As Linc drove up the rutted lane to the house, he silently agreed with Kit. It probably wouldn't be too hard to be married to Billie. At least as long as it lasted; it was the ending that would do him in. He thought of how she'd looked standing beside Marc Thornton today. He wondered if she truly was getting as much money as Kit had heard. With that amount of money she'd surely be leaving, he thought, and a giant hole seemed to open up, threatening to swallow him.

He'd be better off if she left now, he told himself angrily.

During dinner he waited for her to mention the money, but she only explained to the children how this Jonathan Bledsoe had stolen from her. When Ronnie gave her the third degree about Marc Thornton, Billie told how they had grown up together and what a big-time lawyer he was, relating, to everyone's avid attention, details of a few outlandish cases he'd been involved with.

Linc hung around the table after the meal, idly working the crossword puzzle in the Sunday paper, until the children, one by one, at last disappeared upstairs.

"So—are you goin' to be getting much money back?" he asked very casually.

"Maybe. It appears that I still have bonds that Jonathan wasn't able to cash in. And it also appears that the IRS owes me. Imagine that." She laughed as she closed a cabinet door and glanced around to him.

"You'll probably be getting enough so that you won't have to be worried about workin'," Linc said, stretching slowly to his feet, setting the newspaper aside. "Will you be going back to Reno?"

Their eyes locked.

"Why should I do that?" For once her expression was unreadable.

Linc shrugged. "I just figured you might want to."

He felt off balance, wished he'd never opened the conversation because it made him feel as if he were standing there buck naked. *And, damn it all to hell, it would help if he didn't remember so clearly her naked body under his!*

"It doesn't matter how much money I get. I have no reason to quit working here—or go back to Reno. Unless you've decided you want me to go." Her voice dropped to a hoarse whisper, and her eyes darkened with hurt.

Linc cursed himself and shook his head. "No." He stepped across and took her by the upper arms. "We want you to stay as long as you will. *I* want you to stay."

And then, tossing practicality to the winds, he leaned down and kissed her. Hard and proper, with no effort to hide the fire burning inside.

He was shaking when he broke away, the taste of her lingering on his tongue. She was shaking, too, and her eyes were glistening with hot desire. And happiness so plain it cut right into Linc as she smiled up at him.

"Oh, Linc . . ." she said huskily and leaned her forehead against his chin.

It took every fiber within him not to drag her into her room and put his hands all over her. *Man, how he wanted her!*

And then giggling sounded from behind him. Linc whirled to see not only Tommy and Toby, but Ronnie close behind them, all of them bug-eyed. The sight was equal to a dousing of ice water. Linc almost pushed Billie from him. But then he stopped.

"Oh, brother," Ronnie said, rolling her eyes, her face red as an apple. Lips twitching into a grin, she pivoted and ran away up the stairs.

"Is there somethin' you boys needed?" Linc asked, finally dropping his hands from Billie. His face was warm, hers was pink. She stepped forward and knelt in front of them.

"Ronnie couldn't find the bubble soap," Tommy said. Both boys moved wide-eyed gazes back and forth between Billie and Linc.

"There's a new bottle in the hall closet. I'll come help you."

"No." Linc stepped forward, reached for the boys' hands. "I'll help you guys tonight. This was supposed to be Billie's day off."

He led his sons out into the hallway and didn't look back, though it was pleasing to know Billie watched them go.

"D-do y-you like Bil-lie, D-dad?"

"Yep, Toby. I do."

Linc wanted knowledge of his relationship with Billie to remain at home, but he knew that was impossible. He figured Sam Tate had already blabbed about seeing him and Billie together in Lubbock, and the kids would say something to someone. And sure enough, Kit did. He told Fred.

"Heard there's courtin' goin' on at your house," Fred said. At least he leaned over and spoke directly into Linc's ear, didn't blurt it out for everyone's information.

The usual crowd filled the café, which was by unspoken tradition an all-male domain in the mornings. The men were having coffee and visiting before a day's work—Joel Heavener, Rick Moreno, Carlos, Theo, even Wes was there, in the corner booth with Larry—all Linc's neighbors. The portable building was smaller than the old café had been, the booths seemed skinnier, tighter. Linc sat waiting for Eldon in a back booth, and his skin crawled with the feeling that people were right on top of him.

"Where'd you hear that?" Linc asked innocently as Fred slipped into the opposite seat.

Fred gave him a patient look. "Sam told it around last week that he'd seen you two at that restaurant, and Kit says that Sunday evenin' you and Billie were caught kissin'—suckin' face, he called it. Good grief, where do kids come up with this stuff?"

Linc inclined his head and remained noncommittal. He'd always gotten on with Fred, been closer to the old man than just about anyone, though Linc had never been one to have a confidant.

"Well, it sure as hell took you long enough." Fred leaned forward and spoke in a hushed voice. "For a while, I was afraid you had sawdust for brains. And now that you're finally started, you'd better get busy to make up for lost time. That was some fancy fella Billie was in here with last Sunday."

"He's just a friend. They've known each other since they were kids."

"That sounds cozy." Fred moved to the end of the seat, then paused and pulled at his ear. "When Denise hit the road, you turned into a real clam, Linc. You've pushed everybody away and lived your life alone, not trustin' to share with anyone. Well, no man is an island, some fella once wrote. You try to be, but you ain't. Now, my advice to you is to open up. To Billie, to your kids—to your neighbors a mite, too. I know you can't abide people being nosy, but a lot of that would stop if you'd just come out and go about your business in front of them. Now, that's all I have to say."

"I hope so," Linc said. Fred's voice had risen and a couple of the men turned to look.

Tugging on his red suspenders and shaking his head, Fred walked away.

Even while he often thought the old man a fool, Linc had always held a certain respect for Fred. And this time he couldn't get Fred's words out of his mind. By noon he'd finally come to the conclusion the old man knew a thing or two this time.

"Put on your coats," Linc commanded when he came in the door. "I'm taking you and the kids for a hamburger at Fred's."

Billie stared at him as if thinking he'd lost his mind. The boys were already wriggling down from their chairs, yelling, "Zip-a-Dee-Doo-Dah!"

"But . . . we were just going to have alphabet soup," Billie said, gesturing at the bowls on the table. "It's heated and . . . everything."

"You can have soup any day, can't you fellas? Come on. We'll even get Cherry Cokes. I've been a good boy." He winked and shot Billie a deliberately salty look. He felt his chest expanding. He wasn't quite certain what had come over him, but he liked it. "Get your coat."

She stepped away, then halted and cocked her head. "Are you telling me or asking me?"

He straightened his face. "Askin', ma'am."

"Oh . . . okay." And that smile that lit up a room crossed her beautiful face.

Oh, Lord, save him from a beautiful woman. But not too quickly, he added, laughing at himself.

It was the middle of the lunch hour at the café and women were allowed. Gracie Hendricks and three of her blue-haired cronies sat in the one corner booth. Joel Heavener was back again, sitting with his bookkeeper, Chrissy, and Sam Tate, and there were a couple of the guys who worked at the gin, and the parcel delivery woman. And Ginny was there with a couple of her friends—Linc spoke and nodded politely to her. Just about everyone in the café looked at him and Billie, though they were careful about it. Except Ginny, who stared close enough to write a report on what she saw—or what she thought she saw. Surprise even crossed old Fred's stony face. Then he was smiling all over himself and calling a greeting as if he hadn't just that morning been talking to Linc.

Linc paid it all no mind. He was simply a father taking his sons and housekeeper out to lunch and trying not to get catsup all over himself—which wasn't too easy when sitting in a booth with four-year-old twins.

During the following days Billie experienced the most wonderful change in her relationship with Linc. The most amazing, amusing, awe-inspiring change, bringing times she wouldn't have missed for the world.

Linc dropped in to share lunch with her and the twins one day—and he brought her a single Twinkie. Another evening he came and presented her with a bouquet of flowers.

"They had 'em sittin' by the checkout at the Save-on-Foods store over in Lubbock," he said with a shrug, rubbing the side of his nose as he did when self-conscious.

She hadn't known what to say, could only stand there, clutching the stems, staring at the colors.

The night he announced that the Snow's cotton was in was a time of family celebration. Linc lit a fire in the living room fireplace, and they all gathered together. Toby and Tommy and even Ronnie for a few minutes sat in Linc's lap, while Billie sat beside him. Their shoulders brushed, her thigh tingled against his. They shared a bowl of popcorn, and Linc was persuaded to join them in singing Christmas carols.

Friday afternoon he came home excited, eager to share the news of finding a car he thought perfect for Kit. He wouldn't purchase it before she'd seen it, too, so Saturday morning, they went off, alone, to have a look. Billie was astonished to find he was considering a restored 1957 Chevrolet—a choice she would have thought more her style than his.

"Well," he said with that adorable self-conscious shrug and absurdly young look that came over his hard features, "I figure you and Kit have more the same tastes. Besides, I had one of these when I was a kid. Though mine was a piece of junk."

After arrangements were made to pick up the car the following week, he took her to Fred's for a Cherry Coke before going home. "We promised Kit to return in a couple of hours," Billie reminded him.

He took her hand, right there in the café, and said, "A few minutes of celebration are in order—and now that you've got me started on this celebration business, don't stop me."

Oh, she didn't intend to stop him. She savored his attentions and strove to give in return. She brought him coffee when he worked in his office and joined him for quiet conversation during the early morning time alone before the children rose. She worked very hard to serve him his favorite foods—even if she couldn't cook them herself—and to keep the shirts and jeans she knew were his favorites washed and ironed.

Their touches were infrequent, cautious. They both knew the danger. At times Billie thought she would burst into flame if Linc so much as took her hand. Yet sometimes she just *had* to touch him. She would dare to lay a hand lightly on his thick hair or rest it on his shoulder. She would stand close enough for her shoulder to brush his and to inhale his scent...and to dream of what could be.

Oh, Wilhelmina, really! She was acting like a love-struck schoolgirl.

Yes! Yes, she was, and she enjoyed the experience. She delighted in singing with the boys or alone, while she did laundry and cleaned house and decorated for the coming wonderful, beautiful holiday. She spent hours thinking of gifts to buy, ordering a number of things by telephone. Even Marc and Lisa were enlisted in her hunt for the perfect thing for each person on her gift list. Sometimes her joy came out as she danced around the house with a mop or stopped to pick up each of the boys. Oh, these were days of heaven, and Billie thought little of them coming to an end, only how they could get better.

But they did end, as early as Sunday afternoon, when Denise Snow arrived.

Chapter Thirteen

Linc had taken Kit and the boys out for Christmas shopping, and Ronnie was spending the afternoon with a friend, giving Billie a rare day alone in the house.

"Enjoy a day off at home," Linc had teased. "Maybe that way a few things will be saved in the stores for other people to buy."

Perhaps by Linc's conservative standards she did go a little overboard on Christmas buying, she thought as she put the finishing touches on a gift box for Ronnie—but it was so darn much fun! And mostly, except for a few special items, she didn't spend all that much, and she received a thousand times over in enjoyment. Besides the children, she bought for Linc and Fred and Gracie and Don the mailman, and Sue, her favorite clerk at the grocery store, and Ronnie's teacher, and John, Kit's good friend. And of course Eldon, and just a can of chewing tobacco for Con, which didn't count at all. It wasn't as much fun to buy for Wes and Ginny and their children, but she did it anyway, in Linc's name, with his money, to encourage peace. Which was the reason for the season, she reminded him when he said he didn't care to buy for his brother's family.

She set the box atop others piled beside the couch in the living room. She gleefully anticipated Ronnie's delight in opening the package on Christmas morning and finding a denim duster like Billie's. Instead of decorative beading, it had the painting of a prairie wolf on the back. Lisa had arranged to have it specially made up in Reno.

Twice more she and Linc had gone into Lubbock to shop. Both times he'd relied on her advice in choosing gifts for Kit and Ronnie. She'd had to tell Linc that Kit wouldn't wear a sweater, hated them. Kit preferred T-shirts, the louder the color and design the better. She'd also pointed out that more than money could buy, Ronnie would most like a dog. The poorest mongrel from a shelter would do. So far Linc had refused that suggestion, but Billie retained hope.

He'd been amazingly adorable when he decided he wanted to buy Ronnie a gold locket. With his eyebrows knotted, he'd peered into jewelry cases, and his work-roughened hands had been clumsy in holding up the tiny chains with delicate lockets. Her heart had filled to overflowing with love for him, so much that it'd been almost painful. She could hardly believe a person could feel such emotion and still live.

Scattered memories of the past weeks sent an inner joy spreading like warm honey through her body. She and Linc held back, didn't dare risk touching too much because they each knew what could happen. Good heavens, they were like firecrackers just waiting to go off! It was at once the most agonizing and extremely pleasurable situation Billie had ever experienced.

She was ready to make a commitment to Linc. Inwardly, she already had. But Linc wasn't ready to do that. And the thought that he might never be brought a chill to her happy warmth.

Casting such blue thoughts aside, she adjusted the red bow at the corner of the mantel and glanced about the room with satisfaction. Real holly with red berries graced the mantel and stockings hung on either side. Evergreen bows arched above the doorway, giving off a lovely fragrance, and red and white candles sat everywhere. She was one excellent decorator, if she did say so herself, she thought as she continued into the kitchen.

At the sight of the figure standing beside the round table, Billie came to an abrupt halt, frozen with the shock of seeing another person in the house. An intruder. She hadn't heard a car in the drive. No knock or doorbell.

The woman brazenly stood there, placing her purse and shopping bag onto the table, setting a suitcase on the floor.

A suitcase?

"Excuse me?" As Billie spoke she took in the dark, belted coat and blond, bobbed hair. Even as the woman turned, recognition hit Billie like a slap across the face.

The woman cocked her head. "Hello." She lifted an eyebrow and smiled slightly as she looked down at her hands and pulled off her tight gloves. "You must be the housekeeper. I'm Denise Snow. Linc's wife."

Her accent was a deep West Texas drawl, her voice husky. Sultry. Her gaze flicked quickly, sharply over Billie, and Billie felt a twinge of displacement. Linc's *wife,* she'd said—not *ex*-wife. Cool, possessing, Denise Snow stood there.

"Billie, isn't it?" she said.

Gathering her wits, Billie stepped forward and stuck out her hand. "Yes, I'm Billie Ballinger."

She did a quick bit of studying herself in that second, noticing that Denise Snow was approximately her height but thinner by a good ten pounds. Her hair style was shorter than her own, but the color was almost exactly the same. Their hands made quick contact; Denise Snow's was cold, soft. Her eyes were a lovely sky blue. Her makeup was flawless, shades of smoky blue about the eyes, crimson on her lips. The fingers that unfastened her coat were long and graceful and perfectly manicured.

"I'm sorry. Linc isn't here," Billie said, running a hand down her thigh, then raking back her disheveled hair. She was suddenly conscious of wearing no makeup. Her fingernails were short, cut off because of all the work she did. She felt young, awkward and stupid.

Oh, Wilhelmina, really! She grasped at her good sense. She wasn't born yesterday, after all—her sweater was a designer original, and so were her legging pants, and she'd enjoyed the company of many prominent, even powerful women. She had a presence of her own! Silly to be letting this woman crawl all over her nerves.

"Oh." Denise Snow shrugged. "I halfway expected it, since it *is* cotton season. Sunday's just another workday."

"Linc and the boys went to Lubbock, shopping. Ronnie's at Stacie's—she's a friend."

"I know who Stacie Graham is," she drawled, and again her gaze studied Billie. Then she began removing her coat, obviously intending to stay.

"Linc will be picking up Ronnie on the way home, but I don't know exactly when he'll return."

Denise dropped her coat across the back of a chair. "Sometime this afternoon, surely. Until then I'll have a chance alone to reacquaint myself with the house."

As Billie noted Denise's formfitting knit dress, she wondered how the woman could consider herself alone when Billie was standing right in front of her. And with a glance at the woman's suitcase, she wondered just how long this visit was going to be.

"May I offer you a cup of coffee?" It seemed the thing to say at the moment.

"Oh, don't bother. I can get it. I'm certainly no stranger here." She gave a throaty laugh as she walked over to the counter where the coffee machine sat. "I certainly don't want to interrupt your schedule. I imagine you have a thousand things to do."

She was already reaching into the cabinet for a cup; she knew exactly where they were kept. Her red-nailed finger trailed down the smooth surface of the cabinet door. "Oh, my. I remember havin' to choose these cabinets. Linc and I deliberated for weeks." Again came that throaty, sexy chuckle.

Billie's stomach turned over. She grabbed the sugar bowl and pushed it across the counter. "Here's the sugar."

"I take it black, thank you."

Just like Linc, Billie thought.

Coffee cup in hand, Denise Snow turned, her eyes taking on the glint of fond memories as they flowed around the room. Billie had the urge to give her two black eyes. Her stomach tightened more. What in the world did a person say in a situation like this? Billie wanted to invite her to leave but figured that, given her true place in this household, that was not one of the choices.

"Would you like to sit down?"

"No," Denise drawled, "I think I'll just look around. I promise I won't get in your way. Please go on with whatever household duties you were doin'."

Just as if she were dismissing a servant. Which of course Billie had to admit she was, and that thought made her irritation rise all the more.

"Today is my day off," Billie told her in her most accommodating and regal voice. "I have plenty of time to visit with you. Is there anything you'd like to know? Perhaps I could tell you about the children."

From Denise Snow's scorching look, Billie knew her words had struck their mark.

The two of them stood there, silently challenging each other.

Then a clever grin swept across Denise Snow's face. "You've been here a few months, and you think you know so much." She shook her head. "Well, honey, I'm the one who lived with Linc Snow for fourteen years. There's certainly nothin' you could tell me about him that I don't already know. And I'm the one who gave birth to those children. I'm quite sure I could tell you things about them, too." She gestured with her cup. "As for anything new I may want to know...I think I'd rather find that out for myself. Which is why I've come. Now you can just go back to whatever housekeepin' you need to be doin'—or whatever a housekeeper does on her day off. Course, from what I've heard, your specialty isn't keepin' house. Maybe you're better at other things?" She raised a speculative eyebrow, looking at Billie as if she was just so much dust under a bed.

Billie's self-confidence seemed to drain out through her toes while hot anger filled her head. How dare that woman insinuate...

But this woman was a guest in the home of the man she worked for—a very special guest. If she'd learned to be as good at her job as she'd hoped, she would behave well now. She'd show this bitch who was truly a lady—and a damn fine housekeeper!

Billie stiffly inclined her head. "Please make yourself at home."

"I believe I will." And again came that damn throaty laugh!

Billie turned and headed for her room. Fleeing, and not proud of it. Her gaze lit on the laundry basket full of clean clothes sitting on top of the washer. Grabbing it, she headed back for the kitchen.

Denise Snow was looking around the family area, like a conqueror surveying her new domain!

"I just think I'll put these clean clothes away," Billie said, passing through without stopping. "Upstairs in everyone's drawers."

As she mounted the stairs Billie admitted what she'd just said and was doing right now was quite hard to decipher, even in her own mind. It had to do with being intimate with and trusted enough by the people of this house to handle their underwear. She was that intimate and trusted—Denise Snow was not. Not anymore. And Denise Snow was a sharp enough woman to get the point.

As she went from bedroom to bedroom, sorting, folding and putting away clothes, Billie seethed.

Who did that woman think she was? She'd left this house, her own husband and children well over a year ago. Did she just think she could pick back up as the lady of the house?

The swift answering thought that maybe Denise Snow could do exactly that sent a sharp pain across her chest.

Billie went into Linc's room last and shut the door behind her. She laughed at herself when she found she didn't even have any of his underwear in the basket. She had jeans, a couple of T-shirts and some socks. She put them away and then made his bed, which he never made himself. Then she sat on it.

She just couldn't pass back by Denise Snow again. And she wanted that woman to wonder why she was up here for so long. And if she stayed in Linc's room, Denise Snow wasn't as likely to come in. Or if she did, she'd find Billie sitting on the bed. All of which seemed a little crazy. But still she sat there.

Ronnie was complaining about not being in on choosing the tree when Linc turned the pickup in the driveway. She'd been complaining since they'd picked her up at Stacie's and she'd seen the big Douglas fir in the back. Added to that, Tommy and Toby were singing "Santa Claus is Coming to Town" for about the hundredth time since visiting Santa at the shopping mall. Linc's skin was beginning to crawl, but not too badly. He was feeling too excited about the tree—and it was one hell of a tree. The only place it was going to fit was in the front of the hallway. He knew Billie was going to love it, and knowing that made even stringing the lights worth it.

About the time he saw the unfamiliar gold BMW in the drive, Kit said, "Someone's here."

All the kids shut up and focused their attention on the car. Linc's chest tightened with irritation as he imagined another of Billie's friends having stopped by. He didn't want anyone here, damn it! He wanted to show Billie his tree alone—or just with the kids, anyway.

"Classy wheels," Kit said, eyeing the BMW with appreciation.

Oh, well, life was rarely perfect. And Billie was still going to delight in this tree. Some of Linc's high spirits returned as he and Kit hauled the evergreen out of the truck and through the front door. He peered eagerly ahead, wanting to get a look at Billie's expression when she saw it.

But it wasn't Billie who stepped through from the kitchen. *Good God.* Linc froze there, holding on to the tree.

"Denise."

"Hello." Smiling warmly, she walked forward, kissed his cheek, then looked at the children. "Oh, my darlin's!" She reached for Tommy and Toby, but they both scampered behind Linc's legs and clutched him around his thighs.

The tree began to tip dangerously, and Linc struggled to hold it and not squash the twins in the process. *Where in the hell was Billie?*

He and Kit managed to prop the tree in the corner, Linc moving with the twins still leeching onto his legs. He normally would have barked at them, but this time he liked their being against him. And he worried over what effect Denise's sudden appearance might have on them.

Kit allowed a hug from his mother, while Ronnie scowled and stomped up the stairs. That was when Linc finally saw Billie. She was coming down as Ronnie went racing up. Her gaze locked on to his.

And there he stood, with his ex-wife on one side of him, a giant Christmas tree on the other, and his two little boys anchoring him to the spot. He felt like a bale of low-grade cotton.

"We got a tree," he said, pointing at it.

Her blue eyes flicked to the tree, to Denise and then back to him. "I'll just go up and see about Ronnie."

"*I'll* go and see about Ronnie," Denise said and took a step toward the stairs.

But Linc grabbed her arm. "Let Billie talk to her."

Denise turned on him, and he recognized her gearing-up-to-argue expression. But then she nodded. He let go of her arm and thought, damn it all to hell!

She bent down and peered at the boys. "Toby...Tommy. I'm your mama. I'd like very much to give you a hug."

"Don't you even care about the way she's just waltzed in here?" Ronnie said, her face a mask of anguish. "That she's trying to make up to all of us—to Daddy?"

Billie nodded and thought how much it all hurt. "Of course I care. I'd be lying if I tried to deny it. But when you come down to it, what's wrong with her wanting to make up to you and the boys, Ronnie? Or even to your father?"

"Well, I don't like it."

"You don't have to like it, honey. Not one bit. But the proper thing to do is to be polite. She is a guest—and your mother. She's entitled to respect."

Ronnie frowned and shrugged. "I can't pretend what I don't feel."

"I'm not saying you should. I'm saying to be polite—if for no other reason than to make *me* look good. I don't want people thinking I haven't taught you manners."

The girl rolled her eyes but nodded.

Billie touched the child's sleek braid. "I'm not trying to convince you to forgive, or accept your mother back, Ronnie. Just don't make the situation more difficult than it already is. And try...try not to judge too harshly." And that wasn't an easy thing for her to say.

Ronnie came down quietly and helped Billie prepare supper, while Linc and Denise and the boys talked in the living room. That Linc could so easily talk to the woman set Billie's teeth on edge. More than once she heard Denise Snow commenting, "Remember the time..."

The woman had not come unprepared for bribery, either. She had four grocery sacks full of gaily wrapped Christmas presents. The twins were allowed to open two each right away. Kit opened one, too, but Ronnie shook her head.

That's my girl, Billie thought, and was immediately ashamed. She *must* put aside her own selfish emotions, she told herself sternly. But it was so hard! She was caught between her own deep desires and what would be best for the children.

She wasn't happy about the meal, either. There was only one thing to be served—frozen pizza. She'd planned to go shopping the following day. She cursed under her breath now, hating Denise Snow to know what a poor cook she was, but there was no way she could pretend to be a woman who could whip up something from odds and ends in the pantry. She'd probably end up poisoning them all if she tried.

Ronnie appeared to have taken her instruction to heart. Though the child said nothing to her mother unless directly asked, at least she didn't glower or scream at the woman. She always answered, "Yes, ma'am" or "No, ma'am."

Actually, Billie decided, Ronnie's politeness managed to border on extreme rudeness. Oh, what a crackerjack rascal she was—and Billie admonished herself for the small satisfaction she derived from Ronnie's clear partiality toward her. It helped her not to feel so alone, though. And Kit's and the twins' mindfulness of her helped, too.

Linc's reaction she couldn't quite gauge. He appeared highly irritated with the lot of them—and at least in this Denise Snow was no exception. While he didn't ignore Billie, he didn't display any undue affection toward her, either. He was cautious, guarded, as he'd been when she first came into this house. She didn't understand, and it made her angry. And frightened.

All through the meal Linc thought about Denise's suitcase sitting in the kitchen. His stomach was so tied in knots, he could hardly eat. He tried to keep his eyes off Billie, because what he felt for her wasn't any of Denise's business—wasn't anyone's business.

But when he could catch glimpses of Billie's face, she put him off. She wouldn't look at him, kept her attention focused on the kids. Kept herself withdrawn. It occurred to him that this was the way she reacted on those rare times she became angry.

When everyone had finished and Billie and Ronnie started clearing away the dishes, he asked to speak to Denise alone. On their way to his office, they passed the Christmas tree, still lying against the corner of the hallway.

"That tree's goin' to get sap all over the wallpaper, Linc. It won't take a minute to set it up properly..."

"Not now, Denise."

"But it's foolish to ruin the wallpaper. And the children would love it. Wouldn't you boys?"

Immediately Toby and Tommy joined in the campaign to set the tree up.

"I'll take care of it later," Linc said sharply, shutting everyone's mouth. Taking Denise's arm, he urged her into his office. The time he'd taken Billie in here for a talk passed through his mind. Closing the door, he caught sight of Ronnie about halfway across the hall, Kit coming after her.

"You two get the hell out of here." They both did an about-face.

Linc sat back in his old oak rocking desk chair and surveyed his ex-wife. "You're lookin' good."

"Thank you," she said in a husky, breathless way. "You're not lookin' too bad yourself."

They studied each other for a long second. She was the same beautiful woman he'd been married to for over fourteen years. Yet there were things very different about her, too; things he'd either not noticed or had developed since they'd parted. Things such as the way she spoke and looked at him—it was deliberately calculated to be sexy and made her seem oddly cold. The way she tilted her chin upward a fraction or the way she couldn't seem to sit perfectly still. He recalled when the gleam of her hair used to set his blood to warming. It did nothing for him now. Had he really waited impatiently all those nights for her to finish with her hair and come to him in bed? That time seemed to belong to someone else. And when it came down to it, he supposed it did.

"You must be doin' all right with the telephone company. Drivin' a BMW now."

"You were very generous in our settlement—and I got it secondhand at a real bargain."

"I didn't give you anything you didn't ask for."

"You didn't fight it."

"You'd earned it." Again they gazed at each other. "You should have called before comin', Denise."

She stood and moved about the room, looking at things. "You wouldn't have welcomed me, would you?" She lifted a book, looked at it, then at him.

"No. Probably not."

"But it hasn't been so bad, me comin'. Has it?" Her gaze moved slowly from his face, slipped down his chest, lingered at his crotch and came back up.

"It's been okay."

She set the book back on the shelf, moved to the tall file cabinet and picked up his snake-head paperweight. "Mercy, Linc. Ginny said this housekeeper you hired wasn't all that good at the job, but surely it couldn't be too difficult for her to learn to dust. She *is* supposed to be keepin' house, after all."

"You've been speaking with Ginny?" Suspicion slipped across his shoulders. He knew damn well what Ginny had told Denise about Billie's presence in the house.

She blew dust off the paperweight and set it back in place. "Yes. We've kept in touch right along. Just because you and I divorced didn't mean I had to turn my back on my entire life."

"I thought that was what you wanted. To be away from everything out here."

Her gaze rested on him. "I thought that at the time. Now, I'm not so sure." She sat in the chair beside the desk.

"What do you want, Denise?"

Her blue eyes grew darker; she wet her lips. "I've missed the children, Linc. I've missed you." She paused, and the hair on the back of his neck stood up.

Linc stared at her. "You could have visited anytime. You know that."

She looked away. "I was just so mixed up. So damn mixed up." Her eyes came up to his, pleading. "I made a big mistake, Linc. I know that now. Lord, I was so crazy! I don't know what happened to me—yearnin's were tearin' me apart so that I couldn't see straight. And I'm so sorry. I want you to know that."

Linc shifted uncomfortably. "It's all over now, Denise." And he'd just as soon not talk about it.

"Maybe. But I . . . I'd hoped that maybe I could make it up to you."

His pulse quickened, and he wondered what she was getting at.

"Make it up to me?"

She averted her eyes. "Well, to all of you—you and the children."

"How?"

"Oh, Linc . . ." She shifted, looking self-conscious and sad. He hoped she wouldn't cry. "I want to try to get close again. I'd like to stay for a while. To have time with you and the children. I've arranged for a leave of absence from work until after the first of the year. And after that, I'll be transferrin' to the Lubbock offices, so I can be within commuting distance."

Linc stared at her and took a deep breath. "You just show
up with a suitcase and expect to stay? Where do you plan to
sleep?"

She smiled hesitantly. "I don't mind sleepin' on the
couch."

"Maybe the rest of us would mind you sleeping there."

She stared at him. "Linc, I want to see my children.
Please don't deny me that, not at this time of year." She
blinked. "I promise I won't be any trouble for you
and . . . Billie, isn't it?"

He couldn't quite believe she wouldn't be any trouble. She
gazed at him imploringly, but it wasn't her expression that
made him consider the idea. It was the fact that she was the
children's mother. And his kids had a right to know their
mother—as well as possible. No matter the personal problems this gave Linc and Billie. This could be the only time
Denise was ever willing to give to the kids. If he denied her,
he would be denying them.

"You can stay five days—until Saturday. Take it or leave
it."

Anticipating Ronnie's reaction, Linc dreaded telling the
children. But telling Billie was ten times harder. He wondered what she'd think of him. Would she be mad enough
at him to leave? Or worse, maybe she wouldn't even care.

Since everyone was gathered in the living room, he told
them at once and got it over with. The twins, sitting on
either side of Billie, showed little concern. Ronnie looked as
though she'd suddenly gotten a mouthful of mud. Kit tensed
but tried to look pleasant.

And Billie. She looked at him with no emotion at all,
which hurt more than if she'd screamed at him.

So here he ended up, with his ex-wife and lover in the
same house. Lover? Was that what Billie was to him?
No . . . she was more. She was a good friend. She was someone he didn't want to lose. She was someone confusing the
hell out of him.

Seething inside, he went to get blankets and a pillow, intending to be the one sleeping on the couch. It would put him closer to Billie—and wasn't that a stupid thought!

But in the end it was Kit who took the couch, giving his room over to his mother. He even emptied a drawer of his dresser for her. Linc knew it was best to keep his own room because of Tommy and Toby's habit of joining him in the night. And because it kept things perfectly proper, leaving no room for people to get ideas.

He was just stepping out of his shower when he heard his bedroom door open. Towel wrapped around his waist, he came out of the bathroom. "What is it, boys..."

Denise stood there, leaning against the closed door. Her shiny blond hair waved over her cheeks. With bold eyes, she slowly looked him over, then glanced around the room. "We had some good times in here," she said in her deliberately sexy voice.

"*Had* is the key word." He stalked over, grabbed her arm and jerked her away from the door, opening it.

"I only wanted to thank you, Linc," she protested as he shoved her out. Then she chuckled. "Not everything has died, if you can react like this, honey."

He shut the door—didn't slam it for anyone to hear—in her face.

He supposed he should be flattered. But he wasn't. He was disgusted. She'd always used sex, he thought tiredly, as a reward, as a relief from boredom, as a bribe. There'd been love between them; he knew that. But somehow it'd never progressed beyond the you-make-me-feel-good stage. And he didn't think Denise could ever go beyond that.

Maybe he wouldn't have ever known anything more existed, if he hadn't met Billie.

He got into bed and lay in the darkness. The five days stretched ahead like some awful nightmare, and he had the creeping feeling that he'd made a big mistake in allowing Denise even that long. A lot could happen in five days.

His thoughts turned to Billie. She had a right to want to chop his head off. His mind drifted back to their time together. He thought of how it'd been that one time with her. He wanted to go down there and be with her now. To lose himself in her. When he'd had sex with Billie, she'd given, freely. Oh, damn, how the woman gave. It would never be just sex with her. It would always be a celebration of life.

Billie was up before dawn as usual, and was extra quiet making the coffee, mindful of Kit nearby on the couch. Every cell in her body waited for Linc to come downstairs. But when he did, she didn't know what to say. She felt so awkward, wanting him and not knowing how he felt toward her.

She met his eyes only once, then focused on wiping an imaginary spill from the counter. She wouldn't make him feel sorry for her, wouldn't humiliate herself by letting him see how she felt about him.

Then he tugged her around to him. "Denise wants time with the children," he said. "I can't deny her that. I can't deny *them* that."

She raised her eyes to his. There was veiled heat there, but nothing else that she could read. And she needed something else.

"Why does she have to stay here?"

He took a deep breath. "She's been livin' in Houston and is in the process of transferring to Lubbock. When she arranges that, she can drive out to see the kids, but right now she's arranged for a leave of absence. Look, I know it's..."

He broke off and caressed her cheek. And then he lowered his head and kissed her, hungrily, greedily.

Ignoring the voice inside that called her foolish, Billie savored his lips and the taste of him, the feel of his hard chest beneath her hands.

Her lips throbbed, and she gasped for breath when they broke apart. She studied his eyes, seeing hot desire plainly now.

"And where do I fit into this?" she asked in a hoarse whisper. The longing in her heart was almost too much to bear.

"What do you mean?"

"What am I supposed to do? Step back into the woodwork as the hired help and nothing more? Or maybe that's all I truly am—with a few extra duties to the master of the house thrown in."

Anger sparked in his eyes. "You know that's not the case."

"Then what is the case? What are *we?*"

A veil slipped across his face. He rubbed the side of his nose. "I think that's what we're in the process of findin' out."

"We were, maybe. Now I guess I'm supposed to step back and wait."

"Only if you want to," he said sharply and turned away.

Billie watched his lean back as he stepped out the back door into the dark morning. Then, holding back tears, she hurried to her own room. She'd been selfish to push him, to take her frustration out on him. And she'd been foolish, too.

Billie got beneath the shower and cried. Love made people do such hurtful things. Couldn't Linc see that if she didn't love him, she wouldn't have behaved so idiotically? Or maybe he didn't want to see her love? If he felt love for her, he certainly hadn't made that plain to his ex-wife. His ex-wife—the woman for whom he'd carried a torch for a long time.

When Billie came out to make breakfast, she found Denise Snow at the counter, dressed in a frilly peignoir, making biscuits. From scratch. Bacon and eggs sizzled perfectly.

Linc came through the kitchen from his office about midway through breakfast. Again the taciturn man he'd been when Billie had first met him, he barely looked at anyone, bidding each of the children a gruff good morning before heading out the door.

However, he did stop for two biscuits spread with jelly, made by Denise Snow's hand, to take with him.

Chapter Fourteen

Denise took over the kitchen, but only to cook. Billie got to clean up. She also got to make school lunches and see that Ronnie got off to school. Denise took Kit, allowing him to drive the BMW. The small blessing was that she was gone all morning—while Billie changed wet sheets from Tommy's bed, got the twins bathed and took them with her into Moorestown to do grocery shopping.

When they returned, Denise was waiting to play mother to the boys, keeping them from their nap. Billie put away the groceries and discovered that Denise had also done a bit of shopping.

"Thought I'd make chicken and dumplings tonight for dinner," Denise said brightly. "That's one of Linc's favorites."

And the woman made it all from scratch, stewing the chicken, rolling out dumpling batter on the counter, everything! Billie picked at her food and watched everyone else eat. At least Linc didn't offer compliments to the cook. Of course, the three platefuls he helped himself to spoke volumes.

Billie got to clean up the mess after dinner, abandoned even by Ronnie, who joined her brothers and Denise in watching a movie. She tried not to be petty about Ronnie; the child's happiness was paramount. It would be best for her to be on good terms with her mother.

Linc retreated to his office again. That made Billie furious, and she took it out on the pot she scrubbed with all her might. That woman had managed to dirty every pot and pan and lid in the kitchen, and Billie knew that she'd done it on purpose. While Denise Snow was doing her best to charm the socks off Linc and the children, she was doing her best to make Billie's life hell. And the woman was succeeding quite well at both, too.

She'd just finished cleaning the kitchen when Denise came in and announced she was making everyone popcorn—and not the microwave variety but the old fashioned kind popped in a pan on the stove. Of course, another pan.

"Have at it," Billie said and stalked away to her room.

She would not mope, she told herself. She would not even think of crying. Yet she did both for a few minutes. And she wondered why now, of all times, her good sense kept doing a vanishing act. She certainly wasn't helping the situation by turning into a workhorse shrew—just the thing to push Linc at his wife! Oh, but it was hard to have any sense at all when the greatest desire of her life was at stake.

With monumental effort, she gathered what good sense she could and took a shower. Afterward she put on her best perfume and brushed her fresh-washed hair until it shone like spun gold. Then she dressed in a flowing, royal blue velvet party pajama set, an original made just for her. Surveying herself in the mirror, she decided that there were a few things she could do better than Denise Snow, and she went to do them.

There was quite a ruckus going on upstairs when Billie carried a fresh cup of coffee into Linc's office. She knocked softly and entered at his answer. Her heart leaped at the attraction that flickered in his eyes. She went over and set the coffee on his desk.

They stared at each other. For a magical moment she forgot everything but the memory of his body pressing hers.

Though they didn't move, touch each other in any way, they connected completely.

"A farmer's paperwork is never done," Billie said at last and glanced to the papers scattered about his desk. She had to say something, turn her attention to something other than the heat in his eyes and the stirring in her belly.

"Tax time comin'," he said. His gaze dropped slowly to her breasts, and she felt the telltale tingling there.

"Dad. Uh . . . Billie?"

They both turned to the opened doorway. Kit, looking slightly abashed, stood there.

"Ronnie's mouse got loose again and scared Mom, and Toby got soap in his eyes and is cryin' for either of you. I tried to help him, but he won't have me."

Billie started immediately for the stairs, and Linc came right behind her. While he and Kit helped find Ronnie's mouse, which the girl had no doubt let loose on purpose, Billie went to a wailing Toby in the bathroom. Denise was trying to get both boys out of the tub and having a hard time of it. Toby, who wanted nothing to do with his mother, raised his arms to Billie and quit crying when she lifted him to her. She told herself she should be ashamed of the satisfied look she flashed to a very harried and wet Denise Snow. *But the woman deserved a little of her own medicine!* And it was also quite nice that both boys demanded Billie's exclusive attention.

However, all that attention from the children backfired when Billie was the one left to read the boys a story, and Denise was the one to go downstairs with Linc. Faintly Billie heard the woman's husky voice and Linc's answer.

"I l-love y-you, Bil-lie."

She looked over to find Toby staring up at her, and she realized she'd stopped reading. His cherub face was so serious, so very adorable.

"Me, too! Me, too," Tommy was saying, his angelic, scrubbed-clean face smiling. Her heart swelled too large for her chest.

"Oh, you boys. I love you, too." And she hugged them to her, feeling equal parts happiness and despair. She loved them; they loved her. But she wasn't their mother, and she felt she was losing them—and their father.

Ronnie appeared at the door. "Can I hear the story, too?"

Billie read about Santa and his elves and the way they delivered gifts in Santa's airplane. Afterward she tucked each child in and savored kisses and hugs, even from Ronnie.

When she closed Ronnie's window, she happened to glance down to the lamp-lit drive. Linc stood there, Denise at his side. As she watched, Denise slipped her arm through Linc's.

"She's really too young for you, Linc."

Denise pressed close, and Linc froze. He'd been enjoying the night air and bright stars—and getting away from the turmoil of the house. Denise had been beside him for some time, trying to engage in small talk. He'd answered in one syllable words, keeping his face averted, hoping she'd leave him alone. But this last movement was enough.

"If you're referring to Billie, I don't think my relationship with her is any of your business." He twisted away from her.

"It is my business when my children are involved. When they are exposed to an affair right in their own home. And I care about you, too." Her voice flowed sweet as honey.

Linc took a deep breath and tightened the grip on his anger. "You left your kids without a thought of who would care for them—you left two boys that were less than three years old—and now you're worried about their welfare? Well, I guess it's better late than never, but you gave up your rights in the matter when you walked out that door, Denise. And my private life is none of your concern, either. I don't need it, don't want it."

"Oh, Linc..." Her voice wavered. "She's pretty and young and I know that for a man of your age that can be very attractive." *His age?* "But this is all a lark to her. She'll get tired of taking care of someone else's kids."

"You got tired of your own."

"No, Linc, I never got tired of them. I was overwhelmed by it all. You know the depression I suffered after the twins were born. There were days I thought that I'd pull my hair out if the wind didn't stop blowing, and I couldn't stand the sight of the flat land, acres and acres of it and no other houses or people. I needed to get out and do something on my own. You had your farming—I needed a career of my own, too."

Linc had always considered homemaking a big career. "I agreed to your going to work, Denise," he said. "From the time we got married, I told you it would be fine—great."

"And how was I going to do that when I was pregnant from the start, out here in the middle of nowhere?"

He just looked at her, thinking how stupid it was to start arguing.

"I know it's hard for you to understand, Linc, but if it makes you feel any better, I've paid dearly for my actions."

"It's not what I want, Denise. It's just the inevitable result. And if it makes you feel any better, I've paid, too."

"I'm sorry, Linc." Her voice dropped, and she touched his arm. "All that's behind us now. All I want is a chance to make up for the mistakes. Can't you allow me that?"

He drew away and finally looked down at her. "You can try to make amends, Denise. I guess I need to do a certain amount of that, too. But neither of us can turn back the clock. It just can't be done. We have to live with the situation as it is and make the best of it."

"Oh, Linc, try to understand how it is for me. I'm their mother, and it's hard to do anything with the kids with Billie around. I don't have a chance."

"Well, that's a problem you'll have to work around." He had no intention of discussing Billie. "Good night."

He walked off into the dark adjacent field, leaving her and the entire household behind. He didn't want to hurt Denise, and wished he didn't feel so damn responsible for her. When would that feeling pass? Probably never. She'd been his wife; he'd given a vow to take care of her, and that wasn't something that faded easily, even if they'd decided to go their separate ways.

He wondered again how in the world he'd gotten into such a predicament.

The following day was a repeat of the first. Billie had approximately twenty minutes alone with Linc, twenty minutes in which they both seemed to walk on eggs with each other, before Denise put in an appearance.

She gave her usual innocent expression. "Oh...I hope I'm not interrupting. Kit just loves my homemade doughnuts, and I thought I'd make them this morning. But for that I need to get an early start. They take a bit of time." And she was off, turning the kitchen into a disaster area.

Linc left early again—after a fair helping of the doughnuts—and didn't show his face the rest of the day. Billie once more got to spend the morning cleaning the kitchen, washing Tommy's wet sheets and Tommy, too. Denise was again gone all morning, visiting Ronnie's teacher and guidance counselor at school, Billie discovered when the woman returned.

"Ronnie is in desperate need of a stable home environment," Denise announced and looked pointedly at Billie. Billie thought that Ronnie *had* a stable environment until Denise had showed up.

That afternoon the woman proceeded to go through closets and the attic at will, even changed around Billie's Christmas decorations. She made dinner, too—T-bone steaks cooked to perfection and chocolate soufflé for dessert.

After dinner everyone decided to decorate the Christmas tree. Billie stood back and watched, got everyone drinks, made popcorn in the microwave for stringing. She'd lost her Christmas spirit and didn't really care that Denise directed everyone. Once she realized Linc was looking at her with a quizzical expression. She should have been glad for even a little attention from him but felt almost too bruised to feel anything. When she saw Ronnie talking civilly with Denise for a change, she was ashamed to almost break out crying.

She excused herself and went to her room, only coming out later to kiss the children goodnight and assure herself they were safely and snugly tucked into bed. She paused and looked at each of them for a long minute after she turned out the lights. Her children, Marc had called them. But they weren't, and that was a fact to be dealt with now.

Linc was in the kitchen when she came downstairs, and she had to pass by him on her way to her room. She tried to do it without looking at him, but he grabbed her arm.

"What is it?"

"Nothing." She whispered hoarsely past the lump in her throat, glancing to where Kit lay on the couch.

"It's something." Linc whispered, too. "You hardly said two words tonight."

She looked at him, her eyes stinging. "I didn't need to say anything. I need to stay out of the way." She tugged her arm from his and raced to her room.

She jumped when she heard tapping at the door. Tears spilled down her face, and she choked back a sob as she turned the lock.

"Billie," Linc whispered, knocking again.

She remained where she was. She couldn't talk to him, didn't want him to see her the way she was—so jealous and hurt. She wouldn't have his pity. *She was a housekeeper in this house. She had no right to possessive feelings.*

"Billie... let me in." The doorknob turned. "Billie..."

She sat on the bed and clutched a pillow. She wanted to let him in, wanted to feel his arms around her. But she loved him more than her own wants and needs. He shouldn't be put on the spot. He had his children to consider. And by damn, she had her pride!

Certain he'd gone away at last, she gave way to crying into the pillow. The sobbing grew in her chest and exploded like a volcano, exactly as her father had always described it. She imagined him and what he would say to her in that moment. She was so sorry, so very sorry for her self-pity—for he'd certainly tell her it was useless. And he'd hold her and pat her back. Oh, Lord, how she needed her father right then!

She reached for a tissue and damned that Denise Snow for making her cry—making her nose stuff up and causing wrinkles on her face!

Denise Snow was the real wife, or at least she had been. She was the real mother. Billie was the housekeeper. The temporary stand-in.

Billie Ballinger a housekeeper? That was the root of the problem. There was no way in the world Billie could ever have become a real housekeeper, a professional in that realm. Maybe she'd been hired as that, had called herself that, but deep inside she'd been in the business of saving hearts—her own included.

She'd been looking for a home and a family. She'd been in desperate need of being needed and had found that here. She had not taken on a simple job, never that. The children had needed a mother, and she'd tried to be that. Linc had needed a caring woman, and she'd tried to be that. She'd done it all well and could be proud.

But now the situation had changed. Denise Snow was ready to mother the children again, was ready to be a wife again. And maybe this family could get back together—a happy ending to a fairy-tale story. And Billie would certainly be the wicked witch to wish that wouldn't happen.

To leave would tear her heart out. But maybe that was what she had to do.

Linc would be all right without her. He didn't really need a woman; he'd made that plain from the first. Yet should he choose, with her out of the way he would have the room to turn to Denise. The woman who'd first held his heart.

But the children weren't ready for her to leave, she thought, panicking. They weren't! What would happen to Ronnie? What would happen when the twins cried for her? Who would make certain they got their naps and had stories read to them? And it was Christmas. *Oh, Lord, what was she going to do?*

Things had gone too far, Linc thought as he quietly mounted the stairs. He was tired, his feet lead weights with each step.

Billie had barely said an entire sentence all evening. And he couldn't remember her laughing since Denise had arrived. There'd been no singing of "Zip-a-Dee-Doo-Dah" or

Christmas carols, either. The children were in an uproar, and the very house seemed about to blow up.

The look on Billie's face minutes ago brought a tight ache across his shoulders. *She was going to leave them. He was going to lose her.*

He stopped at the bottom of the stairs and looked over to Kit's door. He thought he could see light at the bottom. He listened for sound, heard nothing, but went over to knock on the door anyway.

The door opened, and Denise smiled up at him. She wore a flimsy pale gown, showing plenty of cleavage. "Come in, darlin'."

Linc stepped inside and took the door from her hand, closing it behind him. Her smile grew, her eyes brightened with expectancy. He hated what he had to say, but there was no way around it.

"It's not workin' out, Denise. You're gonna have to leave."

Shock flowed over her face. "What's not working out? The children are okay with me. Ronnie's even beginnin' to talk to me."

"I admit Ronnie's getting better. But I suspect she talked to you tonight while Billie was in the room in an effort to please Billie. If you'll notice, it was when Billie left the room that Ronnie spilled her drink on you. And I really don't think that was an accident any more than her mouse ending up in your slipper was. Kit's on edge and has half a dozen pimples. Tommy and Toby are higher than kites. Your being with the kids is a good idea, Denise, just not all at once. And this isn't a particularly good time."

Her eyes flashed. "Not a good time for whom? You and your lover?"

"Denise, you can't change the last year and a half in one short week of concentrated attention and piles of presents. You're welcome to visit during the day when you can, maybe even spend weekends sometimes. But you can't stay here like this."

"I'll go to court, Linc, and point out how you're living here with a lover right in front of the children."

"You don't have a leg to stand on, Denise. Not only did you leave the kids, but I know you've been livin' with some guy in Houston."

Her face went white. "Oh, Linc, that didn't mean anything. I was just so lonely without you."

She stepped forward, put a hand to his chest. He just stared at her. *Oh, damn, she was gonna cry.*

"How can you do this to me?" she said in a hoarse whisper.

It suddenly occurred to him to wonder how she could do this to all of them. Denise wanted what Denise wanted, regardless of the effect on her own children.

"I'm sorry, Denise. I'll work with you all I can regarding visiting the children in the future. But I want you to leave tomorrow."

"So everyone will know you're throwing me out?" Her chin came up and her eyes sparked.

"Not from me."

"And then I'll look like I'm running out."

"Give any excuse you want—give no excuse. I just want you gone by tomorrow afternoon."

"You're throwin' me out of a home I helped build!" Her voice rose, and she stomped toward him.

"I'm askin' you to leave a home you're tearin' apart." He opened the door and slipped out, closing the door as well as having it pushed shut behind him. He went to the sanctuary of his own room, his back tingling, as if an arrow was about to pierce it.

All he wanted was for the great days before Denise had showed up to return. Was that too much to ask?

He was barefoot and taking off his shirt when his door cracked open. He prepared to snap at Denise, but, seeing nothing at eye level, his gaze slipped downward. It was Ronnie, clad in her footed pajamas, rubbing her sleepy eyes.

"Can I sleep with you, Daddy?"

He thought that the last thing he wanted was to have one of the kids bugging him, and how serious this must be for Ronnie to come and ask that.

"Sure, babe..." He hadn't called her that in three years, but she looked very young and precious in that moment. "Come on and get under the covers before you catch cold."

He tucked her in, put on pajamas himself and got in on the other side. She scooted over and curled up against him. Tentatively he slipped an arm around her.

"Okay, now, babe?"

"Mmm..."

Certain of having a stiff neck in the morning, he fell asleep holding his little girl. He recalled how it was he who had walked the floor with her during those long nights of colic. It occurred to him that, while Denise had given life to the children, she'd been a haphazard mother at best, taking care of her children when it suited her. And while his love for her had faded in the end, his commitment to her and their family hadn't. But Denise had never been committed, not to him, to their life together, to her own children.

Billie didn't come out of her room the following morning until it was time for the children's breakfast. Denise, in her sheer peignoir set, was doing her best to wreck the kitchen, of course. Biscuits again this morning, sausage gravy, eggs, and hash brown potatoes. And grease that Billie would have to clean up spattered on everything in a four foot radius.

The twins were up and rowdy, and Kit was already at the table, explaining that John was dropping by for him early. Linc wasn't there, and Billie wondered where he was. No doubt he would come to get his biscuits!

A few minutes later he came in from the hallway. "Ronnie's stayin' home today," he said, his face showing mild concern.

"What is it?'" "What's wrong with her?" Billie and Denise both asked at once. Glancing at Denise, Billie backed up a step. Ronnie was this woman's child, she reminded herself, bracing against the pain.

"She's okay. She's not even runnin' a fever. She just doesn't feel like goin' to school, and I told her she could stay home. She needs the rest." He looked at Billie. "She's in my bed. I told her you'd bring her up some toast in a little while."

Billie nodded.

"I'll take her up some biscuits and jelly," Denise said.

"She only wants toast—and for Billie to bring it."

Denise clamped her mouth shut and turned away. Billie felt sorry for her, and said, much to her own amazement, "Maybe we could both go."

The look Denise gave her would have wilted even a sturdy cactus.

She felt Linc's lingering gaze. "Aren't you going to eat?" he asked.

"Later." She simply couldn't look at him again. She started washing the dishes, trying to keep herself out of the way.

After Linc and Kit had gone and the twins were watching morning cartoons, Denise disappeared upstairs. Billie put together a tray for Ronnie—sweet hot tea and toast with smiling faces drawn on it with grape jelly.

She'd reached the top of the stairs when she heard voices coming from Linc's room. She knew instantly that Denise was with Ronnie. The two were arguing. Uncertain, but driven by an uncontrollable protective instinct, Billie continued down the hall.

Denise's voice, high-pitched and angry, reached her. "... you have become one smart-mouthed brat, little lady! Well, maybe you don't want anything to do with me, but you're no prize either. And I'm your mother. You *will* learn to show me some respect!"

Billie went cold at the words.

"I don't want you!" Ronnie screamed just as Billie reached the door.

Ronnie caught sight of Billie, and Denise's head swung around. Her face was flushed, her eyes sparking.

"Well, here is your *precious* Billie," she said sarcastically and swept from the room, her pale gown blowing out behind her.

Trembling, Billie walked with assumed calmness across the room and set the tray on the night table. She sat down on the side of the bed. Ronnie crossed her arms on her bent knees and rested her forehead there.

"What was all that about?"

Ronnie remained silent.

Billie laid a hand on the girl's silky hair. "Do you want me to get your father? Do you want to talk to him?"

Ronnie shook her head.

Billie reached out and gathered the child into her arms. Ronnie's tears wet her sleeve, and Billie's heart cracked.

"I'm not a brat," Ronnie said in a small voice.

"No, honey. You're not."

"I'm sorry... I'm sorry..." she sobbed. "I didn't mean to cause more trouble..."

"Oh, Ronnie, it's not your fault. Not any of it." Tears stung Billie's eyes.

She stayed with Ronnie until the girl had eaten a bit and drunk half the tea. Then she tucked her once more beneath the covers and sat and sang "Away in a Manger" until Ronnie had closed her eyes. Then she went to find Denise.

She met her in the hallway at the foot of the stairs. Denise was dressed now in wool slacks and satiny blouse, her hair and makeup perfect.

"That was a vicious thing to say to that child," Billie said, the words bursting forth almost before she had a chance to think.

"It's time Ronnie had a bit of firm discipline. And she was the one who started it."

"She's barely eleven years old, for heaven's sake! You are the adult!"

"Maybe she's only eleven years old, but Ronnie knows exactly what she's been doin'. The girl's been allowed to disrupt this family long enough."

"It was not necessary for you, her mother, to call her a brat."

"That's right—I *am* her mother. Somethin' that both Ronnie and you have seen fit to ignore. And if you weren't always around, steppin' in between me and the children, maybe they'd come to me." Her voice rose and she jabbed at Billie's chest. "You may have an angel face, darlin', and you may have everyone convinced that you are an angel, but I know better. You're doin' everything you can to keep Ronnie from likin' me. You're a home wrecker. You're the reason this family can't get back together!''

Chapter Fifteen

Billie put her one bag into the Thunderbird before going to speak to Ronnie.

"You're going away?" Ronnie's face paled.

"Just for a week, I said. I'm only going for a week, and then I'll be back."

The child's disbelief was quite plain.

"All my stuff is still down in my bedroom, if you want to go look. Ronnie..." She took the girl's hands and looked straight into her eyes. "Have I once lied to you since we met?"

After a second's thought, Ronnie shook her head.

"Your mother needs time here alone."

"But we don't want—"

"I know that. But it's...best. And I promise you, I will be back next Wednesday. I'm going to stay with Marc—that's his number on the paper I gave you. You can reach me there any time you want to call. And I'll call you tonight from my hotel. Okay?"

Ronnie looked down at her fingers. "What if she beats us?"

"Oh, Ronnie." Billie had to grin at the child's sheepish expression, even though it was all she could do to keep from crying. "I imagine you're a match for anyone on that score."

"Yeah. Guess so." She lifted her face. "You'll be sure and be here Wednesday? The school's Christmas play is on Thursday. I'm goin' to play an angel. I was savin' that as a surprise."

"I promise to be here. I wouldn't miss seeing you as an angel." They grinned at each other, then Ronnie flung her arms around Billie, and they clung to each other.

"I will see you in a week, sweetheart," Billie said and turned away before she broke down crying.

She did cry when she hugged the boys. "For a week, my loves . . . only for a week."

"You b-be ba-ck for C-ch-rist-mas?"

"Of course. Santa will bring my presents here. Now you two be good."

"You can tell Linc I'll call tonight to speak to him," she said to Denise, who stood back.

Denise nodded. "I'll tell him."

As she drove away from the farm, she felt as if her heart was being ripped from her chest. She'd told Ronnie it was only for a week—and come hell or high water, she intended to return the following Wednesday—but she didn't kid herself that she would be staying then. No. There wasn't room in that house for her *and* Denise Snow.

Denise Snow wasn't about to be blasted out of that house now that she'd returned. And she did have first claim. She had been married to Linc for fourteen years. He'd still been agonizing over losing her when Billie came on the scene. She'd borne those children and had every right to want a good relationship with them, no matter what she'd done. And, Billie admitted, Denise had every right to seek a reunion with Linc, too. All's fair in love . . . so they said.

She blinked back the tears and looked at the road and countryside through blurred vision. Bits of cotton remained caught in the grass and field stubble and blew across the road, bright white beneath the sun.

Oh, Linc! Oh, Lord, Linc. She thought of him, and the pain was unbearable. She wondered how she could go on breathing, how the sun could go on shining.

She'd been a coward not to speak to him directly, but she simply hadn't been able to do it. He would have seen her pain, would have felt obligated. He may not be the best tempered man, but he was so damn honorable!

This week she was gone would give them all time to adjust.

When she entered Heaven, the gin was going full out. She pulled in front of Fred's café, sniffed and wiped away mascara smudges. A tinkling Christmas bell rang when she opened the door. At least it was the midafternoon lull. The café was empty and Fred was reading the paper when Billie entered.

"Heard about the visitor out at your place," Fred said when he plunked her Cherry Coke in front of her.

"It's not my place," Billie said thinly and swizzled the straw around the ice cubes.

"Oh, rubbish!"

Billie looked at him. "I'm going away for a week. I'll be back next Wednesday."

"You lettin' that woman push you out?"

She shook her head. "It's just better if I'm not around. The kids keep looking to me and not to their mother. As long as I'm there, Ronnie won't ever give Denise a chance."

"So—who cares?"

"Oh, Fred. She's their mother."

"Could have fooled me. What about Linc?"

She focused on the drink in front of her. "He's caught in the middle of us. Now he won't be. He can have some room to make up his mind. And maybe everybody won't be pulled in a thousand directions. You know—too many cooks."

"Oh, hell, gal! Denise and Ginny were in here just the other day, and even this old fool could see the writin' on the wall. Denise got a whiff of Linc gettin' interested in another woman for the first time since she left, and she couldn't stand it. She didn't want him or the kids until some other filly come sniffin' around."

"I wasn't *sniffin'* around, Fred."

He scowled, pointed at her, then ran a thumb beneath his suspenders. "Now maybe I ain't ever been overly fond of Denise, but it's only the truth talkin' when I say she didn't never give Linc or her own kids what you've given them these past months. And you may be thinkin' you're doin' all this for them, but I think you're just lettin' your pride get the better of your head."

She shook her head and laid three quarters on the counter. "I'll stop in when I get back."

"You'd better do that, gal." He came around the counter and grabbed her to him in an uncharacteristic hug.

Billie caught the scent of fried beef and onions clinging to him, felt the warmth of him. "Thanks, Fred."

She drove out of Heaven the way she'd come, heading west in the direction of Billy the Kid's grave. She felt nothing at all like the Good Queen of the World.

"Where's Billie?" Linc demanded as he burst through the kitchen door.

"She left," Denise said, her eyes wide with surprise.

"I thought you were supposed to be gone."

"I couldn't very well leave the children alone, could I?"

"What did you say to her?" Without waiting for an answer, he tossed his hat to the table and stalked off through the house, calling for Ronnie. "Ronnie called me on the radio. Where is she?"

"She's upstairs in your..."

Ronnie came pattering down the stairs and threw herself into his arms. "Oh, Daddy!" He held her trembling body a minute, glanced up and saw the twins standing at the top of the stairs.

He pulled back and looked at Ronnie. "Where'd Billie go?"

Ronnie's lower lip trembled. All traces of the cocky rascal were gone and pure tearful child remained. "She went to stay at Marc's. She said she would call you tonight. She said it was only for a week, Daddy, but . . ."

He put her down. "Go upstairs and watch your brothers while I talk to your mother. Don't argue."

Grabbing Denise by the arm, he hustled her into his office. By damn, he'd had enough of life and everyone else running all over him!

"What happened?"

"She decided on her own to leave, Linc. I didn't have a thing to do with it. And she's only gone for a week. She said she'll be back on Wednesday and to tell you she'd call tonight. I can easily stay until Wednesday, darlin'. It's no catastrophe."

"What did you say to her?"

"Nothin', Linc. For goodness' sake. You have been workin' her like a slave, what with the harvest and everything."

Out of the corner of his eye, he saw Ronnie push open the door he hadn't completely closed. Seeing the way she looked at Denise, he didn't order her out. Denise looked at Ronnie and wet her lips.

"You didn't tell Billie you were leavin' today, did you, Denise?" He watched the edginess slip over her face, and his stomach turned.

"I didn't have a chance," Denise said righteously. "She up and decided to leave first. And I don't think my actions are any of her business."

"What did you say to her?" Linc persisted. In the back of his mind he cursed himself for not making everything clear to Billie.

Denise looked at Ronnie, who stood there staring at her, and frowned. "We . . . we had words, darlin'. It wasn't anything too terrible."

Ronnie continued to stare at her, and Linc knew that his daughter had heard. He wouldn't put her into the position of having to tell, though.

"What words?" he demanded of Denise.

She brought a hand to her hip. "I just pointed out that as long as she was here the kids wouldn't have much to do with me. That she was comin' between us."

"Damn you, Denise!"

Making a fist of his hand that itched to slap her, he turned away, raking that same hand through his hair. Holding himself in tight control, he told Ronnie to leave the room. She instantly complied.

"It's true what I told her, Linc, and you know it."

He turned, and she stepped back. "*Partly* true, and twisted to suit your purposes. I don't have a problem with you wantin' to come back into the kids' lives, Denise. Hell, I'm thrilled about it! For them and for you, too. I was married to you for fourteen years. I can't wipe that out of my life as if it never were! I still care about you, always will. But any further commitment died when you left and insisted on a divorce. When you didn't come to see these kids for months and months."

"I want to make up for that," Denise cut in, tears glistening in her eyes. "Okay—if you don't want me back, please don't keep the children from me."

"You can make up for it, Denise, but the hurt goes too deep to be erased in a few days. You've come bustin' in here, upsetting everybody's life to get what *you* want. That's all you're really thinking about, n . the kids, but *you*.

"You've got to be there for them, encourage them, Denise, but not force them. It simply won't work that way. And Billie wasn't trying to take your place with them. She didn't have to. She's forged her own place with them. And with me."

"You think you have all the answers," she told him angrily. "That you know it all. You've never understood me. Never!"

"I guess that's true. And right now I hope you're right about me knowin' it all because I've got to know what to do to bring Billie back."

"She's only gone for a week, Linc. She'll be back."

"I'm going to make sure of that," he said, starting from the room.

"It would have been nice if you would have made such a fuss about me leaving," she shot after him.

He paused and looked back at her. "I did, but you were too busy to notice. And maybe I learned then that I should make more of a fuss—a mistake I don't intend to repeat now."

He left her and went upstairs, taking the steps two at a time and calling for Ronnie. "Get dressed, while I get your brothers ready to go. I'm goin' to need you guys." When she opened her mouth to question him, he hollered, "Hop to it!"

Kit would be home within ten minutes, and they could leave. To go after Billie. He didn't know if that was wise or not, and he didn't give a lot of thought to pride. He only knew that he wasn't prepared to let Billie get away without a hell of a fight.

He had the twins and Ronnie downstairs putting on their coats when Kit came in from school. He tossed Kit the farm truck keys. "Go down to the tractor barn. Look on the south side and you'll find two little pups in a pen there. Bring them in the dog carrier and put them in the back of the Suburban."

"Pups?" Ronnie gaped at him, and Kit echoed, "Dogs?"

"Yes. Now go get them. I'm takin' all the ammunition I can. I don't think she can resist all of you and the pups, too," he mumbled. And he felt no shame in the idea of bribery.

When they were all piling into the car, Kit prodded him. "Dad . . . uh, Dad?"

"Yeah?" Linc checked to make certain he had everyone.

"What about Mom?"

Linc remembered Denise then and looked up to see her standing there in front of the kitchen door. His conscience pricked, and he called to her, "You're invited to Christmas dinner—Christmas afternoon. You'll have to eat what Billie cooks, just like the rest of us."

She lifted her hand and shot him a dry smile.

They headed off down the drive, and Linc thought how totally unromantic this was—taking his children along to persuade the woman he loved to come back to him. It just might scare her away.

"*Two* puppies, Dad?" Ronnie said from the back seat.

"One is for you, one for Billie. They're your Christmas presents." He felt so stupid. "You said she was headin' for Marc's?"

"That's what she told me. She was goin' to stay with him. Here—she gave me his telephone number."

"How long ago?"

"About an hour and a half now."

He pressed harder on the accelerator and checked to make certain all the kids were fastened into their seat belts. He knew if Billie had come this way, she wouldn't have stopped without speaking to Fred. And he was right, he discovered when he stopped and the old man raked him over the coals.

"We can't miss her," he told Kit when he got into the car. "How many '55 Thunderbirds are we likely to come upon on this road? Here—Fred sent these." He tossed an armload of Twinkies onto the seat.

He had to find her. Oh, Lord, he had to find her. Surely she would go the same way she had come—but with Billie, a person couldn't be certain. It was hard to figure how Billie thought. Damn her, anyway! A week, Ronnie had said. Wouldn't it be easier to simply wait for her to return on Wednesday, instead of taking off on this wild goose chase?

They were barely twenty miles down the road when they had to stop for Tommy to pee. Ronnie started complaining about Toby smearing the creamy filling from his Twinkie all over her coat. Linc thought that he absolutely had to have Billie back—immediately—for more reasons than one.

"Listen up, kids. When we find Billie you have to give her your best pleading faces. You know—those looks you give me when you want me to take you to the show, or want money. Or you want to keep another stray, Ronnie."

"How's this, Daddy?" Ronnie showed her face in the mirror.

"That's the one."

He'd muffed this whole thing up pretty good right from the start, he figured, recalling his treatment of Billie. He hadn't told her how he felt—but damn, he wasn't good with words. So right now he was going to use every asset he possessed.

Billie was sitting in the Thunderbird on the side of the road in New Mexico, with the sun far to the west when she saw, at last, a car approaching in the rearview mirror. She jumped out and stood uncertainly beside the opened door while a cold wind blew around her.

Oh, Lord, she thought, halfway raising her hand, don't let it be a killer, or a rapist. Or someone just barreling on by—there aren't that many people who travel this road. Oh, Lord, let it be a nice old lady or man who...

Oh, Lord, it was Linc!

The realization froze her in place, gaping at the sparkling brown Suburban as it pulled off the road behind her. It was Linc—*and the children.*

She watched him slowly get out of the car. He leaned on the open car door and took off his sunglasses, staring at her. Then he stepped around and came toward her. The setting sun glowed golden on his dark cowboy hat. His face was shadowed. There was anger in his deliberate stride.

He stopped in front of her, and they stared at each other. She was both ecstatic and wary. She could see his eyes now, and he didn't exactly look glad to see her. Why in the world was he here? She was afraid to believe the answer that sprang to her heart.

"It seems we met this way once before." His voice was low and gruff, his jaw tight.

"Yes."

"What's the matter with it this time?"

Humiliation washed over her. "I ran out of gas."

"Aw, Billie!" He jerked off his hat and pointed it at her. "This is a damn lonely highway to be travelin'. You could have been out here all night!" He cocked his head and peered at her. "You didn't think you should have talked to me about leavin'?"

"I left a message."

"And you think a message was enough? Damn it, Billie! I never expected you to be the leavin' kind. And don't I rate more than a message?" He gestured with his hat, then rubbed the side of his nose.

"Yes, I guess you do, but I thought it would be easier if we didn't discuss it. I *was* coming back."

"So I was told." He looked away, then back at her. "What in the hell happened? Were you tired of us? Was that what was too hard to tell me?"

"No, of course..."

"Did any of us—not counting Denise—insult you?"

"No, no one insulted me. I just thought a week away might be of benefit."

"To you—you needed time away from us."

"No. I—"

"Then what exactly did you think you were doing?"

"I thought you and the kids needed time alone."

"We weren't alone—Denise was there."

"That's just the point. I thought it would be better for all of you if I wasn't in the picture."

"So you took yourself off for me and the kids? What did we do to make you think we didn't want you with us?"

She shot him a look of disgust. "It was plain to see you were caught like a sardine in a sandwich. I'm not deaf and blind. And I've never in my life fought over a man—I'm certainly not going to start now."

"So it was me? What did I do? Did you catch me makin' eyes at Denise? Kissin' her? Feelin' her up?"

His sarcasm was fuel for her temper. "You ate her biscuits!"

His mouth fell open. "I ate her biscuits?"

"Yes!" she cried, flinging up her hands. "And you were mooning over your wife when I arrived two months ago. And wasn't I a pretty picture—blond and blue-eyed just like her?"

His eyes widened. "I was not moonin' over Denise when we met. I haven't mooned over her in a year—if I ever did! And you may be blond and blue-eyed, but you're nothin' like Denise. Did I ever tell you I thought that? What did I say to make you think that?"

She approached, poking her finger at his chest. "Nothing! It was what you *didn't* say or do! You didn't tell me how you felt. And you sure as hell didn't tell Denise how you felt about *me*." She jabbed her own chest. "You wanted our relationship kept a secret. Thought I should back up—we don't really have a relationship. At least not one that can be defined, other than employer and housekeeper. I think it was perfectly logical on my part to deduce that my housekeeping services were a bit in the way with the ex-wife back in the house."

"You've rarely had a logical thought in your life, lady, so I don't know why you should start now. And you damn well know that from the minute you decided to stay in our house you were more than a housekeeper—for all of us. And for your information, I told Denise last night that she had to leave because she was interferin' in *our* lives—meanin' you and me."

That shut Billie's mouth. "You did?"

"Yes. I told her to leave this afternoon. She just thought she'd play you around and get you to leave first."

Billie understood that Denise had played her for a fool, but paramount in her mind was that *he'd* told Denise to leave. She recalled the way he'd come to her door, had pleaded with her to open it. He must have told Denise after that. And he'd done it for her, Billie. It suddenly flashed through her mind that this was the exact way they had begun—fighting alongside this same highway.

The next instant Linc grabbed her arm and was tugging her back to the Suburban. He put a hand on her shoulder and bent her level with the windows.

"Look. Look at those faces. You can't leave them, now can you?"

Eager smiles vanished from the children's faces as each one strove to look solemn, something they came by naturally anyway. Then Toby grinned at her—and held up a little puppy!

"We've added two puppies to the brood, and one is yours if you come back with us," Linc said near her ear.

The tears came instantly. She straightened and looked at him. "You think I should come back for the children?"

"Yes." His voice was husky.

"And only for them?" She could hardly squeeze the words past the lump in her throat. She blinked, struggling to see him through the blur.

"For me, too." And then he grabbed her to him. "Oh, God, I love you, Billie. I can't live without you. I'll turn into a mean old man if you won't have me. The kids will leave me . . . I'll lose the farm . . . I'll take to drink . . ."

She started laughing through her tears. She held him and he held her.

"You got me a puppy?" she mumbled in his neck.

"Uh-huh."

"Oh, Linc . . ." It was the same as when she'd carried their clothes up to their rooms in front of Denise. A small, minute act that held all the importance in the world.

And then his lips were on hers, passionate, hungry and demanding. She returned the kiss with equal passion, seeking to tell him how much she loved, needed, and wanted him.

When they broke apart, Billie's head was spinning so that she had to cling to Linc. He smiled softly at her.

Then came clapping. Oh, my, the children! Billie only then remembered their audience, only a few feet away.

"Zip-a-Dee-Doo-Dah!" Tommy cried.

"A-nd to all a g-g-ood night!" Toby added.

Epilogue

Christmas night

Billie looked at the yellow band on her finger. The intricate carving in it caught in the lamplight. Had she truly been married to Linc for nearly two weeks? It didn't seem possible.

With a sigh that was a mixture of rapture and relief, she lifted her head to gaze around the room, her fingers still holding the yellow band on her left hand, as if it might disappear any moment.

It had been Linc's bedroom. It had become their bedroom. Hers and his.

Their first night as man and wife they had spent in her room—the guest room, everyone was calling it again. It'd been their honeymoon night, and the twins were directed to go to Kit for any emergency nightmares. The very next day, Linc had taken Billie on a shopping trip to purchase furnishings to completely redo his bedroom into *their* bedroom.

Billie had chosen new linens and curtains; Linc had insisted they keep the old trunk and had purchased a Navaho rug to set it on. They had matching nightstands, lamps, even clocks. Billie's robe lay across the bench at the end of the bed; Linc's hat hung on the tall bedpost. The puppy Linc had given her slept nearby in a round basket with a large, partially chewed, Christmas-red bow.

She caressed the sleek post of the bed they had chosen together. What a time they'd had! They'd had to visit four stores in Lubbock before finally coming to an agreement. There was a new dresser, too, for her, and a new armoire for Linc. He said he couldn't pronounce *armoire* and grumbled about remembering which drawer contained his underwear. Billie adored his grumbling.

She ran her hand over the polished surface of the chest. His underwear was in the first drawer behind the doors. And it was there, too, she knew, that he'd placed his picture of Denise.

"I thought I'd keep it for the kids," he'd said, when he'd looked up and found her watching.

"You should keep it for you," she'd told him and knew he'd been relieved at that.

Denise had been expected to spend the entire Christmas day—to join them for Christmas dinner, which Fred was cooking. And Billie had determined to bite her tongue and do anything and everything to make the woman feel wanted, a part of the family. Denise had assured them all she would definitely be there—and would of course be bringing her fabulous Texas Tornado cake, which was Linc's favorite in all the world, and her own cranberry sauce mixture. But then she simply hadn't shown up.

Ronnie had been the one to look repeatedly out the window. Tommy and Toby had asked about their mother. Linc had called Denise's apartment several times. Finally at about one o'clock, Denise had telephoned.

She couldn't make it, she'd explained. She was with friends and they'd all decided to take a quick trip up to New Mexico for skiing. The conditions were perfect then and might not be again. She would definitely be coming for New Year's day, she told Linc when he mentioned that the children had missed her. Linc had told Billie not to tell the children about Denise's promised New Year's visit.

"She's done this all before," he'd said tiredly. There'd been no more time for discussing it, for Tommy had bounded into the room, demanding they listen to him play "Jingle Bells" on his harmonica.

Billie smiled, thinking of it. She was a part of this family now, and being constantly interrupted had suddenly become precious.

Her stocking, now empty, lay tossed across Linc's on the dresser—a perfect symbol of their lives. And a banner still stretched across the ceiling of one corner of the room, proclaiming: CONGRATULATIONS BILLIE AND DAD!

They'd had as rushed a wedding as any couple with a shotgun behind them. Plain, in front of a justice of the peace. But Billie held it dearer than a million dollar service. The children and Fred had been there, and afterward they'd returned to the house and all had Twinkies for a celebration. And all the time Linc's eyes had rested upon her...*oh, his eyes!*

The door opened, and Billie whirled around.

"Everyone's asleep."

Linc stopped and smiled at her, then slowly, carefully, closed the door. Their gazes held as he sauntered over to his chair, sat and began removing his boots. Billie went to help him. Though he didn't touch her, he ran his eyes over her like hot, greedy caresses.

"Puppy asleep, too?" Billie asked.

"Puppy, too," he replied with a mock frown and glanced around her at the puppy in the basket. "I don't know how I managed to allow not only one but two of those things in the house."

"Because you're a very wise man, Mr. Snow. You know how to keep your women happy."

"And you're a good con artist, Mrs. Snow." His gaze turned sultry. "Keep wearing that gown at night, and you can have anything you want."

Heat rushed through her body, and she allowed her eyes to speak of her desire. Yet, still, they didn't touch.

He stood and began unbuttoning his shirt. Billie sat on the bed, watching his deft fingers, remembering the feel of them on her skin, catching the faint scent of his cologne. When he frowned and looked away, she knew other thoughts had crossed his mind and sensed what those thoughts were.

"I'm sorry about Denise."

He paused, reached out and touched her cheek. "None of it is your fault."

"I suppose she didn't want to come here because of me."

He looked at her and raised an eyebrow. "Now do you really think that Denise would let your being here bother her if she really and truly had wanted to come? Would anything have stopped *you* from visiting your children on Christmas—especially when you'd promised to show up?"

Seeing the truth of it, she shook her head. "I guess not."

"Denise has simply decided to cut her losses and turn her energies elsewhere—like back with the guy she's been living with for the past six months. He drives a Jaguar and has his own plane."

He grinned then, and she grinned in return, both of them communicating without words as a man and woman in a household of four children learn to do.

Denise will always be a thorn in our side.

I don't care.

Neither do I—because I love you like hell, lady.

And I love you.

He took her easily into his arms, and his eyes grew bright. Then he swept her up into his arms and headed for the bed.

She laughed and kicked her feet. "Don't you dare drop me!"

He grinned and kissed her, then dropped her onto the mattress, leered wickedly and began unbuckling his belt, slowly, enticingly.

Rising up on her knees, she moved to help him and to run her fingers over his sleek chest. "Fred's bringing out dinner tomorrow night, and he wants to talk about giving us a combination wedding celebration-New Year's party at the café.''

He unbuttoned his jeans. ''Hope he's bringing chicken and dumplin's.'' He jumped as her fingers brushed his belly as they moved to his zipper.

''He is. And I'll learn how to make them, too.''

He stripped out of his jeans. ''Oh, lady, you don't need to learn anything more than you already know.'' He rubbed against her, and she answered in kind.

''Since I'm now married to the Good Queen of the World, am I the Good King of the World?'' he whispered as he kissed her neck.

She chuckled. ''Oh, yes.''

''I thought so. I sure feel like it.'' He sat and pulled her across his lap.

She ran her hands up and down his back, feeling his sleek, hard muscles. He drew back and gazed at her. She saw the longing in his iridescent eyes.

''I love you, Linc.''

Joy replaced the longing.

They kissed, nibbled and tasted each other until Billie was quivering all over. They moved up to lie on the pillows and snuggled beneath the covers.

''We'll have a proper honeymoon,'' he said huskily into her hair, ''before wheat harvest.'' He kissed a trail to her breasts and slipped his hand beneath her gown.

''Are all events arranged around the crops?'' She lost her breath at his touch.

''Umm, pretty much. But, man, what there's time for in between.''

He kissed and licked her neck, and his hands were everywhere at once. Faint memories of their first time kept ricocheting about her mind, adding fuel to the fire burning inside.

He pulled back and took her face between his hands, gazing at her for long seconds. She saw the conflict going on behind his eyes and forced herself to wait for him to reveal what was bothering him. It wasn't easy, the waiting, but she'd come to know it was what he needed at these times.

His brows wrinkled. "I get pretty stubborn sometimes; I know that. And I know I'm not an easy man to live with."

When he paused, as if waiting, she said, "You are a very special man—especially to put up with a wife who can barely cook or clean. You're the man for me."

"Just don't ever leave me, Billie." His voice cracked. "No matter what kind of fights we get in. No matter how mad you get with me. Don't ever leave."

She touched his dear cheek with her fingertip and thought of all the nights she would make love with this man. Of all the mornings she would wake beside him and all the afternoons she would wait impatiently for him to come home.

"I promise you, Linc, I'll never leave."

And then their lips came together, and the passion that had long been growing burst forth, full and ripe.

*   *   *   *   *

Silhouette Special Edition®

proudly hails

WOMEN OF GLORY

from Lindsay McKenna

Soar with Dana Coulter, Molly Rutledge and Maggie Donovan—Lindsay McKenna's WOMEN OF GLORY. On land, sea or air, these three Annapolis grads challenge danger head-on, risking life and limb for the glory of their country—and for the men they love!

May: NO QUARTER GIVEN (SE #667) Dana Coulter is on the brink of achieving her lifelong dream of flying—and of meeting the man who would love to take her to new heights!

June: THE GAUNTLET (SE #673) Molly Rutledge is determined to excel on her own merit, but Captain Cameron Sinclair is equally determined to take gentle Molly under his wing....

July: UNDER FIRE (SE #679) Indomitable Maggie never thought her career—or her heart—would come under fire. But all that changes when she teams up with Lieutenant Wes Bishop!

SEWG-1

Bestselling author **NORA ROBERTS** captures all the romance, adventure, passion and excitement of Silhouette in a special miniseries.

THE CALHOUN WOMEN

Four charming, beautiful and fiercely independent sisters set out on a search for a missing family heirloom—an emerald necklace—and each finds something even more precious...passionate romance.

Look for THE CALHOUN WOMEN miniseries starting in June.

COURTING CATHERINE
Silhouette Romance #801

July
A MAN FOR AMANDA
Silhouette Desire #649

August
FOR THE LOVE OF LILAH
Silhouette Special Edition #685

September
SUZANNA'S SURRENDER
Silhouette Intimate Moments #397

CALWOM-1

 *Silhouette Books®*

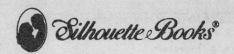 *Silhouette Books*®

SILHOUETTE BOOKS ARE NOW AVAILABLE IN STORES AT THESE CONVENIENT TIMES EACH MONTH*

Silhouette Desire and Silhouette Romance

> May titles: April 10
> June titles: May 8
> July titles: June 5
> August titles: July 10

Silhouette Intimate Moments and Silhouette Special Edition

> May titles: April 24
> June titles: May 22
> July titles: June 19
> August titles: July 24

We hope this new schedule is convenient for you. With only two trips each month to your local bookseller, you will always be sure not to miss any of your favorite authors!

Happy reading!

Please note: There may be slight variations in on-sale dates in your area due to differences in shipping and handling.

*Applicable to U.S. only.

SDATES-RR

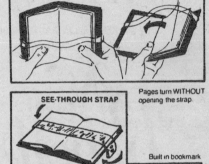

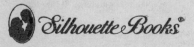